EVERYTHING WE NEVER KNEW

a novel

JULIANNE HOUGH &
ELLEN GOODLETT

sourcebooks
landmark

For young Julianne,
who did what she needed to do to survive and protect
herself to get her to the place that she is today. Knowing that I will
have your back and I will be there for you no matter what—so a
little dedication to my younger self.

Published by Sourcebooks Landmark, an imprint of Sourcebooks
P.O. Box 4410, Naperville, Illinois 60567-4410
(630) 961-3900
sourcebooks.com

Cataloging-in-Publication Data is on file with the Library of Congress.

Printed and bound in the United States of America.
LB 10 9 8 7 6 5 4 3 2 1

CONTENT WARNING

This book contains depictions of drug-related death and miscarriages. It also includes content relating to sexual assault, harassment, parental abuse, difficulty conceiving, and the death of a child, all of which occur off-page.

Chapter One

After the worst year of my life, I deserve tonight's victory lap. The formfitting mermaid dress (for which I seriously over-paid) hugs my curves in all the right places as I sail into my company's annual Holiday Gala. Despite the nondenomina-tional name, the gala is extremely Christmas themed—huge pine trees in the corners, green and red pine garlands every-where. There's even a Nativity scene on the lawn (though it's anyone's guess whether that belongs to us or the hotel itself).

With Shane on my arm, straight-backed as a soldier in his brand-new suit, my chronically polite Utahn coworkers look downright envious.

Not that I blame them. We paint a perfect image: what passes for a power couple here in Garden Vale, Utah. Shane's a whip-smart structural engineer who volunteers at the local firehouse; I'm about to be crowned queen of Garden Vale real estate for the third year running.

Nobody suspects what's behind the shiny façade.

"There she is! The woman of the hour." Don DeKamp, president and CEO of Medina Property, has a voice like untimely fireworks. It booms through the crowd, past several hundred real estate agents, property managers, investors, and guests.

Heads swivel in my direction. I smile and wave as Don hops onto the temporary stage. Every year, he makes the interns erect it smack dab in the ballroom of the only three-star hotel in Garden Vale. Don's responsible for the hotel's current ownership, which I'm pretty sure is the only reason they put up with us.

"Welcome friends, Romans, countrymen!" Don shouts, just like every year. Half the room flinches, because he doesn't seem to realize he's miked. "If you'd be so kind as to take your seats, we'll get this show on the road."

Everyone settles in except me and Shane. We work our way through the bustle toward the stage. Building it used to be my job, once upon a time. Back when my friend Tanya and I were brand new at Medina, eager to work our way up the corporate ladder.

Part of me misses those days. Sure, being Don's lackey involved blood, sweat, and rooting through dollar store craft bins, but at least the only direction to go was up. Now, teetering at the top...

Shane bends to whisper in my ear. "Three o'clock."

I follow his gaze, spot Tanya and her husband absorbed in something on Tanya's lap. Probably a makeshift scorecard—she loves playing Corporate Speak Bingo, checking off a box anytime Don says *synergy* or *assets*.

"Wonder who's winning." Shane's breath tickles the nape of my neck. "Besides me, of course." His hand slips to the small of my back, searing hot through the fabric of the gown. "I'm proud of you."

A spark flares in the pit of my stomach. Not the usual kind Shane elicits. This one is twisted, vicious. Why? it hisses. It's not like I bring any real value to the table.

Shane deserves better. But then, I've always known that.

I lean into his touch, let my body speak instead. My usual move, when I can't trust my tongue.

Don's wrapping up, talking about "an impressive sales record despite trying times"—window-dressing the fact that despite a supposedly booming economy and record-breaking sales last year, our numbers this year sucked.

I try to picture the flashcards I've been rehearsing all week in front of the bathroom mirror, the houseplants, or Shane, depending who's available. Instead, my traitor brain summons the worst possible thought: *today would've been the due date.*

Or maybe not. Maybe it would've been a few days from now, late but still a Christmas miracle. Hard to tell with these things.

Nine months ago, I perched on the edge of our claw-footed bathtub—the one I begged Shane to install because I dreamed of taking long, sensuous baths but that I've barely used since. My heart rose into my throat when the little pink plus appeared. The world's oldest magic trick.

That was the best night of my life. And then, like a closed parenthesis, two months later came the worst.

The blood came first, staining our sheets. Then the cramps. Shane followed me to the toilet, terrified. Later, he said he'd never heard sounds like that. Deep, wrenching howls.

I barely remember. Just flashes. My body a comma around the toilet bowl. Shane cleaning something—me or the floor, I'm not sure. And the cramps, in waves. It didn't physically hurt that much. Not as bad as my first periods, back when I was fourteen.

It should've hurt more. I wanted it to.

"Without further ado…" Don brandishes an envelope like he's hosting the Oscars. Behind him, the floor-to-ceiling windows normally frame snowcapped mountains. Now, after

3

dusk, it becomes a mirror. My pale silhouette overlays the Utah night. "This year's top seller is a familiar face."

What did the therapist say about grounding yourself? List five things you can see, four you can touch...

I forget the rest. I stopped going to therapy after a month. "Don't need it anymore," I told Shane, not fooling anyone. For once, he didn't push.

"Alexis Cole," Don bellows. Cheers erupt, some more enthusiastic than others. Tanya leaps to her feet, whooping. Her husband, Paul, dives under the table, presumably to fetch their bingo cards.

"Lex." Shane's voice calls me into myself, better than any therapist touchstones.

I plaster on a smile so wide my cheeks throb and stride up the rickety steps. "Thank you, Don." I pump his hand— twice, with a tight grip, just to prove I can. I once heard him complain that women have limp-wristed shakes.

He hands me the statue. Same as always: a glass skyscraper etched with our company logo, reminiscent of the kitschy souvenirs sold in national parks. The first year I won, the statue felt heavy with import.

Tonight it just feels heavy, period.

Don passes me the mic. I take center stage beneath a fairy light and snowflake display that'd be more appropriate for a courthouse wedding.

Shane flashes me the middle finger surreptitiously. Our code. *Just you and me. Screw what anyone else thinks.*

Calm trickles through my nervous system. I raise the skyscraper. "Don't see many of these around here," I joke. The tallest building in Garden Vale is a six-story apartment block by the train station. It was built thirty years ago, but you still get old-timers complaining it ruins the view.

A few people laugh. Bless them.

"Seriously, though, it's an honor." I scan the sea of polite faces. Tanya waves. John Wood, my main competitor for top agent, scowls. Otherwise, most people look glazed over. "Don't worry, I'll keep this short and sweet so they can bring out the steaks."

More gracious titters.

A man rises from his seat in the back. He's a bit older than me, a white guy with dirty-blond hair. I don't recognize him. He must work in another department. Or maybe he's someone's date?

"This year's market wasn't easy on us," I say, then kick myself when Don clears his throat. *More upbeat, Lexi. Stay on script.* "We had big challenges to overcome. But that's the exciting part. Challenge is where growth happens."

The man at the back remains standing by his chair. He doesn't flag a server nor does he head for the restroom. He's not even looking at me, just his own hands. There's nothing noteworthy about him, yet he sucks the breath from my lungs.

There's something around him. A cloud, almost, as if the air is thicker. This gray haze drifts in sluggish circles, flowing up from the top of his head and falling over his features, curtain-like.

The longer I stare, the worse I feel. My lungs refuse to expand. My skin goes clammy. Plus it's freezing. Did someone turn the AC on?

I wet my lips, shivering. "We're all here because we love… growth." *What am I saying?* The taste of salt water and seaweed surges up my throat. I very nearly gag.

At the last second, self-preservation kicks in. *People are staring. Act normal.*

"Um…" My voice sounds tinny, underwater. "I just… I wanted to thank…" *Breathe. It's only a memory.*

5

They claw at me sometimes. Surge up from my past when I least expect them. Cracking in public is my worst nightmare—I work so hard to hide the real Lexi. The mélange of fuckups and anxiety. Everyone knows me as the life of the party, the fun one, always up for a dance or another drink. Only Shane has an inkling of how bad it gets, and even he doesn't know the full extent.

My fingertips tingle, a cry for oxygen. I gulp another breath, painfully aware I've stopped talking. The pause stretches, grows claws. I cannot do this—not here, not tonight.

I scan the audience for my husband. Instead, I lock eyes with the strange man. That's when the screaming starts.

At first, I can't make out words. With each passing second, however, the cries get louder. Clearer.

"Someone help! Please," begs a woman's voice. "Save him."

Maybe this isn't in my head? "Sorry, does anyone else…" But one glance at the ballroom tells me nobody hears her. Everyone has gone stiff, their polite smiles strained. Probably all wondering if I'm having a meltdown.

Am I? Because as overwhelming as my past can be, I always recognize the memories that torment me on repeat. This is something else.

It's not my memory.

That's impossible. Insane sounding. Yet the thought lodges in my breastbone. It feels true.

Shane, bless him, vaults onto the stage with a glass of water.

"Thank you," I whisper off-mic, drinking deeply, if only to excuse the weirdness. "Got a little too excited," I say, once I've finished.

Everyone laughs, breathy and relieved. People hate awkwardness, even secondhand.

I brush off decades of nightmares about this exact scenario

and try to haul my speech out of the fire. "What I meant to say is that I couldn't have made any sales without the help of every single person on my team. Not to mention this great company." I hoist Shane's water. "Let's all raise a glass to the Medina Property team!"

Around the room, champagne flutes, martini coupes, and soda glasses rise. Cheers echo from the ballroom ceiling. "To Medina!"

The man at the back remains stock-still. He doesn't touch his glass, doesn't clap. The strange haze still obscures his features, but I swear he's watching me. Like he knows what threw me off. Like he hears the woman too.

Goose bumps prick my arms. The woman's voice returns, louder than before. "Please, Henry, I'm begging you. Don't let go. Save him."

She sounds so close that I can't help it—I glance over my shoulder. Of course, nobody's there. Just my reflection, expression haunted.

I get the strangest feeling the woman is talking to me. That she wants me to follow the man—*Henry?*—and do something. What, I can't imagine.

It makes me angry, all of a sudden. *I have enough to deal with.*

I lift the mic again. "Now, can we please feed these hungry people before they boo me offstage?" Glasses clink once more as I make my way to the steps. Shane meets me halfway, arm extended. I grip so tight I'm surprised he doesn't protest.

Whatever the woman wanted me to do, it doesn't matter. By the time I reach the ballroom floor, Henry is gone. It's for the best. If he'd stayed, I might have been tempted to talk to him, and chasing some poor stranger to interrogate him about a disembodied voice would not exactly prove my normalcy.

You imagined it. That's all.

"What happened up there?" Shane whispers in between handshakes from well-wishers.

"Later," I lie, already knowing I won't tell him the full story. Most of my mother's advice is objectively bad, but there's one thing we agree on: white lies are sometimes the best option.

Throughout dinner, I steal the occasional glance at not-Henry's seat. It stays empty. No coat slung over the back, no uneaten steak on his plate.

A small, superstitious part of me wonders: Was he ever really there?

Chapter Two

Snow has begun to fall by the time the night winds down. *Just* looking outside makes me shiver. I'm dreading the cold, which means my social batteries must really be drained because staying seems worse. A dull headache thuds in my temples, sharpening every time I think about my onstage meltdown. I haven't seen the man again, but I catch myself checking every cluster of faces.

"Please tell me you're not abandoning ship already." Tanya sidles up to me with a Diet Coke. Over her shoulder, a cluster of her fellow BYU-grads-turned-Medina-employees gestures for our attention. "They haven't even played my request yet!"

Every year, we make a game of asking the DJ for the cheesiest songs, trying to one-up each other. "Don't worry." I nod at the corner where our husbands are sequestered. "At the very least, I'm stuck until this war story finishes."

For a moment, we just watch them. Shane gestures so animatedly that, despite his suit and tie, he resembles the teenager I met in college. Tanya's husband, Paul, bursts into his contagious, belly-deep laugh.

Paul used to volunteer at the fire station too, but an accident put him out of commission last year. Now whenever we get together, he requests dramatic reenactments of the latest firehouse antics.

"We should take them on more playdates," Tanya says. "God knows I could use some adult conversation."

"Adult?" I deadpan, as Shane mimes a fire pole slide gone wrong.

"Try singing 'Wheels on the Bus' eight hundred times in a row. Your standards drop real fast."

We grin. Mine fades.

"What's up?" When I don't answer, Tanya purses her lips. "If it's about the speech, trust me, you're the only one still thinking about it."

It's not the speech. Not really. It's everything else: the woman's voice, those weird flashes of cold and drowning, the man who disappeared. The fear that maybe this time, my mind is breaking for good.

I wrinkle my nose. "Half a dozen people came up during dinner to tell me I did 'just great, sweetheart.'"

"That was a whole hour ago. Glenn's unparalleled dance skills have erased all memory of the before times."

Nearby, a circle of coworkers surround the short, perennially happy mail room guy. He's currently facedown, mid-worm. He does not have core strength or any rhythm to speak of, but Glenn never lets that stop him.

I laugh, then side-eye her. "You're still thinking about it."

"I'm your best friend. I don't count." She wraps an arm around my shoulders and squeezes. "Now, are we joining Glenn voluntarily, or do I have to drag you out there?"

Paul's familiar baritone interrupts. "Funny, I was about to ask you the same thing." He loosens his tie, shirtsleeves already rolled up. The two of them met in a ballroom dance class in college and still take every opportunity to show it off. "Unless you're stealing my wife for the first round?" Paul glances at me.

"She's all yours." I kiss Tanya's cheek, lift her arm, and twirl her toward her husband. "Sorry, guys, but I'm beat. Gonna ask my knight in pressed tuxedo to whisk me home." I crane my neck. "Speaking of Shane..."

Paul points. "Coat closet. Said he got a feeling you wanted an early night."

Bless that man. I flash Tanya one last reassuring look. "Have fun, okay? You two deserve it."

"Oh, we know." She winks at Paul, then sobers. "Promise me you won't spend the whole night in your head?"

"Who, me?" I feign shock. "Never."

She looks dubious, but Paul is a hard man to resist. As he draws her onto the dance floor, she calls over her shoulder, "Nobody remembers!"

I snort, wishing she were right. If only I could forget the woman's voice. *Please, Henry, I'm begging you... Save him.*

Shane appears, coats draped over one arm. I rise on tiptoe to kiss his cheek. "You're a goddamn hero. Quick, let's go before Don realizes I'm still here." Our CEO isn't exactly inappropriate, but he gets grandfatherly after he's had a few. I've already suffered one too many uncomfortable hugs for the night.

Sometimes I wish I knew how to shut people down. But politeness was baked into me, my mother's guiding platitude: *If you can't be useful, at least be nice.*

Of course, the rule never applied to her, which is why I currently have five unopened voicemails. I can't bring myself to delete them, but I can't press Play either.

It's fine. My brother would tell me if anything serious happened.

"So," Shane drawls. "We gonna talk about what's been bothering you all night?"

"I'm just tired." I shrug into my coat, a ridiculously thin

11

blazer I had no business bringing out in December. My puffer didn't go with the dress, though.

Shane gives me his usual piercing look. I set my jaw. After a brief contest of wills, he sighs. "If I get the car, will you talk about it at home?"

I squint at the snowstorm, debating. The whole truth isn't an option. If I tell Shane I heard voices, he'll panic. But maybe I can avoid that part. Even before the weirdness onstage, I wasn't feeling like myself.

Besides, in addition to the coat, I paired impractically high heels with this dress. Capitulations must be made. "Deal," I grumble. He turns smug. But before he starts gloating, a flash outside catches my eye. I inhale sharply. "Shane. Is that...?"

Telltale red lights whirl against the fluffy white flakes over on Grant Street, a few hundred yards away. A handful of my coworkers pause outside the doors, gawking.

Shane curses. "Stay here." A volunteer firefighter since college, Shane's used to switching into emergency mode at a moment's notice. "I'll see what's happening. It's probably nothing."

Dread pools in my veins anyway. I watch him push through the doors, heart rate climbing.

He's been doing this for as long as I've known him, yet the anxiety never gets easier. Every time he answers a call, I wonder if he's coming back. Staring at Shane's backside, I think about the man earlier. The woman's voice. *Please, Henry... Someone help.* I recognize her fear. I've been there.

Between one breath and the next, I push through the glass doors in my husband's wake. Shane's already halfway across the parking lot, jogging.

The cold claws at my nose, my throat. Someone calls my name, but I keep my eyes on the ground. These heels are tricky on concrete, let alone ice. Luckily, I grew up ice skating. My nervous energy transmutes into a flood of adrenaline.

As I jog across the lot, I realize I left my award on the dinner table. *Fuck it.* I have two identical ones at home.

The red lights pull at me, magnetic.

The closer I get, the harder it is to breathe. *It's the cold,* I tell myself. Deep down, I know better. It's the same feeling from earlier, like drowning on dry land.

The taste of salt water hits again. I cough, then gag.

Just as I reach the fire truck, two volunteers roll up a gurney with a figure wrapped in one of those reflective warming blankets.

Shane spots me and jogs over, his forehead creased. "I said to wait inside."

"I..." I can't tear my eyes from the gurney. It bumps the curb, and one EMT loses his grip, gasping. The whole thing tilts, the patient sliding, boneless as a sack of flour. I catch a glimpse of his face, and my heart stops.

Henry.

His eyes are open but empty, two glassy voids. The sight hits me like a gut punch. Just a couple of hours ago, he was fine. Oh God, was my terrible speech the last thing he saw?

"Come on. There's nothing we can do." Shane wraps an arm around me, starting toward our car.

I don't budge. The EMTs right the gurney and hoist it into the truck. They slam the doors, blocking my view. But I still can't leave.

The truck idles. Nobody rushes to the driver's seat to speed to the hospital on Elm.

"What happened?" My voice sounds far away.

So does Shane's. "Overdose. One of your coworkers spotted him lying on the side of the road, called it in."

"Why aren't they going to the hospital?"

My husband runs a hand through his hair. Snowflakes dislodge, drift onto his shoulders. "They will."

"They should hurry." What did the woman say? *Please, Henry... Save him.* She was practically begging. And then there was that cloud around him, almost like a shroud...

There's no way I could have known what was about to happen. But I can help now.

"What are they waiting for?" I storm toward the truck, but Shane keeps hold of my elbow.

"Lex...it's too late."

"No." I try to shake him off.

He hangs on. "Trust me. I saw him. He's gone." Then Shane folds those warm, strong arms around me. Normally I'd sink back, let him comfort me.

But I don't want comfort. I want them to do their jobs. I want to save this man I left for dead. I shrug off my husband. "Tell them to go. They have to at least *try*." I'm shouting, but I don't care.

"Lexi." There are tears in Shane's eyes. Only then do I realize I'm crying too. They're spilling down my cheeks, freezing in their tracks. All for a man I never knew, a man I only glimpsed once, for a split second, but—

Save him.

Maybe I could have.

"Henry," I whisper.

Shane's brow furrows. He cups my cheek, thumbing away a tear. "Did you know him?" When I shake my head, his frown deepens. "Then...how did you know his name?"

14

Chapter Three

Monday has been girls' night ever since Tanya and her friend Chloe lured me away from the office for "a quick drink." Tanya now has two kids at home (three, if you count Paul) and Chloe's constantly jetting off on work trips, but we still meet here every Monday we're in town. The corner seat of Murphy's dive bar has the best people-watching view of Main Street.

This bar has witnessed our best and our worst. Bad dance moves, impromptu karaoke, comfort cries, and breakups. It's our constant, our safe place. Every week, we order the same plate of fried pickles (extra crispy), drink the same drinks (barely potable red for me and Chlo; Diet Cokes and stolen sips of our wine for Tanya), and have the same conversations about kids (Tanya), sex (Chloe), and work (me).

The routine used to comfort me. Regardless of whatever else changed, Monday wouldn't. I loved it. Relied on it. But now...

"Lex?" Tanya asks. From her tone, it's not the first time. "Chlo was asking how your big night went."

"Hmm?" Outside, a couple strolls past with twin girls dressed in adorable matching reindeer sweaters. I tear my gaze away. "Oh. The gala? It was good."

Except a man died.

Suddenly, the fried pickles don't smell as appealing. I nudge the plate toward Chloe while my friends frown.

"That's it?" Chloe snatches a pickle. A feat, given that she's sitting with one leg slung over the chairback in the world's most exaggerated pretzel. Her hair is bleached blond this week, with an undercut that reveals dark roots and a series of painful-looking piercings. "Lexi, you've been talking our ear off about the gala for months. At least give me some juicy details. Any weird hookups?" She wiggles her eyebrows. "Ooh, did our girl throw up in the potted plants again?"

Tanya chokes on her soda. "That was one time. And I was pregnant, you jerk. When you two have kids, you'll understand."

My stomach knots.

She doesn't know. I wasn't far enough along to tell anybody when it happened. Still, her words send me spiraling back to that night in the bathroom, curled on the freezing tiles.

At the other end of the table, Chloe gags. "If I ever get knocked up, have me exorcised because a demonic entity has possessed my body, okay?"

"I thought you wanted a big family and a farm," Tanya retorts. "Lex, back me up here." She turns my way, dark curls spilling across her deep-brown shoulders.

Normally I'd crack a joke or mediate a compromise. Instead, my thoughts spiral. Bathroom. Blood. *Think about something else.*

The voicemails on my phone. *No.* The last time I saw my mother and brother, two years ago. They drove out for a visit—and went straight home again the next day, after Mom and I got into a fight. *No.* The whirling red lights in the parking lot. Henry's body.

Shit.

"Yeah, as in, like, a ton of dogs and a goat or something. Not human children," Chloe's saying, oblivious to the interrogative stare Tanya's aimed at me. "I mean, unless Marisol wants to carry a baby. Then maybe."

No lesser statement could have distracted my best friend. But this does the trick. She whirls back to Chloe. "Wait, Marisol as in the girl you went to Banff with last weekend?" She actually bounces in her seat. Tanya's an incurable romantic. "Oh my God, Lexi, our wild child might actually be into someone for longer than—" She breaks off at the sight of me. "Lex?"

All I needed to muster was one half-decent smile. What is wrong with me?

"See? I'm not the only one grossed out by the pregnancy talk." Chloe twirls the crystal pendant she always wears from her first campaign as a paid influencer. "Quick, talk about business strategies. Or promotions."

They're both watching me now. *Business strategies.* Is that really all I am to my closest friends?

I can't do this anymore. I'm not sure where the thought comes from, but I can't shake it. "Sorry. Feeling a little weird." Excuse, I need an excuse. "Maybe something I ate."

Chloe wrinkles her nose at the pickles.

The sensation gets worse. The bar feels too small, the heating too high. *Is this the rest of my life? The rest of all our lives?* "One minute." I squeeze out of the booth. "I just... I need some air."

"Want company?" Tanya asks. She's always been the mom of our group, even before she became one.

"Don't be silly." I wave her off without a backward glance, hurrying toward the exit. *Air.* That's what I need.

In Utah. In December.

Cold hits my face the instant I push through Murphy's

heavy wooden front door. The bell tinkles, a discordant, cheerful note.

Outside it's biting. The wind is so cold my lungs shrink. I breathe in anyway and savor the burn, with its faint scent of approaching snow.

Winter is my favorite season. There's something crystalline about it. I always imagined, growing up, that if sheer energy had a smell, it would be this.

Up the street, in the west, sunset has started. Deep mauve and burnt sienna paint the snowcapped mountains. The center of Garden Vale is flat, a quaint row of matching storefronts cradled in the mountains' shadows. Right now, white lights and heavy pine boughs deck the streets. Twinkling snowflakes dangle overhead, and tinny Christmas music pumps through a speaker hidden among the trees.

It's a postcard. A timeless snapshot, holidays in a nutshell. It reminds me why we chose this town.

We could have moved anywhere. Between my BA in business management and Shane's engineering degree, we had plenty of opportunities. But Garden Vale was our spot. It was the first place we went away together, a couple of months into dating. Shane booked the cheapest Airbnb he could find and surprised me with a romantic getaway. The next winter we came again. A month after graduation, he proposed to me in the little French restaurant on Fifth Street, where we still celebrate our anniversary every year.

When it came down to it, there was no question. Garden Vale was as much a part of our relationship as the two of us.

At least, that's the story we tell. Sometimes, I think we were secretly afraid we'd jinx it if we moved anywhere else. Like if we went to some big city, we'd stop being us, fall apart.

Was that a mistake?

For as long as I can remember, I've had the same vision: a perfect future, all mapped out. And for most of my adult life, it has been steadily coming true. Husband? Check. Hometown? Check. Steady career? Check. Family?

Yet no matter how hard I try, I can't tick that last box. Motherhood is not a sale I can close.

Maybe because family has never been your strong suit, whispers a nasty little voice, one I've spent a lifetime fighting.

Guilt follows hard on its heels. I slip my phone out and scroll to voicemail. The tiny number five glares, accusatory. In preview, a partial transcript of the most recent voicemail pops up.

Alexis, honey, it's your mother. I know you're busy, but I wanted to check in and see if you remember...

The message is dated two weeks ago. My thumb hovers over Play. It's two minutes long. On the short side for her. And it starts out nice. There's a chance it's innocuous. Maybe she really did just want to catch up. I could be blowing this out of proportion, ignoring her for no reason.

There's an equal chance that halfway through, the message will shift into a rant. Either about me, or my older brother, Ricky, or most often about our father. How we're both too much like him.

I wouldn't have prayed for a daughter if I'd known this was how you'd turn out.

Staring at the horizon, my eyes water. I squeeze them shut until the sting goes away. She's not what I'm really upset about. I learned how to deal with her a decade ago.

The scarier thought is that I might be more like her than I thought.

What happened at the gala? I keep pushing it to the back of my mind, convincing myself I imagined everything. But then I snag on Shane's question. *How did you know his name?*

"You have to let yourself feel it," someone says, close enough to make me jump.

I turn to the gardening store on the corner, filled to the brim with succulents, herbs, and potting soil. Mixed among the plants are shelves of crystals, wind chimes with five-pointed stars, stacks of tarot cards, and bundles of dried herbs.

It's the store teenagers sneak into when their parents aren't looking, frequented by tourists and skiers over from California for the season. Locals mostly ignore it, except for the older folks. They tsk and shake their heads when they pass or else cross the street entirely.

Bea's Odds and Ends reads the beautifully painted sign over the front door, decorated with three moons back to back. Nobody calls it that.

It's the Witch's Lair, according to Tanya and Chloe, who used to dare one another inside. They grew up here, childhood friends who left Garden Vale for separate colleges, then boomeranged home after.

The eponymous Bea stands outside Bea's Odds and Ends, a wreath of smoke curling around her frizzy gray curls. The witch of the Witch's Lair.

Beatrix O'Neill has been a fixture of Garden Vale since before anyone I've met can remember. Nobody's quite sure about her age. She's got one of those faces that could range from early fifties to late eighties depending on the time of day, the cant of light.

Now, in the ochre sunset, she looks younger.

I glance around. The street is empty. But she said something, right? "I'm sorry?" Surely she's not talking to me. The only time I've been in her store was when Chloe dragged me once for "backup." She claims Bea has a grudge against her, but to be honest, Bea seemed equally annoyed by all of her customers.

Bea jerks her chin at my stomach. "You have to mourn your loss before you can move on."

On instinct, I stiffen. "I don't know what you mean."

She shrugs. "Sure you don't." She blows out a thin stream of smoke. "Just like I don't smoke." She stubs the cigarette on the wall of her shop, then tosses it into an empty planter. She slides that under her awning and yanks down the chain link grate, bending to lock it.

Most businesses in Garden Vale don't bother with security. Hell, a few don't even lock the front door. But Bea has to. Too many people have broken in over the years, either to steal or to scrawl ugly messages on the walls.

I linger, not entirely sure why. I feel anxious, jittery. A live wire exposed to the elements.

How does she know? More importantly, can everyone tell? Is it obvious just by looking at me where the holes are?

Bea opens a can of tuna to leave on the porch. "For the strays," she murmurs. I'm not sure if she's talking to me or herself. Then she straightens and looks me dead in the eye. "Someone's got to take care of them when they show up."

She pockets her keys and strides away, layered skirts swishing around knee-high boots.

For a second, I feel that tug again. Similar to the pull at the gala, when I first saw Henry, except this time it isn't a bad feeling. A flood of calm trickles from the crown of my head all the way to my toes, which curl inside my office flats. There's a faint scent too. Not smoke or snow. Something lighter, altogether wrong for the season. Almost like... oranges?

"There you are." The bell above Murphy's door jangles. My friends stand in the entrance.

"Who were you talking to?" Chloe peers up the street. "Batty Bea?"

"Don't call her that," I say automatically.

Chloe shrugs. "Whatever she said, don't take it personal. She once told me I was destined for prison."

"Okay, but you did break a statue and then refuse to pay for it." Tanya ushers us back into the dingy bar.

"It was an accident! And no way that piece of junk cost fifty dollars. She just figured she could bully a teenager into overpaying." Chloe flips her hair irritably.

Normally Tanya would argue, but she's still watching me with concern. Tanya's always been my grounded friend. The practical, down-to-earth organizer. We don't talk about our pasts, but I believe they're similar.

You learn to hear the blank spaces in other people's stories when you insert them in your own.

Right now, she probably wants to do what I would in her shoes—fix me. But to be honest, I'm not even sure what's wrong. Is melancholy a diagnosis? I thought they made it up as an excuse to toss women in asylums a hundred years ago.

How about hearing disembodied voices? Voices that tell you a stranger's name. Then you find said stranger dead an hour later...

If I told my friends about Henry, they'd listen. They'd probably even believe me, in their own ways. But then what? Tanya would recommend rejoining the church. Chloe would suggest a séance or microdosing magic mushrooms, whatever kick she's on this week.

Why go through the song and dance?

Besides, I refuse to have a breakdown in Murphy's, of all places. So I let my friends lead me back to our table. There, I scoop up my abandoned wineglass and pepper Tanya with questions about her upcoming family trip. Before having kids, she and Paul used to visit her maternal grandparents in Mexico every Christmas. This will be the first time they're making the journey as a family, and she's been looking forward to it all year.

I really am excited for her. Or I will be, once this fog passes. The last thing I want to do is bring my friends down because I'm having a weird day. *Act normal.* Soon, I'll transform back into the old me, firing jokes at the bartender and lining up songs on the jukebox.

I can't wait to leave this shaken, uncomfortable Lexi behind.

Chapter Four

I spend Christmas Eve cocooned on our couch, a weighted blanket draped over my legs and one of Shane's thick sweaters on. My stomach won't settle, despite copious amounts of ginger tea. *Shouldn't I be over this? I'm almost thirty, for fuck's sake.*

. Yet here I am, counting down the hours until the dreaded phone call. Any other day, I can dodge my mother, but on Christmas, we talk.

It never ends well.

Shane's used to my moods this time of year. He's curled up with me, *Die Hard* playing in the background. Like every guy friend we have, he insists it's the best Christmas movie of all time. I agree, though only because it doesn't remind me of childhood. Excessive on-screen violence was one of my mother's many cinematic pet peeves. Even seemingly innocuous movies like *It's a Wonderful Life* could spur whole rants about one tiny "inappropriate" detail.

For once, however, I'm not paying attention to vintage Alan Rickman. I'm too focused on my own research.

Henry Jensen's obituary was posted in the *Garden Gazette* yesterday.

From it, I learn he has one surviving daughter, Sophia,

and two sons who died young. His wife passed a year ago. Cancer.

Following a trail of links, I locate a news article about his boys. There's a photo attached. This Henry looks nothing like the desperate man I saw at the gala. He smiles broadly, one arm around each of his sons. Their smiles match his, bright and happy. All three have the same bright-blond hair and sunny blue eyes, even lighter than mine.

Tragic Accident in San Francisco Bay Rips Family Apart

My heart beats faster. Maybe I shouldn't read this. But they don't call it morbid curiosity for nothing.

Unexpected swells near the Bay Bridge this Thursday turned a family's dream holiday into a nightmare.

Henry and Carol Jensen from Garden Vale, Utah, had rented a sloop, hoping to teach their sons to sail, but rough seas tossed Mr. Jensen and the boys—Abraham, 11, and Benjamin, 8—into the bay. The boys did not survive.

"That surge would have been difficult even for an experienced local to navigate," said Captain Ken Booker, the harbormaster. "Mr. Jensen had never sailed in the bay before."

Mrs. Jensen told authorities that their oldest son was steering when the first waves hit. By the time the Coast Guard arrived, Mr. Jensen had been thrown overboard along with both of his sons.

Mrs. Jensen, herself an experienced sailor, sustained a concussion but regained control of the sloop long enough for the Coast Guard to board the vessel. The search for Abraham Jensen remains ongoing. Benjamin Jensen was rushed to UCSF Benioff Children's Hospital, but revival efforts were unsuccessful.

*"Drowning doesn't look the way it does in movies,"
warned Petty Officer Beth Marshall, captain of the Coast
Guard ship that answered the Jensens' distress signal.
"There's not a lot of thrashing and screaming. Mr. Jensen
was holding his youngest son when help arrived, but it's
important to recognize the warning signs. If your child goes
quiet, that's when you need to be concerned."*

I stop reading as the story delves into how many children drown in swimming pools right next to oblivious adults. Shivering, I burrow deeper into Shane's sweater.

Back at the gala, when I made eye contact with Henry, it felt like I was drowning. I tasted salt water, my skin went cold and damp, it was hard to breathe... Plus, there was the woman's voice. *Save him. Please, Henry.*

Was what I heard—or felt—related to the accident somehow?

Impossible.

"Are you still obsessing?" Shane's voice startles me so much I slam the laptop shut.

"I was just curious." My face reddens. I'm acting like he caught me looking at porn.

Actually, porn would be normal. This is decidedly not. I don't believe in visions. Not like Chloe, who devours all those ghost-hunting TV shows. And not like Tanya either. She believes in the definition of God we grew up with, in miracles and prophets.

I'm more like Shane.

We met sophomore year at a "party" my friend dragged me to. It turned out to be a youth social to draw wayward members back to the church. Even though I had zero intention of rejoining, I felt rude leaving right away.

I was hiding by the snack table when Shane found me.

We bonded over not realizing what we were getting ourselves into.

We spent the whole event talking. We talked about my mother's version of religion, how she wielded it like a cudgel to get my brother and me to obey her. We talked about Shane's younger brother, who came out of the closet at eleven. At first, Shane's parents didn't react well. Shane was only fifteen, but he wrote a letter to the church the same day, resigning. He told his parents if religion taught them to treat their own kid that badly, he didn't want any part of it.

His mother came around pretty quickly after that. His dad took longer, but by the time Shane started college, the family all supported his brother. His parents have since taken it upon themselves to try and change the church's mind, campaigning for a shift from the inside.

Still, when it came to religion, Shane never looked back. He wanted to focus on the real world. To help people here and now, not obsess over some afterlife fantasy.

Opening up to Shane was so easy. Normally it took me ages to let down my guard, but around him, the walls melted instantly.

Our whole relationship stemmed from that night. Our whole *life*.

The gala was a fluke. Hearing Henry's name, the drowning sensation, it was a coincidence. I reopen the laptop, willing myself calm, and click back to the obit. "I wanted to know what makes someone so desperate."

"The overdose was probably an accident." Shane drapes one arm around my shoulders, as heavy as the weighted blanket. "I've seen relapses before. If someone gets clean for a while, then goes back to using, they often try to take the same dose. But their body doesn't have the tolerance anymore."

I can't imagine what it would feel like if I finally had a child—children, like I've always wanted, two beautiful boys, with sparkling personalities—only for them to die like that. Henry's younger boy drowned in his arms. On a boat trip he suggested.

I don't blame Henry for the drugs. Especially not if that's the nightmare he was escaping. "I should have done something," I say. "Maybe if I'd talked to him, he wouldn't have taken the drugs. Or at least not that specific dose, in that specific place."

When Shane takes my hands, I let him. His palms are freshly calloused, rough but warm. "Lexi, what you're feeling right now? I've been there."

I seriously doubt that.

"At the firehouse, when somebody gets hurt, or worse…I always beat myself up after. Tell myself if I'd gotten there sooner, I could've stopped it."

My chest tightens. I've witnessed those aftermaths. Lain awake and listened to his breathing, jagged and sharp.

"We want to believe we're in control so badly that we convince ourselves everything is our fault. Because the alternative—the world being totally random and out of our hands?—is terrifying." He squeezes my hands. "But that's reality, Lex. There was nothing you could have done. It's called survivor's guilt."

"I don't believe that."

"It's a real diagnosis—"

"No, I mean, I don't believe there's *nothing* we can do. Random cruel world or not, we can still make a difference." I hug one knee to my chest.

"Of course. But you can't get stuck on *what if*. It'll turn you into a big ball of anxiety."

"*What if* I'm already a big ball of anxiety?" I grin.

He doesn't. "Is something else bothering you?"

"This isn't enough?"

"Seeing something like that is a lot," Shane says slowly. "But you seemed off before the accident too."

Resting my chin on my knee, I mumble, "I was kinda hoping you forgot."

"About my wife? Never."

I roll my eyes. "You're impossible."

"You're stalling."

On TV, a sweat-drenched Bruce Willis army-crawls through an air duct. "I guess I was just…questioning things."

Intellectually, Shane is a great listener. He knows when to be quiet versus when to ask questions. He always keeps his voice neutral, and he's quick to de-escalate fights, sticking to facts. But his body is another story. The moment those words leave my mouth, every muscle tenses. He relaxes again with obvious effort. "Life, the universe, and everything type questions? Or something more specific?"

He sounds so calm. If we weren't touching, I wouldn't have noticed his real reaction. "Everything, I guess. I've just done all of this before. The gala, the award. Normally I like it—"

"*Like* it?" He gives me a dubious look.

"Fine, normally I'm obsessed. But this year I knew I was going to win. It wasn't even a challenge. And I don't have anything else, you know? You've got work and the firehouse. Whereas I have…" I gesture vaguely.

"If you want to start volunteering, let me ask Brian for ideas. He and Mina volunteer at the soup kitchen. Or I bet Mom knows some organizations with chapters here."

Knowing Holly Cole, she probably has a whole binder full of options. The thought only makes me feel worse. I should be more like her. She's always busy: hosting visitors, working at the animal shelter, delivering Meals on Wheels, running errands for neighbors. What do I do the minute I get home from work? Collapse face-first on the couch?

I rest my cheek on his shoulder. "Sure, ask Brian."

"Do you actually want me to, or are you just saying that?"

I groan and straighten again. "I don't know, Shane. See, this is why I didn't bring it up. Now you're all nervous and going into problem-solver mode over nothing. It's just your basic ennui."

"Speak for yourself. My ennui is never basic."

I groan.

He grins an apology and loops both forearms around my waist. "Sorry it makes me nervous that my wife is bored with our life."

I soften. "I never said that." I tip my head back until he meets my gaze.

We used to do this for hours. Just stare at each other. On buses, in class. Our friends made fun of us. *You're so obsessed with each other. It's creepy.* We'd laugh, retort without breaking eye contact.

"You could never bore me," I say. Relief bleeds across his face. It echoes in my chest, the mirrored comfort of saying the right thing, lessening your partner's pain. But *never*... Is that a lie? He doesn't bore me now, but how will I feel in five years? In ten?

I used to think we'd never tear our eyes off each other, and yet...

He kisses me and I force the worry away. Maybe all promises are gambles. We're betting against our future selves. An endorphin rush of assurances today in exchange for painful obsessing later if we're wrong.

Pops of gunfire interrupt us. Shane groans and mutes the movie. On-screen, Bruce Willis dodges bullets and broken glass. Shane opens his mouth, ready to keep pushing, no doubt. He never rests until he gets a solid answer, but I've got no answers to give.

So I rest my fingertips on his forearm. Trail over the veins, featherlight, as hairs rise in my wake. His eyes drop to my lips and I tip closer, until we're only an inch apart. "Let's go upstairs."

Cheap shot, but it's been a few weeks. What with holiday events and late nights, we're both exhausted by the time we turn the lights out.

Not to mention tomorrow morning, at an ungodly hour, we'll be driving two hours north to his parents' place. Given how many family members and friends his mother packs into the house for Christmas, the chances of anything happening there are next to nothing.

Shane searches my face. I expect him to call me out, force me to keep talking. To my surprise, he nods. "One condition."

"Are we bargaining?" I plaster on a flirty smile.

He nods at the laptop. "Promise me you'll leave this alone?" Henry's still on the screen, staring up from his obituary, expression borderline accusatory.

"Already forgotten." I slam the laptop shut, then gamble one more time. "Promise."

Chapter Five

I used to adore Christmas. The lights, the anticipation of Christmas morning, the songs on every radio station. Winter had only just begun, so I wasn't sick of snow yet. I'd plan ski trips with roaring fires and Jacuzzis overlooking the slopes.

But in recent years, my enthusiasm has soured. These days, Christmas reminds me of frozen extremities and to-do lists, guilt trips, and eggnog spoiling in the back of my fridge.

Not that my in-laws are to blame. They're generous to a fault—and I do mean to the point where it's a fault. Shane's mother, Holly, has taken in more lost animals than I can count: a whole pack of mismatched dogs, a geriatric cat in a wheelchair.

She takes in humans too, for which I am eternally grateful. Besides me, there are Shane's brother Eric's ex-boyfriends. Holly's practically adopted two, both from phobic families. ("They shouldn't call it homo*phobia*," Eric always says. "Those people aren't afraid.")

Luckily for Eric, he breaks up amicably. If I had to eat Christmas dinner with two of my exes, it would not end nearly as well.

On anyone else, her enthusiasm might seem like overcompensation, but Holly is too genuine.

Sometimes, though, I'll admit I envy Shane. Lounging on one of the many cozy recliners in the Cole family living room, I try not to wish I'd grown up here instead. This is everything family should be.

Shane's three sisters crowd the sofa. Each has a pack of her own, eight nieces and nephews speed-racing from living room to den to dining room and back. The boys shout, the girls squeal, the babies coo in their mothers' laps. In the dining room, Shane's ninety-three-year-old grandmother watches his aunts play Scrabble.

Next to me, Shane's father, Frank, dunks a cookie into his eggnog, one eye on the doorway in case Holly walks by. (She's a strict believer in no desserts before dinner.)

Meanwhile, I'm mentally replaying last year's Christmas phone call disaster. It devolved into a screaming match, followed by six months of stony silence.

How long until one of us cuts the other off and leaves my brother trapped in the middle?

"You look like you could use a distraction." Frank picks crumbs from his beard. He's not much of a talker, but he's more observant than people give him credit for. "Pick a topic."

I laugh. It's a game he plays with his grandkids. Any questions their parents can't (or won't) answer, they bring to Frank. Mostly silly stuff: what's the worst thing their parents ever did; what does a bad word mean. "Pretty sure I know all the swears," I reply.

"You'd be surprised." Frank pops the last piece of cookie into his mouth. "Learned some new ones myself the other day. I made the mistake of reading a comment section."

"Shane warned you about that." We helped Frank set up his social media a couple of years ago, mostly to access grandkid photos.

Across the room, the oldest cousin tussles with his sister.

"Knock it off, you two!" their mother calls, without even breaking stride in her conversation. The siblings race out of the room.

In the ensuing lull, Frank lifts two bushy eyebrows.

He's right. I could use a distraction. The first thought that comes to mind is a question that's been lingering for a while. "You're still active in the church."

Frank nods.

"And you really believe in it? Not all of the church's political stances," I hasten to add, familiar with Frank and Holly's campaign to change hearts from within. "I mean the spiritual aspects."

"Of course." Frank's glasses are half an inch thick, but his gaze remains sharp. It's clear where Shane got his interrogation methods.

"Have you ever seen anything you couldn't explain? Something…weird."

"Define 'weird.'"

I pick at a stain on the La-Z-Boy. "Have you ever known something you couldn't? Like a fact just dropped into your head, and there's no logical explanation for how it got there."

"Sure." A smile touches one corner of his mouth. "The Holy Ghost is always prompting. It's my job to listen."

"So, you literally hear a voice?"

He pauses to consider. "Not like when a person speaks to me, no. It's more a conviction that I'm on the right path."

"But how can you be sure you're not imagining it? What makes you believe?"

He's quiet for another moment. "Never saw reason to question it." He tilts his recliner back. A black cat appears in his lap like a magic trick. Is that a new cat? Holly, I swear.

"Don't the contradictions bother you? I mean, there's scripture, and then there's…" I wave vaguely. "Life."

"There are contradictions in life too." He strokes the cat. "Going to church every week, praying, being with the community…it quiets my mind. Maybe it's only the ritual and the routine, who am I to say. But I can't deny it has an effect."

We fall silent.

In the kitchen, Holly, Shane, and one of Eric's exes belt out Christmas carols. A dog barks in tune. Upstairs, the floorboards creak. I glance over at the couch. The sisters have dispersed. They're probably changing into dinner outfits— strategically loose-waisted pants in stainproof colors.

Ritual and routine I can understand. They're comforting.

Ritual and routine don't explain what I experienced.

"Okay. But what if…" How do I phrase this? "Say you sensed something about another person just by looking at them." I'm wondering about Henry, yes. But I'm also thinking of Beatrix O'Neill, eyeing me on snow-drizzled Main Street.

You have to let yourself feel it.

I shiver, despite the central heating. "Do you think that's possible?"

"Why not?" Frank scratches the cat under one ear. "Some people have that way about 'em. Take Holly, for instance. Woman could spot a being in need from ninety paces. You little brats take advantage, don't you?" he coos to the cat, in the baby voice he reserves for animals. Not even his grandchildren get that much sap from the old man.

The cat purrs, loud as a lawn mower on the fritz.

It's not quite what I mean, but I don't know how else to phrase it. There's only so existential I'm willing to get on a holiday.

Also, I'm worried my cat allergies are going to act up. One feline in the house was tricky enough. Who knows how many more Holly's collected in the couple months since we last visited.

35

I lever myself up from the chair and point to Frank's empty napkin. "Need a refill?"

Frank does a dramatic scan of the room, like he's checking for counterintelligence operatives. He beckons me closer, then whispers, "My study. Second drawer on the left. There's a box of snickerdoodles." He taps his nose. "Don't let Holly find the stash, or I'll never make it to New Year's."

I stifle a laugh. "Your secret's safe with me."

He settles back again. I've almost relaxed, until he murmurs, "So is yours."

After delivering a fresh napkinful of cookies to Frank, I migrate to the kitchen to help Holly chop veggies. Anything to keep my hands—and mind—occupied. But I've barely started when, three full hours ahead of schedule, my phone vibrates.

The knife slips, barely missing the pad of my thumb.

"All right, honey?" Holly reaches for the knife.

I let her take it.

Shane turns from his station at the stove. He notices my expression, the phone in my hand. "Should I come out with you?" He wipes his hands on his apron.

I force a smile and shake my head. "It's fine. I'll be right back."

Shane nods, obviously still worried. When his family looks away, he flashes a quick middle finger. *Just you and me.*

My smile grows a little less fake. I slip out of the kitchen and into my boots. By the time I answer, crunching across the fresh snow of the Coles' backyard, my phone has nearly gone to voicemail.

"Mom."

"Wow, she lives." She sounds too lighthearted, almost a

singsong. "For a minute there I thought I was going to have to send a search party."

"Sorry. It was a bit loud; took me a minute to step outside."

"Ah. Well. Tell the Coles I said hello."

Damn. Rookie mistake. She hates that Shane and I always spend holidays with his family, never mine. Not that she ever invites us. I didn't even know she wanted us to come until the year she sent a passive-aggressive formal printed invitation, complete with RSVP card. Of course, it didn't arrive until three days before Christmas, by which point we already had plans.

"Mrs. Cole was just asking how you're doing," I say. My mother likes when people remember her.

"Was she now?" Mom's volume dips. "And what did you say?"

I think of Henry and his silently drowning son. I walked right into this trap. "I...said you're doing well."

"Not that you'd know." There's a click. The receiver being set down. A moment later, I hear a screw top, then a splash of liquid. "Don't these people wonder what's wrong with us? If my daughter-in-law never visited her relatives for a single holiday, I'd assume they were complete fuckups."

I squeeze my eyes shut. "Please, can we not do this today?"

"Whatever you want. You make the rules. You decide when we can call, when we can see you, *if* we ever get to see you..."

"Mom—"

"I miss you, Alexis."

The sound of my given name forms a lump in my throat. She's the only one who uses it. "I miss you too."

She barks out a laugh, so loud I wince. "You've got a funny way of showing it. The drive's only five hours, you know."

That didn't take long. "I could say the same to you."

"I came to you last time."

"That was years ago, Mom."

"You want to play that game? Fine. When was the last time you came home?"

Every. Damn. Time. I grit my teeth. Explaining it the first time was excruciating enough. Now every year it's the same thing. *Groundhog Day* for the worst conversation of my life. It takes several deep breaths to get my voice under control. "You know why I don't."

She scoffs. "This again. You were perfectly fine living here for eighteen years. Rent-free, I might add."

"I was your child, not your roommate."

"You still are my child, missy. You act like a child too. When are you going to get over this? You can't spend your whole life obsessing."

A sob rises up the back of my throat. I yank the phone from my ear, hit Mute just in time.

"Rick misses you. He'll never admit it to your face, but the way he mopes around all the time…"

There's no warning. One minute I'm fine, the next hot water streams down my cheeks.

"When you first left, I told myself: this is normal, Katrina. This is growing pains. Give her space, let her grow wings, and she'll fly home eventually. But it isn't normal anymore. People talk. 'What's going on with Alexis?' Every time I'm out. You should hear some of the rumors."

It's so cold. I dig the heel of my palm into my eye socket. The damp feels unrelated, somehow. Water from a leaky faucet, not my body.

In the background, my mother drones. *So-and-so told So-and-so, who said…*

I clear my throat hard. There's something stuck, which is

a problem. She'll notice the change in my voice. Tears make her angry, convinced I'm trying to manipulate her. I double over and cough once. Again. Finally, the clump loosens. I gulp a mouthful of saliva, battling my gag reflex.

"Swear to God, you are just like your father. Hello?" Mom barks. "Are you even listening to me?"

With Herculean effort, I tap Unmute. "I'm here." Then, before she carries on. "Is Ricky home?" My voice only sounds mildly stuffy. Success!

"You sound funny."

Or not. "It's freezing. My nose is runny."

"Hmm. Rick is still at work." My brother, forever Ricky to me, has a master's degree in English lit. Yet the only gig he can find lately is driving for a meal-delivery app. "He said he'll call you later."

"Okay, well." *Enough. Get out while you can.* "I've got to go, but it was nice talking to you."

"Was it?" she snaps.

"Yes." I scrub my free hand across my face again. A little clump of snow detaches from the eaves. It looks so big in midair, yet it hits the ground in utter silence. "I'm sorry I didn't call you sooner. I've been really busy at work."

If I shut my eyes, I can picture her expression. She's debating: let me off the hook or claw deeper? I hold my breath.

"You work too hard," she finally mutters.

I exhale so hard it's almost a laugh. "Like you taught me." This is as close as either of us will come to an apology.

"Well, at least you listen to some of what I say."

"I love you, Mom." *Sometimes that's the hardest part. How much I still care.*

"I love you too. Give Shane a hug from me."

"Sure thing." I disconnect.

Huddled under the eaves, I stare at this backyard, seeing

a different one. A smaller plot. No trees, only a couple of winter-bare shrubs. A broken wooden fence in place of the Coles' metal one, a screened-in porch instead of a wraparound. In my mind's eye, I open the screen door, step outside. There's the garage, the pitted driveway. An unfamiliar car, sleek black paint, the driver's side opening. Out of it steps—

"Lex?"

I gasp. Whip around, still half-submerged, only to find Shane in the doorway. His forehead knots in concern. "Oh." I laugh breathily, not fooling anybody. "Hey."

"Was that her?" He nods at the phone clenched in my fist.

I stuff it into my back pocket. "Yeah."

He takes a step toward me. Slow, the way you might approach a spooked animal.

I hate this. Almost as much as I hate the phone calls. He's so tender after; it makes me want to scream. *Why are you okay with this? Why do you put up with me?* It's not normal. I'm not normal.

It's impossible not to worry that someday this will all come to a head. Someday I'm going to have to answer the unspoken questions. Mine and his.

"Need a hug?" His holds out both arms. It reminds me of a parent, beckoning a little kid.

You act like a child. I face the yard, bracing myself on the porch railing instead. "I'll be there in a minute."

He's quiet for so long I almost relent. *I'm sorry. It's not you, it's me.* Or maybe *it's my mommy issues.* I consider cracking a joke, but then the back door creaks and I'm alone again.

Chapter Six

After dinner, we groan and sprawl across furniture in whatever position eases the digestive process. I wind up sandwiched between Eric's current boyfriend, a handsome Black man named Tyrone, and Shane's youngest sister, Clarissa.

"Wait, so you're from New York?" Clarissa is asking. "Like *actual* city."

"Brooklyn born and raised," Tyrone replies, although not before he side-eyes me, amused.

"Why on earth would you move here?" She wrinkles her nose. Clarissa's always been what Holly calls a "flight risk."

It wasn't unusual that Clarissa took a gap year to go on a missionary trip to France. It was unusual that the minute she got home, she started talking about leaving again. She daydreamed about Oxford, Paris. She saved up for years to go to Thailand one summer, then eloped to Playa del Carmen with a German Nigerian man she met on said trip.

These days, she's settled in Los Angeles, where both she and her husband work in film. It somewhat placated Holly, since at least they're on the same continent. (It also helps that, after everyone recovered from their heart attacks over the whirlwind courtship, the whole family came to adore Clarissa's husband.)

Tyrone laughs. "Not everyone's cut out for city life."

Now it's my turn to smile at him, conspiratorial. "Shockingly, some of us prefer peace and quiet."

Although, that's not why I stick to Garden Vale. For me, it's about the outdoors. The fresh air, the mountains, the big lawn that circles our house. I couldn't imagine living in a cramped apartment, all concrete and metal. Not to mention the lack of privacy. By her own admission, Clarissa doesn't know half the people in her building, yet she overhears their sexcapades on the regular.

"Besides, Salt Lake's not exactly the country," Tyrone adds. "Plenty of excitement in a city that size."

"Ninety-nine percent of LA would disagree." Clarissa levers herself from the sofa. "Need any refills?"

I heft a full mug of tea in response. Tyrone shakes his head too. I wait until Clarissa pads away before I glance at him. "Speaking of excitement. You and Eric are the only ones who haven't seen our place since the renovations. You should come by! We're only a few hours' drive." The moment I say it, I hear the echo of my mother. "No pressure, of course."

Tyrone frowns.

Great. It's annoying enough when Mom guilt-trips me—I don't need to pass it on. "Or we could come visit you guys sometime. Or, I mean, if you're busy—" Out of nowhere, a piercing sensation drives through my temple. I gasp and touch it, almost expecting to see blood on my fingertips. Did I bump into something earlier?

The stabbing feeling expands into a steady throb. Weird. I don't normally get headaches. Then again, I don't normally eat half my body weight in Holly Cole's infamous holiday pot roast.

"Wow, I do not feel great." I sink into the couch. "I don't

42

know what's..." But then I glance at Tyrone. He's doing the exact same thing: massaging his right temple, grimacing.

"Migraine?" he asks, noticing my hand on the same spot.

"Oh, I..." The pain intensifies, like someone's rooting around in my gray matter with a knife. "Don't know. Never had one."

"You're lucky." Tyrone leans against the back of the couch. His eyes flutter closed. "This one isn't too bad. It'll pass soon."

"Can I get you anything?" I stand and nearly lose my balance. Spots cloud my vision. When I blink, the living room lights flare brighter. Halos circle each bulb.

"I wouldn't say no to an ibuprofen." Tyrone's voice sounds far away, distorted.

"Sure thing." I smile at him, then freeze.

There's a cloud between us. Or, not a cloud, exactly. It reminds me of hot pavement on a summer day—a faint, barely there haze. It drifts in a slow current around Tyrone, cocooning him. I know at once that it's the same thing I saw around Henry at the gala. But the cloud around Henry was thick, lumpy gray. This is almost clear, save for a few darker spots.

Watching it move makes me nauseous. The back of my tongue suddenly tastes like copper.

"I-I'll be right back."

Tyrone swallows, and I swear my throat contracts too.

I hurry toward the staircase, rubbing my eyelids. Maybe by the time I get back, that mist will be gone.

Do migraines make you see things? What are the chances of spontaneously contracting your first one at the same time as someone else?

Maybe it's something I ate. Red meat gives people weird dreams, right? Or am I thinking of cheese?

Holly keeps the first-aid supplies in the second-floor bathroom, but it takes longer than usual to get there. My legs wobble. Every time I think I've adjusted, the headache redoubles with a vengeance.

Around me, the house bustles. Dogs paw at my legs while a pair of aunts help their grandmother past us to the restroom. Cousins sprint by, nearly tripping me. One of the younger kids has cornered the geriatric cat. She's in the process of picking it up, kitty wheelchair and all.

"Oh, Jean, leave Miss Kitty on the ground, please," Holly calls. Jean drops the cat with a clatter, and it lets out a disgruntled meow. I dodge them both.

The drumbeat in my temple speeds up. *Stab*, release, *stab*, release. I can barely think. I keep picturing that haze. What is it?

Finally, I duck into the bathroom. The lights are way too bright. I shield my eyes and duck into the cabinet. The medicine basket has expanded since my last visit, all the medications jumbled together. I paw through it. After picking up the same packet of cold medicine three times in a row, I give up and grab the whole thing. Someone with less blurry vision can find the ibuprofen.

Or something stronger. Tyrone said this migraine wasn't too bad, but it feels pretty damn intense to me.

How would you know, Lexi? It's his head. I just ate too much at dinner. That, or I'm experiencing some kind of sympathy pain. Is that a thing?

I hurry back up the hall just as a bedroom door flies open, Latin music spilling out. Shane's brother Eric despises Christmas ballads. He runs smack into me and I drop the basket, spilling Tylenol and Tums all over the carpet.

"Damn." I drop to my knees, scooping everything together.

Eric bends to help. "Everything okay?" He grabs a box of Band-Aids. "Mom didn't cut her finger again, did she?"

"No, Tyrone has a headache. He says it's not bad, but..."

"He always says that." Eric eases the basket from my grasp. "I swear, that man's last words are gonna be 'Oh, I'm fine, how are you?'" He produces a packet of ibuprofen. "His migraines have been getting worse ever since—"

He flushes, like he just spoke out of turn.

"That's okay. You don't have to tell me." I stand.

"It's all right. Won't be a secret much longer." Eric rises too, which accentuates his height. He's like a stretched-thin version of Shane. "I asked him not to say anything until after the holidays, since it'll upset Mom. But we're probably moving to Brooklyn."

"Oh." My eyebrows rise. Fall again. "But...Tyrone was just saying how much he likes Salt Lake."

Eric bobs his head. "So do I. It's as big a city as I thought I'd ever live in, and Ty hates East Coast winters. Says he'll take heaps of snow and sunlight over freezing rain any day."

I laugh. "Same, to be honest." When Eric doesn't join in, I go quiet.

I'm not the most intuitive person. Shane does enough people-reading for the both of us. But even I can tell there's more to the story.

Distant laughter and music drift up the stairs. Somewhere, a dog barks. A couple more join in, and the doorbell rings. One of the Coles' neighbors, no doubt. There's been a steady stream all day.

Eric gazes fondly in the direction of the ruckus. "We always talked about going someday. Ty's mom is older than my parents; she won't be able to live alone forever. None of his siblings are nearby, and he's the oldest, so he feels responsible. We were planning to move in five or six years, but then our landlord notified us he's hiking the rent, and I lost my job, so—"

"Hang on, when did that happen?" For a minute, I forget the headache. Shane didn't mention this. Eric loved his job.

"Last week." His shoulders hunch. "Anyway, I should go make sure Ty's okay." He starts toward the steps, then pauses. "Don't tell anyone? We haven't decided for sure."

"Of course. If there's any way I can help..."

"Actually, yeah." Eric flashes a wry smile. "Help get Mom on board after we break the news?"

"Get her on board with another child moving away? It'd be easier to move a glacier."

"Global warming's managing," he shouts and bounds downstairs.

I linger, kicking myself for not taking one of the ibuprofens. But halfway down the stairs, the headache vanishes as suddenly as it arrived.

By bedtime, I've forgotten all about the incident in the living room. I help Shane's middle sister tuck in her curly-haired twins. Then we sneak out while her husband reads the girls to sleep.

Downstairs, Shane and Eric are deep in an animated discussion with Victor, Clarissa's husband. I hover in the doorway. Shane usually goes to bed when I do. For once, though, he doesn't notice me. Victor's showing the others something on his phone. Shane tosses his head back, laughing harder than I've heard in weeks.

Beside him, Eric is near hysteria. "Nooo, I can never unsee this!" he moans. "Play it again."

Victor taps the screen. A high-pitched kid's voice babbles. They bust up again. I watch Shane, heart aching.

Did Eric tell him about the move yet?

It's not like we see Eric and Tyrone often. Christmas, Easter, the odd long weekend in Salt Lake City. Functionally, their move won't change our lives. But Shane's like Holly in more ways than he cares to admit. He doesn't deal well with change. He prefers safety, security. Everything and everyone where they belong. That way, if anything goes wrong, he can leap to the rescue.

I pad upstairs without saying good night. The whole family's under one roof tonight. Shane should enjoy it.

In Shane's old third-floor bedroom, I unearth my toiletry bag. When we aren't in residence, this is Frank's makeshift darkroom. Artsy self-portraits of Frank study me from the walls, some frowning, others grinning. The odor of developing chemicals lingers.

Okay, maybe the headache wasn't completely mysterious.

I exit the bedroom just as the door to Eric's old room across the hall opens. Tyrone emerges in a pajama set and the brightly colored socks Holly got us all. He starts toward the bathroom but stops when he sees me. "Ladies first."

"Oh no." I wave. "You were here before me."

"Pretty sure we tied."

When Tyrone doesn't budge, I lean against the wall. "How are you feeling? Any better?"

"Much. Like I said, wasn't a bad one." He smiles, and I hear Eric's echo. *He always says that.*

I peer at Tyrone. If the haze I glimpsed earlier is still there, I can't see it in the dark. But I'm aware of that taste again, like I licked a stack of pennies. Is it Frank's chemicals?

I must be staring, because he raises an eyebrow. "Do I have something in my teeth?"

"No, sorry." I laugh, a little breathless. "I'm a space cadet

47

today. Go on." I gesture at the bathroom. "I'm going to take forever, spare yourself."

"I'm fighting a losing battle here, aren't I?"

"If you think you can out-polite a native Utahn, then heck yeah you are, sugar." I wink, and he raises both hands.

"All right, I concede defeat." He steps into the bathroom. "Night, Lexi." He flicks on the light. *There.* It's only an instant. In the next, he shuts the bathroom door. But for a second, I could have sworn I saw the fog again, thicker than before.

"Night," I call, a beat too late, trying and failing to suppress the worried twist in my gut.

Chapter Seven

It's not Monday, but Chloe lures me to Murphy's with the promise of post-Christmas specials. "First, mulled wine to fortify us. Then, a shopping spree. Hopefully I can trade a few sponsor gifts for store credit." Chloe deposits two tote bags next to her bar stool with a resounding thud.

She's always getting free stuff in exchange for posts on her travelgram. Even more, now that she's close to a hundred thousand followers.

"What'd you get this time, bricks?"

"Close." She nudges the tote with a chunky combat boot. "Pilates weight sets. Plus some kind of all-in-one nutrient meal." She grimaces. "If I'm gonna drink my calories, it better have an ABV of at least five."

"Don't make me interrupt Mama Tanya's vacation to lecture you about nutrition."

"It was a joke!" Chloe waves her napkin in surrender. "No need to tattle. Sheesh. You're the worst big sister."

"Aren't you older than me?"

"Shh, not in front of my paycheck!" She mimes covering the tote bag's ears.

I snort. "Speaking of mama, any updates?"

"Not since the group text. That view was stunning. I've

got to ask what part of CDMX they were in; it'd make a killer background."

"Weren't you just in Mexico City?" Our drinks arrive, trailing steam. The mulling vastly improves Murphy's house red—it's hard for anything to taste bad with this much honey and cinnamon added.

She heaves a sigh. "Yeah, but none of the places I shot were off the beaten path. It's getting impossible to find destinations that a zillion other people haven't photographed to death."

"Since when did international travel become blasé?" In college, I only knew a handful of people who'd been abroad. Hell, my country count is four: USA, Mexico, Canada, and one whirlwind business trip with Shane to Ireland.

"Since the invention of long-haul budget flights?" Chloe shrugs.

A chant breaks through the general bar noise. It's busier than usual this afternoon. The Christmas decorations are still up, strands of icicle lights dripping from the ceiling. Through the front windows, this narrow strip of downtown churns with people. Families dressed in winter coats cradle armfuls of packages, either hunting sales or exchanging gifts.

The source of the chanting is a bachelorette party on the opposite side of the bar. A brunette woman in a crown stands on her seat. Her friends raise shot glasses around her tulle skirt.

Chloe elbows me. "What's her style, you think? New Year's Eve wedding, Winter Wonderland theme?"

I take another sip, pensive. The woman sways her hips to more cheers. "Nah. Definitely a destination wedding. They leave tomorrow for the Bahamas."

"Ooh, I like it." Chloe purses her lips. "Cuts her guest list in half, but she'll still get points for inviting everyone. Now them." She juts her chin at an older Asian man beside a boy who frankly doesn't look old enough to be in here. The older man holds a beer menu and talks so animatedly, his entire upper body moves.

They have the same angular chins, matching slim noses.

A strange little ache settles behind my breastbone. "It's the son's twenty-first birthday. Dad's buying his first beer."

"That's cheating." Chloe sticks out her tongue.

"What? How so?" I laugh.

"You recognized them, obviously." At my blank expression, she points again. "Andrew and his son? They live next door to me? They came to that barbecue party last summer!"

Andrew must sense our attention, because he looks up. Catching sight of Chloe, he smiles and waves. We wave back, too far away for a real greeting.

"You mean the party where you served vodka in a watermelon keg?" I ask. "You mixed me a cocktail so strong Shane had to drive me home before the food was even served. Remember?"

"Now that you mention it, that does ring a bell." She grins, unrepentant. "Well okay, Little Miss Psychic. His oldest turned twenty-one today."

I steal another glance at the pair and shake my head. "I read their body language, that's all."

"Sure, witch."

Sudden discomfort makes me squirm. I can't help but think of the other not-so-normal things I've experienced lately. I haven't told anyone. The closest I came was my almost-conversation with Shane's father.

But if anyone in Garden Vale would have advice about weird experiences, it's Chloe. And she won't judge me. She loves all things inexplicable.

"Hey, random question."

"Hold that thought." Chloe fumbles a vibrating phone from her pocket. *Marisol*, reads the screen. All the color drains from Chloe's face. "Oh, shit." She practically leaps off the stool.

"What's up?" I frown, worried. Marisol has lasted longer than anyone Chloe's dated since a bad breakup two years ago. Hopefully there's no trouble in budding paradise.

Chloe gestures me quiet and picks up. "Hey, babe. Yeah, I'm on the way. No, of course I didn't forget! It's just really loud in here, hang on…" She elbows her way toward the entrance.

I fish out my wallet, sensing imminent departure. By the time I've counted out cash for our tab—plus a holiday-spirit-sized tip—Chloe is back, breathless and flushed.

"I can't believe I forgot," she moans. "Marisol's been planning this white elephant party all week. I mixed up the days in my head…"

"You're going to a party together?" I try to keep my voice light, despite a surge of excitement. Normally Chloe doesn't meet the friends of anyone she's dating. She doesn't introduce her friends either.

"Mar's hosting. Attendance is kind of required." Chloe curses and scrubs a hand through her hair. "Do I look okay?"

"Photo-shoot ready as always," I promise. It's true. In her dark jeans, slouchy leather jacket, and off-the-shoulder top, she looks like a model.

"Sorry to drink and dash." She pulls me into a jasmine-scented hug. "Rain check on the shopping?"

"Of course."

Five minutes later, I'm on the sidewalk outside Murphy's watching the taillights of Chloe's car fade. I parked a few blocks up the road, but something makes me turn in the opposite direction.

A fat pine wreath decorates the door to Bea's Odds and

Ends. Otherwise, Bea eschews holiday decor. Her riot of plants has moved inside, probably because of the snow. Without them, the storefront looks bare. Lonely, somehow.

Granted, it's miles cleaner than Murphy's, whose windows haven't been scrubbed since the Great Recession. I shiver and pull my coat tighter.

Chloe isn't the only person in Garden Vale who might have answers...

A much older couple stroll past me, hand in hand. As they pass Odds and Ends, the wife mutters something. The man tuts sadly, as if the store were a grandson who just declared an art history major.

They are a reminder: leave this alone. Go back to my real life. *Forget about Henry.* But I've been trying to do that for days. It's no use. I wake at odd hours, unable to sleep until I've ducked under the covers to search *drug overdoses* or *predicting death.* At this point, my search history's probably been flagged by a three-letter agency.

The door to Odds and Ends jangles.

I leap aside, mentally drafting excuses. But it's not Bea. A middle-aged woman with light-brown skin gives me a pleasant smile. My brain connects the dots a second later: Cassie Jones. She bought a split-level from Tanya a while back. Nice woman—cute family, sweet dogs, a job that impressed Tanya, although I can't remember what.

And now she's coming out of Bea's with a brown paper shopping bag. "Hey there!" She beams. "Long time, no see. Merry Christmas."

"Merry Christmas!" I keep my smile plastered on until she crosses the street.

See? It's only a store. If Bea really were a witch, Cassie Jones wouldn't be caught dead shopping here. I think back to the one time I went in with Chloe. We laughed at some posters, and Chloe bought a necklace. I don't know why I'm acting so jumpy now.

You have to mourn your loss.

How did Bea know? The same way I guessed that boy's birthday at the bar? Body language?

Doesn't matter. I don't have to talk to Bea. Last time, she ignored all the customers until checkout anyway. I'll just browse. Who knows? There might be something helpful, like *Interpreting Hallucinations for Dummies.*

My breath fogs, reminding me of the haze I keep seeing around people. It gives me the final push. Head bowed, I duck inside.

The scent hits first—incense, heady and sweet, mingled with the spice of dried herbs and a hint of wax. To the left, candles burn atop a makeshift altar. Each candle flickers within a tall glass jar, beautiful paintings emblazoned on the glass. A woman with a dagger in one hand. A man wearing a crown of ivy. A Virgin Mary, hands folded in prayer.

"One minute," shouts a voice from the back.

I flinch and scan for the bookshelves.

The back of the shop is partitioned off behind a gauzy curtain. Next to the candles are crystals. Some I recognize—deep-purple amethysts and big, chunky quartz. Others I don't, like a square black rock, so matte it seems to swallow the light.

Tearing my gaze away, I weave between trails of ivy dangling from the ceiling. Glass terrariums burst with air plants and an entire wall of succulents towers on my left. They look thoughtfully arranged, which only makes the adjoining bright-red signs funnier. NO TOUCHING. YOU BREAK IT, YOU BUY IT.

In the second aisle, I nearly trip over a fat tabby. He's splayed belly up in front of—*aha*.

The books.

I've barely started to scan the spines when footsteps approach.

"Apologies again about the poinsettias, Rose. The supplier promised they'd be in by Tuesday, but—" Bea breaks off as she rounds the corner, cradling a cardboard box. "Oh. It's you."

For a moment, Bea looked almost welcoming. Now, a mask snaps over her pale face. Without another word, she sets down the box and starts unpacking figurines. I watch her unwrap a statue of a many-armed elephant-headed man, then a different Virgin Mary, this one crushing a hissing serpent.

Okay.

I should go back to browsing. Scan the books and then get out. But something about Bea's attitude irritates me. She doesn't treat everyone like this, clearly. She was nice to Cassie and whoever Rose is.

Why doesn't she like me?

I crouch to Bea's level and offer a hand. "Lexi Cole. I don't think we've properly met."

Bea glances at my hand. "I know who you are." She unwraps another statue. "Monday night specials next door."

Heat trickles up my neck. "Sure. I mean, I've seen you around too. Adorable shop, by the way. I don't think I told you that the last time I was here."

"With your influencer friend? No, you were too busy laughing at the tantric display." Bea cuts me a look. "Don't worry. Lots of people act like teenagers about sex."

Be nice, I remind myself. But my ingrained politeness takes longer to summon than usual. "I apologize if I offended you."

"You couldn't possibly." She places the last statue and fishes one final item from the box. A romance novel, of all things, complete with a half-naked Scottish Highlander on the cover. Then she heads over to a settee, pointedly ignoring me.

Most Main Street shop owners fawn over customers, upselling until they're blue in the face. I knew Bea wasn't like that, but this is worse than I remembered.

I hover, not sure what to do. Keep browsing? Leave? Ask why she hates me?

Bea turns a page. Sighs loudly. "If you're having trouble sleeping, try the lavender and chamomile blend. Couple of drops in a diffuser before bed." She waves at an essential oil display without looking.

I resist the urge to check my reflection in the nearest decorative mirror. *How does she know I'm not sleeping?* Then again, makeup only goes so far when the bags under your eyes have carry-on luggage of their own. "That's not why I'm here."

Bea adjusts her cat's-eye reading glasses. In the pleasant yellow glow of the store, she appears to be in her late fifties at most. Her hair is in a top knot, gray streaks sparkling like highlights amid her curls. The only real signs of age are her crow's-feet and what seem like laugh lines around her mouth.

That can't be right. Frown lines, maybe.

"Whatever you need, I have a website. You could've saved yourself the trip. And the embarrassment."

My cheeks go hot. "If you treat all your customers like this, no wonder your store is always empty," I snap before I can stop myself.

To my confusion, Bea finally looks up. And *grins.* "Good. You're not a complete pushover."

I gape as she snaps the book shut and surges to her feet. "Excuse me?"

"Let me guess." Bea approaches, and I tense. But she just picks up a nearby watering can and crosses to a hidden sink near the succulent wall. "You're a Libra. Probably some Aquarius in your chart. The moon sign?"

"Oh, no, that's..." This is exactly what I wanted to avoid. If Shane heard me talking about this, he would drag me bodily into therapy. "I don't believe in that stuff. Astrology and all."

Bea shrugs. "Some people don't believe in Australia. Does that make it any less real?"

I laugh. When she doesn't join me, I sober. "That's different. That's a physical, provable fact."

"Now we can prove the earth is round, yes. We couldn't always. What's science for, if not to expand our understanding? Explain the heretofore unexplainable." She finishes filling the can and sets about watering a row of snake plants.

"But you're talking about astrology, not science."

"Who says they're mutually exclusive?"

"Pretty sure science would." I shake my head. We're getting off track. "Look, I only came in here because..." *Because what?* Because I thought she'd have answers about whatever's wrong with my head?

Bea pauses midwatering. Waits.

All at once, I feel ridiculous. What am I doing? She's a grumpy shopkeeper, not some wise woman. This was a mistake. "Never mind. I should—"

She cuts me off. "What did you see?"

For the first time since I stepped inside, I have Beatrix O'Neill's full attention. Immediately, I wish I didn't. Up close, those dark eyes are far too perceptive.

"It must have been intense," she says softly. "To bring someone like you into my store."

I bristle. "You don't know the first thing about me."

She arches a brow. "So you don't mind if people see you talking to Batty Bea?"

Shit. I didn't think she heard that. "I'm sorry. That was a bad joke. My friends and I, we sometimes—"

Bea gestures dismissively. "I've heard worse. Your friend resents me because she treats spirituality like a fad diet."

"It's her life," I say, defensive.

"That it is. So go on. You were telling me what brought you in."

I don't know why. Maybe because Bea mentioned astrological signs the way other people discuss the weather. Or maybe because there's no past between us, no relationship to preserve. Sometimes, the better people know me, the harder it is for me to open up.

Whatever the reason, I open my mouth and the whole story spills out. Henry, the gala, Tyrone, even Chloe's neighbors in the bar just now. All the things I'm too embarrassed to tell my husband, I share with a complete stranger.

It's a relief to voice it. But by the time I finish, my cheeks are burning. Bea still hasn't said a word. "I know, it's ridiculous. I'm probably imagining things, overreacting."

"You don't seem the type to overreact."

Without warning, my eyes sting. Horrified, I bury my face in my palms. "Sorry, I–I don't…"

Something wooden scrapes along the floor. Then Bea grips my shoulder. "Sit." She presses me down onto a plush chair. I rest my elbows on my knees, cradling my forehead, and gulp shuddering breaths.

Bea waits until my breathing slows. "You're waking up."

I lift my head. My eyes still ache, but my cheeks are dry. At least I didn't make a complete fool of myself. "You believe me?" I hate how pathetic I sound.

Bea looks like she's battling a smile. "I went through something similar. How old are you, twenty-seven, twenty-eight?"

"Twenty-nine. What's that got to do with anything?" Besides the big 3–0, approaching like a car crash you see coming yet can't avoid.

Bea pulls a poster off the wall. The image reminds me of a protractor: a sectioned circle, numbered in twelve quadrants. A key next to it lists unfamiliar symbols, and colored lines bisect the chart, connecting some symbols to others.

"It's called the Saturn return." Bea taps a cross-like symbol with a squiggly tail. "It's different for everyone, but sometime between the ages of twenty-seven and thirty-four, Saturn returns to the same position in the sky as when you were born. Saturn governs responsibility and duty, as well as facing your fears. Death and rebirth."

Death. Despite the warmth of Bea's shop, goose bumps rise on my forearms. "So, what, Saturn's a planet-sized reminder that we all die someday?"

She laughs. "Maybe. Is that your biggest fear? Death?"

"Isn't it everyone's?"

"I can think of worse things." Bea traces the Saturn symbol's orbit. "Saturn disrupts the status quo. Makes you rethink your life, whether you're on the right path. It's a chance for your nature—the way you were born, back before life got its claws in you—to reassert itself."

"Sounds like a quarter-life crisis."

"If that's what the kids are calling it these days."

Right before going up onstage at the gala, I remember wondering if my life plan no longer worked. But doesn't everyone feel that way now and then? "Okay, say for some reason I believed a planet millions of miles away could influence my life. What does a quarter-life crisis have to do with..." I wiggle both hands in my best imitation of the haze. "The stuff I keep seeing." *Or hearing. Or tasting.*

"When we're born, we haven't been influenced by the

world yet. By other people's opinions, our own experiences, or biases or fears we learn along the way. We're wide open, able to absorb everything—not just physical reality, but the energetic world too. Saturn returns us to that natural state, meaning it reawakens the energetic abilities we're all born with but that most people forget as we age."

I want to point out the gazillion scientific flaws in this explanation, yet something stops me. Not belief—what Bea's saying is pretty out there, even for Chloe. It's just…it sounds familiar. Like a story I heard as a child but forgot until today.

"When you say 'energetic abilities,' you mean…?"

"Perceiving and influencing energy. Our own, or other people's." At my blank stare, Bea reaches for the chart again. She flips it over and grabs a pen from the register. "Every living thing has a physical body and an energetic body." She draws a stick figure. "Our auric field is the energetic body. It extends beyond our physical one." She sketches a series of concentric circles extending from the stick figure. "We're all made of energy, powered by it. When you're healthy, your energy flows around you." She adds a series of arrows up through the stick figure, out the crown of its head, then circling back to the ground. The loop reminds me of the water cycle drawings we made in school. Lakes evaporating to clouds, clouds raining to earth.

At the gala, I could barely make out Henry's face through a dark haze. *His auric field?*

"If someone is physically or spiritually afflicted, their auric field will appear cloudy. Sometimes you'll see blocks that disrupt the flow." Bea adds scribbles around the stick figure.

My heart rises into my throat.

I don't believe what she's saying. But she's drawing exactly what I saw. The marks in the air around Henry, and Tyrone too. "Once you have a…a block. Can you fix it?" My voice goes tight, remembering the woman's voice. *Save him.* "Could I have helped?"

For the first time today, Bea no longer looks imperious, annoyed, or even amused. Just sad. "Possibly. But it takes a lot of practice to heal another person. And although healers provide a helping hand, at the end of the day, the only person who can fix you is you."

You. Something inside of me flinches. She thinks I need help.

Don't you? hisses a familiar voice. For a second, I'm in the Coles' backyard again, phone digging into my ear, my mother spitting on the other end.

That's not why I'm here. I came to figure out what happened to Henry. I came because of Tyrone. Because I can't bear standing by while something bad happens again. Right now, life feels strange and wrong-sized, so even though none of this makes sense, my gut screams at me to stay.

When was the last time I listened to my gut?

"I want to help. I want to learn about this stuff in case it happens again."

"I can teach you," Bea says, and my heart leaps. "But you won't like it."

"How would you know?"

"You were so embarrassed you could barely walk in here. What happens when people find out you're studying with me?"

Oh.

I wish I could say I was only concerned about my coworkers' reactions, or people like that old couple on the street. Really, I'm thinking of Shane. Of the first time he kissed me, beneath the big campus maple gone red for autumn. I knew it was coming, had shut my eyes in anticipation. He skipped right past my mouth and buried his face in the crook of my neck. "You are such a relief," he whispered.

My laugh came out low, unintentionally sultry. "How so?"

"You think like me." His lips blazed a trail along my carotid artery. "I thought I was the only one."

I swallow around an unexpected lump. Shane would not like me being here. He'd say it was fine, but it wouldn't be. Not really. "We could keep it a secret," I say.

Bea rolls her eyes.

Fair. Out loud, the suggestion does not sound quite as mature as I thought. "Sorry, that came out wrong. Or, not wrong, but… It's just, my husband is super practical. Salt-of-the-earth type. He doesn't trust religion."

"So? Neither do I."

Is there a polite way to say, *My husband would think you're a scam artist?*

Bea takes pity on me. "If you want to bend over backward hiding things, that's up to you. But training requires time and effort. It's hard work. Can you handle that?"

Clearly she hasn't met me. Effort is my middle name. And a new challenge is just what I've been craving. I need to funnel my energy into something besides my husband, my dwindling job satisfaction, *half a dozen plastic sticks with no plus signs.*

If there's a way to study what's happening to me, to master it, then I'll do whatever it takes. And if nothing else happens? At least I'll know it was all in my head. Either way…

"I want to try." My pulse flutters. I'm not even sure what I'm agreeing to, just that I can't walk away now.

Bea continues to look dubious, but she reaches for a calendar. It depicts a series of moons: black circles that crescendo into white globes, then shrink again. Beneath each one is a date, although the calendar doesn't begin on January first.

Some countries and religions follow the lunar calendar. I wonder if Bea's faith does. Or…does she have one? She said she doesn't trust religion.

"Sleep on it," she says. "If you really want to do this—for yourself, not to appease me or anybody else—meet me at Dallen's Creek trail next Tuesday. Midnight, on the new moon." She touches the image of a pitch-black moon. "You know where the east meadows are? Past the trailhead, before you get to Valleybrook Lake."

"Sure." Shane and I have been hiking at Dallen's Creek plenty of times. Though never at night. "Why there?"

"Because I have other business besides teaching half-hearted rookies." With that, Bea plucks her romance novel from the counter and resumes reading. From this angle, the kilted Highlander smolders right at me.

Was that a dismissal?

Bea plops onto a pouf and turns a page.

Guess so.

I pull out my phone, add a note to the calendar. Tuesday at midnight. Already, my logical brain regrets this. *I'll give it one lesson.* Just to see if there's anything to it. Most likely, Bea is feeding me superstitions. Once I'm sure, I'll quit.

Before Shane gets suspicious.

I start toward the exit. The fat tabby rolls into my path and bats my ankle. I crouch to pet him, allergies be damned. Behind me, cloth rustles. When I turn, Bea's watching me over the top of the book.

"Bring something from childhood when you come."

When. Not if. The minor vote of confidence raises my spirits. But... Something from childhood? It's like Bea guessed the most difficult item she could ask me for.

You can still back out.

But I know myself too well. I love a challenge. And Beatrix O'Neill is the biggest one I've met.

Chapter Eight

Shane's in the middle of a story about the guys at the station, but I've lost the plot. Instead, I study the kitchen. Our favorite room in the house, it's a carefully negotiated combination of our tastes. Open plan for Shane, with ultramodern appliances and a high ceiling. We threw in old-fashioned oak cabinets and matching wooden ceiling beams for me, plus a decorative fireplace. I wanted the real deal, but Shane refuses to allow open flames inside the house. Even the cooktop is induction.

Given everything he's seen, I get it.

Normally, our dinners feel cozy. Tonight, lingering oven heat thickens the air. The oak cabinets I insisted on loom like trick walls in a Halloween house. I imagine them sliding inward, the ceiling lowering to crush us.

"So Brian's up on the roof, can of tuna in hand, when the woman yells that she found the cat. Of course we're all thinking, *What's Brian's feeding, then?* Now, keep in mind he wasn't wearing his glasses…"

Condensation drips down my untouched glass of white wine. I force myself to take a sip. Ugh. So sweet. And I've only managed three bites of my tagliatelle. I pick up my fork, spear another piece. "What was on the roof?"

Shane's been waiting for his cue. He grabs his phone and brandishes grainy footage: his friend Brian shaking a can of tuna. The video zooms in on a furry lump near his feet. Striped tail, big gray bristles.

"Here, kitty, kitty," Brian coos at the raccoon. The camera quivers with Shane's repressed laughter.

"Please tell me you warned him."

"Eventually." Shane smiles, boyish.

Dual impulses seize me. I want to hug him, coddle him, protect him from the world. At the same time, I also want to shake him. *We aren't kids anymore. We have to grow up.*

But my current mood is not Shane's fault. I swallow another bite of pasta and try to ignore the ringing in my ears.

"How about your day?" His gaze lingers on my almost-untouched wine. The hope on his face is unbearable.

I can't bring myself to look at him directly. "It was fine." Last time, our first clue was my nausea, even before the missed period. So I scoop a bigger forkful. The pasta sticks to the roof of my mouth, but at least it saves me from speaking.

"Anything exciting?"

I volunteered to hang out with a witch? "Not really. Oh, Chloe's still dating that girl, Marisol. Seems like it's getting serious. And Tanya's back from their trip. Looked incredible."

"What about you?"

"Well, I'm not in Mexico," I joke.

His eyebrows contract. "Are you still feeling the way you mentioned before Christmas? Unhappy?"

"I never said that."

"Okay, sorry, not unhappy. But you said you were bored, and ever since we got back from my parents' house, it's like something's hanging over you. I can't help you if I don't know what's going on."

I nudge pasta around my plate. "What if it's not the kind of thing you can help with?"

"At least let me try."

What did I tell Bea? *I want to try.* The words are on the tip of my tongue. The same explanation I fumbled through in Bea's shop. *I saw something. The night Henry Jensen died.*

Scooping up my wine, I drown the temptation. Telling Shane would be selfish. He's already worried; he'd straight-up panic if he knew I heard a disembodied voice. Plus, it only happened once. Until I have a better handle on what's happening—until I can explain everything rationally—he'll be happier in the dark.

We put truth on a pedestal. But so often growing up, I wished my mother had cared enough to lie.

"Dunno. I guess Mom got under my skin worse than usual." *You can't spend your whole life obsessing. When are you going to get over this?*

As if it's that easy. As if she lifted a pinkie to stop it.

"What did she want?"

I twirl the stem of my wineglass. The remaining amber liquid swirls. "What else? She wants me to come home."

"I don't get it. She knows why you refuse to visit. How can she not understand? You're her daughter."

My hand twitches. I push the wineglass away. "She says I should be over it by now. She thinks I'm obsessing."

He goes quiet for a moment. "Are you?"

Do you really think I'm that breakable? "Of course not. I just refuse to set foot in that house." Picking up my plate, I head for the sink. It's easier to talk when my hands are busy.

Accustomed to my habits, Shane collects cooking utensils and meets me at the double basin. "If you don't want to go back, don't."

"It's not about wanting to." I soap a sponge and scrub

crusty red sludge from the saucepan. Tomatoes taste so delicious, yet smell so disgusting when you have to clean them up.

Shane braces his forearms against the counter. "Would you go? If not for, y'know, what happened?"

"In an alternate reality where I had a peachy keen childhood, sure, probably. In this one..." I hold out the clean saucepan and shrug. "I'm the terrible daughter."

He accepts the pan and hunts for a dish towel. "Well, if you decide to go home, it should be on your terms. Not because she's guilting you."

"It's not even about the guilt trips. I just want her to *acknowledge* it. She never takes responsibility. It's all about how she feels, what she wants, her opinion. We were the kids, you know? It wasn't our job to manage the adults."

"No. It wasn't."

I groan. "Maybe she's got a point, though. Every time she calls, I replay our conversations over and over. It is a bit obsessive. Most people don't fight with their parents this much, either."

He laughs. "Trust me, I fought mine plenty when I was in high school."

"Oh yeah?" I offer him the next plate. "Please, describe high-school-era Shane. Starting with the hairdo, because I've seen photos and it requires an explanation."

He flicks water at me. "Pictures cannot capture the true glory of the frosted tips."

Pulling a face, I towel off my shirt. Shane's voice relaxes me, the cadence as familiar as the stories he tells: the time Frank caught him out past curfew and took the tires off his car, the homecoming dance he missed because Holly found condoms in his backpack. (She didn't believe he got them from sex ed class.)

"Our worst fights were about church, of course," he says as we reach the last plate. "Mom thought I'd suffer without religion. I thought she was suffering more because of it."

"How did you resolve that?"

"We didn't." His gaze drifts to the window. Something must have moved in the yard, because the motion sensors come on, illuminating a patchwork quilt: white snow and brown mud. "We stopped talking about it."

"And...are you okay with that?"

The motion lights snap off again. He shrugs. "My point was, I get stuck on parental stuff too. It's normal."

"That or we're both weirdos." I smile, glad now that I didn't bring up Henry or the stuff with Bea.

Shane snags my waist and I let him draw me close. My shirt, still damp where he flicked water at me, sticks to my abdomen. Through it, I feel the press of his thigh, the hard clip of his buckle. My breath quickens. I long to sink into our bodies, out of my head. But Shane pauses, mouth an inch from communion. "I'm good with weird. As long as you and I are the same."

He kisses me, slow and sweet. But after that, his every touch carries a static aftershock of guilt. Because I'm no longer sure we are.

Chapter Nine

I've hiked here a dozen times, but never at night. The parking lot is pitch-dark—they must turn off the streetlights once the trails close. One step out of the car and I'm already shivering. Hopefully the hike will warm me up.

The lot is half a mile from Valleybrook Lake, overshadowed by pine trees. What Bea called the "east meadows" must be the big field right before the peak.

Luckily, we keep a flashlight in the car—along with a blanket, granola bars, and a hammer. The roads on the outskirts do get treacherous in winter, but between Shane's emergency experience and my anxiety, we probably overprepare.

Flashlight in hand, I cross the lot. It's deserted save for one other car, a beat-up sedan with a Coexist bumper sticker. Gotta be Bea's. It looks even older than her.

Snowy gravel crunches underfoot. My breath fogs. At the transition from parking lot to trail, I pause. The sun melted the snow earlier, but nightfall has frozen it once more, leaving me to tiptoe over slicks of black ice.

It's peaceful, though. This far up in the mountains, there's a hush. Just me and the pines.

My heart rate picks up. I'm accustomed to altitude—I was born higher than this—but it always takes a few minutes to reacclimate. At the crest of the first hill, the pine trees abruptly end. The world opens all at once, like a stage with its curtain torn away.

In summer, this whole expanse would be vibrant green. In fall, blue and yellow wildflowers dot the green.

Tonight, it is sheer, glistening white. Beyond the field looms the mountain, glacier nuzzling its side, lake curled at its feet. In the dark, it is only visible as a jagged absence of stars.

So many stars.

For a moment, I tip my head back and savor the view.

Freshman year of college, I planned to major in stars. I wanted to study astrophysics, had imagined myself in a lab coat puzzling over dark matter and black holes. But college physics was a lot harder than high school. It didn't help that every time I called home, my mother seeded more doubt.

How much money do stargazers make? Be practical, Lexi.

Plus, I was one of only two girls in class. The idea sounded cool and groundbreaking, until I was actually there. Eyes tracked me to my seat every morning. I started wearing baggy pants, shapeless hoodies. One afternoon before my father left replayed in the back of my mind: I was sprawled on the living room couch, ten years old, nose buried in the type of science-fiction novel I'd eventually grow embarrassed to like. My father glanced at the spaceship-riddled cover and sighed.

You're so smart. Life would be easier if you weren't.

Funny. I haven't thought about that since I switched majors.

I squint toward the east. On the far side of the white expanse stands a figure. Backlit by stars, Bea seems more sketch than person.

My boots crunch in the snow as I approach.

She must hear me coming—the only other sounds are the occasional hoot of owls and the crackle of glacial ice settling. But she doesn't look up.

Nearing her, I slow down, not wanting to interrupt.

She's cleared out a perfect circle of snow. Inside it, she stands on brown grass pockmarked by unlucky wildflowers frozen on their stems. Slowly, she extends her arms skyward.

Is she meditating? Casting a spell?

Without warning, Bea folds in half and slams both palms against the earth. She pushes up halfway, her mouth wide, tongue splayed. Finally, she rolls upright and opens her eyes.

"Knew you'd come," she says, as if I didn't walk in on her mid-...whatever that was.

"I didn't," I admit. In her store the other day, this seemed simple: I wanted answers, and Bea might have them.

Binging reality TV with Shane this weekend, it felt less cut-and-dry. Was meeting Bea really worth the risk? Shane would be upset. And if there is something to all this—the Saturn return, auric fields—do I want to know? Am I pulling a Pandora, tempted by knowledge I'll wish I could unlearn?

And yet...

Saturn returns us to our natural state. Makes you rethink your life.

Bea's explanation struck a chord. It was enough to make me invent a late-night catch-up with Tanya, then drive all the way out here to meet a witch on a mountain in the dead of night.

The witch smiles. "Second-guessing yourself is a good sign. It means you're taking this seriously. That's step one."

I hug my torso. "What's step two?"

She sits and pats the frozen ground. "Step two is keeping an open mind. Can you manage that, Ms. Let's Keep This a Secret?"

I'd blush if it weren't so cold. Stepping out of the snow-bank, I drop to the grass beside her. Good thing I wore long johns under my jeans. Damp soaks through the outer layer immediately. "I can try."

"All I ask." Bea slaps her thighs. "Okay, so, starting with the basics. How much do you know about the elements?"

"You mean the periodic table? Or, like, the *Fifth Element* kind?"

Bea's mouth twists in amusement. "Actually, that's not far off. Fiction reflects reality." She gestures at the sky. "There are five basic elements that underlie everything in the known universe. All you see up there, as well as everything down here. Humans included."

Following her gaze, I spy a perfect dark circle: the new moon, suspended in earth's shadow.

"Each of us has a different mix of elements. The pro-portions affect our personality. For example, take air—our breath, our mind, our ideas." Bea exhales a stream of fog. "People with a lot of air tend to be good communicators and creative thinkers."

She waits for me to nod, then slaps the ground again. "Then there's earth: our roots and daily routines. Where we come from, how we plan our future. Earthy people are grounded and practical."

I think of Shane.

Meanwhile, Bea scoops up a handful of snow. "Water powers our subconscious. Emotion and compassion, dreams and imagination. A great listener who's in touch with their emotions probably has a lot of water in their constitution."

Except, that also sounds like Shane. "These are all so general." I wave a hand. "Let me guess. Fire's next?"

Bea side-eyes me. "There's a reason it sounds familiar." She digs through her satchel for a lighter. "This knowledge lives in our collective subconscious. Once you start looking, it shows up everywhere. In nature, in mythology, in art…these elements underlie the stories we create and the ways we define ourselves."

The lighter sparks. Flickers. She cups a palm to shield it from the wind. As the flame grows, it casts shadows into the hollows of her cheeks. "The fourth element, fire, is action. Willpower, drive, inspiration. It's what gets us out of bed in the morning and what powers our body throughout the day. People with a lot of fire are highly motivated, passionate leaders."

She lets her hand fall. The flame winks out.

Behind my eyelids, its afterimage lingers. "You said five."

"The fifth one is less tangible." Bea touches her chest. "Aether. It's the combination of the other elements. It creates your spirit or higher self. It's what makes you greater than the sum of your parts."

"Basically your soul."

"Some people call it that, yes."

My hand drifts over my heart too. "You say five elements make up everything. But scientifically—"

"Science divides those five into smaller component elements." Bea nods. "That's more useful for studying the material world. But we're not here to study your physical body. We're here to learn about your spiritual self. Who she is, how she connects to the universe."

"Okay." I rock on my sit bones, not entirely convinced.

Bea doesn't seem to mind. She speaks like she's had this conversation a million times. Her confidence reminds me of Holly or Tanya, both so sure of their faith.

Sometimes I envy them. *How do they know?* Late at night, alone with their brains, what convinces them? Maybe they have an extra sense I'm missing. Maybe they feel it— whatever it is—in a way I don't.

"Aether will come in its own time," Bea says. "The other

73

four I can coach you through accessing. But first, I need to determine your elemental constitution—how much of each element you have. It determines what you like and dislike, your strengths and weaknesses." She sizes me up.

I frown. "But people have so many strengths or weaknesses. And there are so many different personalities. We don't all fit into four boxes."

"Of course not. Nobody's entirely one element or another. A politician could have a lot of air and fire, or a nurse might have both earth and water. Some people have an equal balance of all four."

Not me, I think.

Bea's smile widens, almost like she heard me. "I'm going to tap into your energy field. Do I have your permission?" She watches me expectantly until I nod. "Good. Sit still, okay?"

Easier said than done. Suddenly I'm remembering the sensory-deprivation tank Chloe once dragged me and Tanya to. Forty-five minutes of torture, locked inside a hot salt bath. Every time I tried to relax, a new itch started. By the time the aide let us out, I was convinced I was allergic to salt water.

Bea settles in. Her breath slows until her chest barely seems to move.

The cold ground seeps through my long johns. I reposition. Immediately, my nose itches. I scratch it quickly, then plant my palms against my thighs, determined not to move again. Except, the heavier my body grows, the more aware I am of the cold. And of a hard protrusion under my butt. Rock? Root?

I shift as little as possible, so Bea won't notice.

Bea. Her eyes are open, unblinking. She doesn't seem entirely here anymore. As if her mind has shuffled away, left her body behind.

I'm tempted to check her pulse. She wouldn't still be upright if something went wrong. Right?

My nose itches again. I slide my hands beneath my thighs instead. This is why I quit yoga. Doing the flows was fun. But afterward, lying on the mat, I could never stop fidgeting.

Finally, after what feels like eternity, Bea returns. She doesn't move, so I'm not sure how I know. Her body just seems fuller, all of a sudden. A light switches on in her eyes again.

It makes me uncomfortably aware of the tenuous connection between mind and body.

Bea massages the back of her neck, head bobbing. "You have a lot of fire. You thrive under pressure—you probably sought out a fast-paced job because you found it rewarding. But you need to feel passionate about your work. Lately, that hasn't been the case."

I try not to let my surprise show. But that must be an easy guess—most people are dissatisfied at work.

"You also have a decent amount of air," Bea murmurs. "You're prone to overthinking and anxiety. You get stuck in your head, second-guess yourself all the time..."

Don't all women?

"But you're curious. That's why you came tonight. You still don't know if you believe what you experienced, but your mind is open to change. That's rare, you know. Most people have already decided what they believe. They stick to their worldview regardless of conflicting evidence. Not you."

That one hits a little too close to home. "Great. So the indecisiveness is a feature."

Bea shakes her head. "Flexibility. And it's not a weakness, Lexi. It's one of your biggest strengths." I open my mouth

75

to argue, but she clicks her tongue. "We're not passing judgment. We're just getting to know you better."

"I thought this was about learning to help other people. Why the focus on me?"

"Physician, heal thyself." Bea taps her temple. "You need to understand your own energy before you can even think about meddling in other people's."

Makes sense. Still, it's hard to fight my rising anxiety. I don't want to poke around in my own head, let alone allow Bea inside. But I've come this far. And she's right, I am curious. I want to know if there's more to the world.

"We should start with air. I'm sensing a block, but it seems minor. Since air is your primary element, it should be easy to work through."

There's no one else here, I remind myself. And Bea's a low-risk person to act weird around. However strange I am, Bea is unabashedly ten times odder. If it gets too much, I can always leave. "Okay."

Bea holds out a hand. "Did you bring something from childhood?"

There weren't a lot of options. I escaped my childhood home for college with only two suitcases, eager for a fresh start. Once it became clear I was volunteering during summer and winter breaks to avoid visiting, my mother sent photos of the things I'd left behind: stuffed animals, old outfits, baby toys. *Come get your crap or I'm tossing it.*

I told her to throw everything away.

But after a long search, I found one object that survived my transition to college, and the next move from college to Garden Vale. Every time I come across the shiny, gold-colored penny at the bottom of my change drawer, I consider tossing it, but something always stops me.

"We made them in middle school science class," I explain.

The experiment was a simple chemical reaction: add zinc to copper. At the time, the result seemed like pure magic. "Is... this the right kind of thing?"

"It's not about right or wrong. If the penny has meaning for you, that's what matters." She points. "Lie back and hold it in your hand."

Bracing myself, I lie flat, knees bent. Thankfully, my jacket insulates my torso, so it's not as cold as I expected.

"I'm going to walk you through a light meditation. A block is a snag in your energy field—it's not dangerous, but your energy will flow better once it's removed. You may feel a sensation around your throat or in your head while we work."

I remember the stabbing headache at Christmas and my whole body tenses.

Bea touches my shoulders. "Relax." She pushes me to the earth. "This won't hurt. But if you get uncomfortable, raise a hand or sit up, and we'll stop. How does that sound?"

"Okay." Forcing myself to swallow, I look past Bea at the sky. For a second, the enormity dizzies me. I imagine floating up and off this fragile planet.

"You're in your head. I need you here, in the present. Close your eyes."

I squeeze them shut.

"Relax," she admonishes again. "And breathe."

Cold air tickles my nose.

"That's it. Feel the ground beneath you."

A rock digs into my shoulder, another at my hip.

"Don't fight it. Melt into the sensation."

I become aware of my hands, pressed against my stomach. Of the penny growing warm in my palm. My breath shushes, in and out. After a while, the sound morphs into ocean waves.

"Breathe in," Bea murmurs. "And out. Feel yourself growing heavier."

I can still feel the rocks. But the longer I lie still, the more my body molds around them. My skin and bones conform to the planes and divots of the earth.

Behind my eyelids, the world is dark.

"In and out... In and out..."

Bea's voice becomes a rhythm, a mantra. Aside from my own breath, she's all I hear. I lose track of time. Space. I don't feel the rocks anymore. I'm barely aware of having a body at all. Only the breath remains.

"Now, I want you to move backward. Think about the memory you formed with this object."

The penny burns like a tiny sun against my skin. Middle school. What class was it? Science...

I picture the building. Redbrick exterior, linoleum floors. Narrow hallways, my old locker. The science classroom with its wide black desks and metal stools, a burner at each station.

"Don't just visualize. Smell it, taste it. Engage all your senses."

Formaldehyde tickles my nostrils. The fluorescent lights make the backs of my eyelids throb.

"Be there."

I sit at my usual desk. The metal stool is cold, hard. I wriggle, unable to get comfortable.

"How do you feel?"

Happy. But why? About what?

"Don't question. Experience it."

I twist the stool side to side. *I'm happy.*

"Remember why you chose this memory."

*I'm happy because...*MaryBeth is my lab partner. She's the most popular girl in our class. I've admired her since grade school. I studied her in the cafeteria, trying to figure out how she fits in so effortlessly, when for me it's a constant struggle. I'm always saying the wrong thing, laughing when no one else does, and not understanding jokes that come easy to everyone else.

If I could just be MaryBeth's friend, this would all get easier. Now we're lab partners. I have a whole year to make it happen.

Every day, I stride into class, confident that today I'll start a conversation. And every day, MaryBeth spends the whole hour texting friends underneath her desk, while I wonder what it must be like to have friends so close they text you again minutes after you wave goodbye.

Or what it would be like to have friends, period.

I had one friend in elementary school: Katelyn, who lived two doors down. Our parents carpooled us to school and we spent summers half-naked in sprinklers. But when middle school started, she joined the soccer team. Her teammates warned her I was weird. They said if she kept hanging out with me, people would think she was weird too.

To her credit, she told me this verbatim. *It's nothing personal. You'd do the same in my shoes.*

Maybe she's right. Maybe I would have.

At lunch, I sit with a group on the outskirts of the cafeteria, but none of us are really friends. The only thing we have in common is that we don't fit in anywhere else. Our lunchtime conversations alternately bore and confuse me.

Still, I keep sitting there. What am I going to do, eat alone?

"Stay in this memory," someone says. She sounds old and far away. "Ground yourself."

I touch the smooth surface of the lab table. I hear another voice, a man. Faint and underwater-sounding. Looking up, I watch a blurry man in a lab coat draw on the board. My science teacher.

That's right. It's the penny experiment today.

For once, even MaryBeth is paying attention. "I hear this is the coolest one all year," she whispers. The teacher keeps writing, but I'm not looking at him anymore.

She's talking to me. It's happening. "I heard that too," I murmur, even though I didn't. One little white lie and voilà: we have something in common.

We get our supplies, set up the zinc solution to soak the pennies.

"I like your shoes," I tell her, emboldened.

"Thanks." She grins. "I like your backpack. I've been meaning to tell you."

It's bright red. What I don't tell her is that I badgered my mother into buying it because MaryBeth had a red one last year. This year, hers is black. I've been kicking myself ever since. Right up until now.

At last, the floodgates unlock.

We start talking—really talking. About clothes, then bands, then boys. I agree with everything she says. Who am I to argue with the class tastemaker? Eventually, our pennies are silver all over with zinc. Time for the best part.

MaryBeth doesn't like using the burner—it freaks her out—so I offer to do it.

I take the tongs, hold the penny over the flame. We both gasp, even though we know what's coming. In a blink, silvery zinc transmutes to brilliant gold.

It's not real gold. Our teacher explained that at length. Still, we are transfixed. I drop the penny into a glass of water to cool. It sparkles all the way down.

"You could start a jewelry company, making these," MaryBeth says. "I'd buy a necklace of them."

"Let's do it," I declare, brave from basking in the glow of a middle school legend. "Together."

The moment the words are out, my whole body goes hot. I've moved too fast, missed a step. I always do. *She doesn't want to hang out with you; she's just being nice because you're stuck in this class together.*

But MaryBeth laughs. "Deal." She passes me the glass, penny within. "You keep this one. Put it toward our stockpile of future supplies."

I practically float home, high on success.

For a few glorious weeks, it holds. MaryBeth and I whisper through every class. She doesn't bother to text her friends. Or if she does, she shows me the phone and whisper-complains about whoever's on the other end. Other girls, mostly. Occasionally a boy texts, and she asks if I think he's cute.

I know enough to say, *Yes, but he's not my type.*

Her life seems so full. I don't text anyone but my parents and, even then, only when obligated. It's so nice to be included. For once, I'm not on the outside gazing in.

It doesn't last. Of course not. And as usual, I'm the one who screws it up. I approach MaryBeth in the lunchroom, ignoring the stunned expressions on my usual lunch mates' faces.

"Could I sit with you?" I ask. It doesn't seem strange to me. We've shared so much. Stories, crushes, daydreams, gossip. Why not lunch?

The rest of her friends all look up at once, a startled flock of birds. Then the laughter starts. MaryBeth turns bright red.

I've messed up again. Why can't I be normal? Everyone else understands how this works. They know what to say, and when, and how. They weave delicate friendships while I blunder through, wrecking everything.

"Don't be a freak," MaryBeth finally replies. She has to. Her friends are bordering on hysteria. "Of course not."

I drag myself away from her table, excruciatingly slowly, even as my mind yells at me to run, *get out of there.*

"Deep breaths," someone is saying. "Ease out of it, Lexi." Bea, that's right. "Come back to your body slowly."

She sounds so calm. It infuriates me. *How can she be calm right now?*

I bolt upright, gasping. There's not enough oxygen in my lungs; my heart races. The penny—that stupid fucking penny, why did I save it?—feels white-hot. *Fuck this.* I throw it as hard as I can. It hits the snow without a sound. Completely unsatisfying.

"Lexi." Bea reaches for my arm. "What you're experiencing is normal. You hit the block we're trying to release. That's a good step. It's unpleasant, but only because you haven't processed it yet."

I surge to my feet. My hands shake. "I can't do this."

It's not just MaryBeth's rejection. It was the entire school's rejection. Katelyn before her, so many attempted friendships after. It was middle school rumors that followed me to high school, because in our tiny town, there were no do-overs. The weird kid from middle school morphed into the shy, awkward high schooler. By then, the rumors had grown teeth.

I hear her dad ran off with a stripper.

My mom says her mom's got anger issues.

Her brother's a stoner. What about her? Gotta be something.

Crazy's genetic.

It was more than one incident. It was everything, my whole life, not having any real friends until I went to college. It was living in the same small town with the same small people, unable to escape. Someone decided I was weird before I was even old enough to understand the word, and that was it.

I thought by now, as a grown-ass woman, I'd figured out how to fake normal. But look where I am. I followed the town outcast to a mountain like she's some sort of guru. What am I doing? If my friends see me here; if anyone sees me...

"Lexi, you need to ground yourself." Bea doesn't sound reassuring anymore. She's nothing but a sullen old lady, messing with people's heads.

I have an ugly urge to tell Bea everyone in town is right. But the politeness gene kicks in at the last second and saves me from acting as bad as MaryBeth. All I say is, "This was a mistake."

Then I sprint out of the circle, surging through snow-drifts. My last glimpse of Bea, she's no longer smiling or even annoyed. It's worse, because I recognize that look. I've been on the receiving end too many times.

She pities me.

Chapter Ten

The next morning is my first day back at the office. Adjusting from the vacation temporal shift is hard enough without spending half the night before on a mountain. Even after crawling into bed beside Shane, middle school memories kept jolting me awake, my chest heaving.

Gonna be one of those days.

My desk is buried in a sea of paper. Contracts, invoices. Above it all, someone stuck a Post-it: *Email system down.*

I need coffee.

In the break room, I brew a double espresso and try to focus on the positives. At least I don't have to think about MaryBeth or any of that bullshit again. I was curious, I tried it, and now I know: like yoga and sensory-deprivation tanks, Bea's work is not for me.

Even if there might be something to it. The memory Bea called up felt so visceral. The visuals didn't surprise me, per se—my dreams have always been vivid, and I've heard hypnosis can induce intense memories.

The strangest part was that last night, for a few minutes, I wasn't me. Grown-up, successful, stable Lexi was gone, replaced by the little girl who'd been undone by one not-even-friendship unraveling. I used to be so damn fragile.

Deep down, I'm afraid I still am.

The espresso machine beeps. I take my cup, then open the fridge to hunt for soy milk. There's one carton, but it's expired.

Why would Bea want me to relive ancient history? She said I had "blocked air," something tied to that memory. But I learned my MaryBeth lesson years ago: play the game. Make friends with the right people. Don't expose your weirdness or you'll drive everyone away.

I'm not that lonely little girl anymore. So what's the point in rehashing those years?

"If it isn't my favorite space cadet." Tanya's voice startles me out of gazing at the kitchen sink like it contains the secrets of the universe.

Shaking myself, I take a sip of coffee. "Morning."

"Late night?" Tanya retrieves the tea kettle to brew her favorite, a lavender-chamomile blend.

"Had trouble sleeping." Not a lie. "By the way, if Shane asks, we hung out last night."

Tanya's eyebrows climb her forehead. "Everything all right with you two?"

"It's nothing." Still, I make sure no one else is in earshot before adding, "I just had an errand to run. Something he wouldn't approve of."

Tanya frowns. "Lying to your partner isn't a great sign."

"You never fib to Paul when girls' night runs late?" I give her a pointed look. "Really, it's no big deal."

"If it's not a big deal, talk to him."

My knee-jerk reaction is denial. For once, though, I ask myself why.

Maybe Tanya has a point. After all, I didn't tell Shane about my experiences earlier because I wasn't sure what I thought about them. Now that I've decided not to work with Bea anymore, would there be any harm in mentioning it? If nothing else, Shane will convince me that walking away was the right call.

Why is my first instinct to keep everything to myself?

Don't be a freak.

What did I learn from MaryBeth? How to make friends and act normal? Or how to hide the real me? To put on a mask because the truth drives people away.

No. That's ridiculous. No way some middle school incident has anything to do with my marriage.

Is there?

By late afternoon, I'm seriously flagging. Words and numbers blend into alien script on my computer screen. An email from one of my clients pops up, and I close the invoice I was working on with relief to skim it.

Then I reread the message, pulse hammering. "*Asshole.*"

I don't realize I've spoken aloud until Don's secretary leans her head past my doorway, eyes wide. "Everything okay?"

I never swear at work. "Sorry. Got some...unexpected news." With that, I spring up and march past her, across the main floor.

My target is the coveted corner office. It's supposed to be tied to sales, occupied by the highest earner. But John Wood has worked from that office for a decade. When my sales surpassed his, the higher-ups told me they felt bad kicking him out.

I told them it was fine. No big deal. The spot bonus and awards were enough for me. Asking for more seemed petty, especially because my office is perfectly fine.

After three years of biting my tongue, this is how he repays me?

John's office door is closed, as usual, but the light is on.

I barge straight in. "Did you poach my client?"

John reclines, feet kicked up on his desk, an iPad in his lap. He's handsome in a conventional way: broad-shouldered and tan, with a full head of dark hair, no grays yet. He's never said so, but I get the impression he doesn't like me. I've caught him glowering at the top-seller awards on my desk.

Still, I never imagined he'd sink this low.

"If you wanted the Vernons' commission, you should have worked harder," John replies, without looking up from his iPad.

"We aren't supposed to poach from each other. What would Don say?" Our CEO maintains a strict noncompete policy among our agents.

"Don would probably agree you've been slacking." Finally, John lifts his gaze to mine. The moment our eyes meet, a rushing sound starts in my ears. Far away at first, but it's growing louder by the second. "You should have closed days ago. Instead, you left the Vernons waiting."

What is that sound? I shake my head. *Focus.* "I just got back to the office. We spoke about it before I left for the holidays."

John shrugs. "Those of us willing to go the extra mile deserve the rewards. What's our number one priority here at Medina?"

The rushing sound is deafening now, as loud as the train tracks when a high-speed Amtrak whizzes past our sleepy little stop.

"We take care of our customers." I speak through gritted teeth. The noise must be in my head, since he's not reacting. "Like the couple I've been showing around town for months. You can't swoop in right before I close and take credit."

"Can't I?" John smiles. It doesn't reach his eyes.

My breath catches as a sudden ripple appears in the air.

Traces of...not haze or fog, exactly. More like the dots that swim across my vision when I've been staring at the computer too long. They cluster around his face, his shoulders, his torso.

The longer I stare, the more dots appear.

I look away, blinking. Maybe it's residual screen fatigue. But the dots vanish at once and only reappear when I turn back to John.

Suddenly, I remember Bea's drawing. The stick figure and the scribbles she drew: blocks in an auric field. For a moment, my anger subsides. Maybe he's in a bad place, like Henry. "Listen, John..."

He rolls his eyes. "It's already done. If you want to cry foul to Don, be my guest. But he doesn't appreciate being dragged into petty squabbles. At the end of the day, a sale's a sale."

I don't know how to shift tacts from *what the hell* to *are you okay*. As I hesitate, his gaze wanders down my body—not so much a leer as a predator sizing up a meal. Prickles race along my spine. He's still smiling, but it's taken an ominous turn.

I shouldn't have closed the door. Old, familiar panic raises the hair on my arms.

Stop it. My coworkers are right outside. One shout and the whole office will hear. But it's hard to remember that now. I know how I react in these situations. If he comes toward me, I'll freeze. I can't help it.

While I still can, I take a sliding step backward and grope for the doorknob. *Get out of here, Lexi.*

John tilts his head. "Leaving so soon? I take it you agree; I'll be handling the Vernons from now on."

"No, we do not agree." My voice shakes, which makes me want to kick myself. But the panic has grown too intense to ignore. "I'll be speaking to Don about this."

"You do that." John waves a dismissive hand.

At the same instant, sharp pain hits my gut. I double over, gasping, all my wind knocked out. It feels like he punched me. I scan the floor, certain he threw something. But there's nothing nearby except the worn carpet.

John leans forward, the very picture of false concern. "What's wrong?"

I blink, and for a split second I glimpse his real face: a twisted, laughing mask. "I..." Finally, my hand strikes the doorknob. I yank it open.

John's eyes crinkle in amusement. "If you need help..." Yet he hasn't moved a muscle, not to offer me a chair or anything.

For that, at least, I'm grateful. The sooner I get out of here, the better. "I don't want anything from you." I practically trip into the hallway, and his office door slams behind me. Did I close it? Did he? Either way, it was too loud. Colleagues startle and sniff disapprovingly.

I beeline for the one safe place I can think of: the women's room. John can't follow me there.

You're being ridiculous, the rational part of me says. *He didn't even come near you.*

But my gut knows what happened.

In the bathroom, I fling myself into the first stall. I lean against the door, chest heaving. Fight or flight takes it out of you. Based on previous experience, I'll be dealing with the jitters for days to come. But adrenaline has never made my stomach hurt this bad before, a sensation like the worst cramps of my life.

I tilt my head back against the cool metal stall door. After a minute or two, I've steadied myself enough to untuck my shirt. Gently, I peel it up.

Right below my rib cage, there's an angry red mark,

purpling at the edges. A bruise. The mark is round, with four ridges along the top. I curl my fingers up and position my knuckles over it.

Sure enough, the bruise is the exact shape of a human fist.

Chapter Eleven

At home, I channel my excess adrenaline into cooking a nice dinner. Potentially too nice.

"Wow, what's the occasion?" Shane finds me in the dining room adding final touches: fresh parsley for the garlic scallops, chimichurri drizzled on the rib eye.

"Trying something new." I smile, hoping he can't tell that my pulse is still racing, even hours later. I spent the whole drive home jumpy, triple-checking the mirrors. Every time I look at my stomach, convinced I imagined everything, the bruise remains, more vivid than ever.

What the hell was that?

Whatever John did felt targeted. As if he'd known how to hurt me—and that I wouldn't be able to stop him.

"Smells incredible." Shane rounds the table to kiss my cheek. "Is this a great-first-day-back meal or a blowing-off-steam dinner?"

"Let me grab the wine," I say.

"Well, shit." He makes sympathetic noises while I slip into the kitchen.

I meet him back at the table with a bottle of leftover white. He pours while I serve. "Do you remember John Wood?" I spoon scallops onto Shane's plate. "Guy in the corner office."

"Ah yes. Deposed Sales King Refuses to Vacate Throne." He trades me a glass for his plate. "The magnanimous new queen was too nice to toss him out on his ass."

"Kind of regretting that now." I push my hair off my forehead. "He poached my buyers today."

"Doesn't Don hate that?"

"Yep. But Don also hates interoffice drama. You can only complain so often before it pisses him off, and a new year just started... God, John was probably banking on that," I mutter, just realizing it now.

"So what if it annoys Don? It's his policy." Shane skewers a scallop. "You've gotta stop letting people walk all over you, Lex. First the office thing, now this."

"It's not my fault he's an asshole."

"No, of course not. But you have to stand up for yourself." Shane plants his forearms on the table and raises a middle finger. "We're fighters. Give the asshole a piece of your mind."

Speak my mind. Make waves. Put myself out there. *Get laughed at all over again in the middle school cafeteria of life.*

I shake my head. "It's not even about the sale; it's the way he acted. Like he only wanted to screw me over. It was so... violating." My hand drifts to my stomach again. When I press, the bruise throbs.

"If you won't confront him, at least report him to Don. Remember when the architect on my last build kept pushing for a design I knew wasn't safe? He wouldn't listen 'cause he's got more experience, so I went to the head of the firm—"

"That's different. No building's gonna collapse just because John Wood stole a commission."

"But it will drive you nuts if you ignore it. You're like me; when you care about something, you make sure it's done right."

"Maybe that's the problem." I cut into my steak. Medium-rare, the way Shane and I both prefer. For some reason, tonight the pink flesh turns my stomach. I set down my silverware and scoop up the wineglass instead. "I'm not sure I care."

Fine lines crisscross my husband's forehead. "So...you're still feeling bored?"

"I guess."

Outside, a car door slams. I tense.

Shane eyes me worriedly. "You said you aren't being challenged anymore. Maybe this is an opportunity in disguise."

"I meant I wanted to learn new skills, not fight with a coworker."

"Fighting's a skill!" He grins. When I don't return it, he sobers. "You've worked so hard to get where you are at Medina. Don't let anyone take it from you."

What do I actually want?

I don't know.

Which is terrifying, because I've always known. I only applied to one college, early decision. Within our first year of dating, I knew I wanted to marry Shane. I fell in love with Garden Vale on our first visit. Even when it came to dropping my astrophysics major, once I made the decision, I never looked back.

Maybe Shane's right. Maybe today is an opportunity in disguise. Just not the opportunity he thinks.

I graze a hand over my navel again. Half an hour ago, I was staring at the bruise, wondering how the hell to explain it to my husband. Now... "Actually, there's something I've been meaning to talk to you about."

Is this a terrible idea? But he asked. And I need to speak up more, he's right.

"It started at the gala. When Henry Jensen died—or, actually, before he died. Remember how I lost my place up onstage?"

Confusion clouds Shane's expression, but he nods.

"Well, I...I think I sensed something bad was going to happen. I saw this cloud around Henry. And I heard..." *Do we want to admit to hearing voices, Lexi?* I swallow hard. "There was a moment where he and I connected. It was like I remembered memories that didn't belong to me. I tasted seaweed and salt water; I couldn't breathe. Someone kept shouting his name. I thought I was imagining things, but then... I was searching for his obituary and I found another article. A long time ago, Henry was in a boating accident with his sons. They both drowned."

Shane goes very still. "That's terrible."

"I know." I force myself to meet his eyes. "It's weird. Believe me, I know. But I'd never met Henry. How could I pick all that up from across the room?"

My husband's expression shifts from worry to something more like bemusement. "Phantom smells are common, Lex. They don't mean you're living someone else's memories."

"But how did I know his name?"

"You worked at the same company. Maybe you met him in passing and forgot. Come to think of it..." He picks up his wineglass, swirls it thoughtfully. "That could explain the boating accident too. People around the office must have talked about it. You could have overheard them sometime. It's wild how much information our brains pick up, even things we aren't consciously aware of."

"Pretty sure I would remember gossip about a horrific sailing accident involving a colleague."

"Dunno. You get pretty laser-focused in work mode." He grins, clearly trying to lighten the mood.

For a moment, I'm tempted to let him. To laugh it off, slide this back under the table. But for the first time all evening, my stomach has stopped hurting. And there's a looseness around my throat, like a muscle cramp you don't notice until it suddenly releases.

Keep talking.

"It's not just Henry. Since the gala, it's happened a couple more times. I've seen clouds around people and sensed things. At Christmas, I got this horrible headache at the same time as Tyrone, and then today, at the office—"

"Honey."

My jaw snaps shut. Shane never "honeys" me.

He doesn't seem to notice my glare. "You've been under a lot of stress. Maybe we should give the counselor another call."

"You mean the woman who diagnosed me with daddy issues while I was grieving our child?" I snap.

We both freeze.

It's been so long since either of us has said that word. *Child.* At one point, it felt like a third presence in the house. Every conversation, every plan for the future revolved around that dream. Then our hopes shattered, and we took it out on each other, fighting about everything and nothing—dishes, laundry, therapy. We were mad at the world, but since we were the only ones here to blame, we let each other scream.

I thought we'd finally climbed out from under that nightmare's shadow. But it comes roaring back now, all our disappointment and heartbreak.

"There are other counselors," Shane finally says, voice thick.

I stare at my plate. *What did I expect?* This, verbatim. "It's not a grief thing."

"I'm not suggesting it is. But until you know what's going on, it might help to talk to someone about what you're... going through."

Entire dissertations could fill his pause. "I have been talking to someone." I steel myself against the relief on his face. "Beatrix O'Neill, down at Odds and Ends."

"The Witch's Lair?" He laughs. Then scrutinizes me. "You're serious."

"She knows what's happening to me. She explained it."

"Lex, psychics are frauds."

"She's not a psychic—"

"They're good at people-reading, and they use that to take advantage of anyone vulnerable. Shit's been happening since the Victorian era. Come on, you know all that stuff is bullshit."

For a second, I feel her inside me. Old Lexi, middle school Lexi, who bent to everyone else's whims in a desperate bid to fit in.

I'm not that little girl anymore. "I do, Shane. And you know me. I'm smart; I'm practical; I believe in reason. I wasn't out looking for some mystical answer to the universe. I trust both science and reality."

He opens his mouth, but I bowl over him.

"Which is why I thought maybe, just maybe, I'd earned a little credibility. Do you think I haven't been telling myself everything you just said for weeks? I've tried so hard to ignore this stuff, but it keeps happening. Today, at work? John did more than just poach my client."

I grab the hem of my shirt. *This is it.* Proof. Or as close as I'll ever come. You can deny a lot of things, but not a fist.

Shane watches me with that too-careful expression I hate, the one he always gives me after shit goes down with my family. *My poor wife, dealing with her poor shitty parents.* His pity grates on my last nerve.

"I saw the same cloud around John. Bea says it's his auric field, or his energy. When I was leaving his office, he threw the energy at me, somehow." With all the triumph of tossing out a trump card, I yank my shirt up. "It left a mark."

There's another pause, longer this time. "What mark?"

I follow his gaze, heart rising into my throat. Half an hour ago, the fist-shaped bruise was dark purple. The kind that takes weeks to fade, going blue-green en route to yellow. Now my stomach is bare. A little on the pale side—thanks, winter—but otherwise unremarkable.

Fuck.

"It was there earlier," I say, knowing how it sounds. "A fist, right..." I plant my knuckles over my diaphragm, as if that will make the bruise reappear.

Shane exhales very slowly. "Lexi."

"Don't."

He raises both hands. "I wasn't." When I don't reply, he scoots closer. "You're going through a lot. I get it."

"But you don't believe me." I stare at the ceiling, surprised by the sudden burn in my eyes. I knew this was coming. I put off talking to him for weeks because I knew how he'd react. I don't understand why it still hurts.

"I believe you believe it. And to be honest, that's what worries me. The mind is a fragile thing."

I set my jaw.

"Put yourself in my shoes," he says. "If I came home one day saying I saw a ghost at the fire station..."

"That's not the same thing." I swipe angrily at my cheek. *Why, why am I crying now?* Right when I most need to appear rational.

"Imagine it."

I picture Shane cooking me a fancy dinner. Sitting me down. Carefully explaining his paranormal experience. Who would the ghost be? Someone he failed to save? His grandfather, whose death hit Shane hard in college?

Our child? No, enough specters tonight.

"I'd believe you," I say. "Because you're you."

"Well, I thought you were practical too, but—" As soon

97

as the words leave his mouth, his face reddens. "I didn't mean—"

My chair legs screech as I stand. The scallops have clumped into unappealing nimbuses on the serving platter. I reach for the platter, but Shane catches my wrist. "Let me clean up." His grip softens, fingers tracing the underside of my wrist. "I'm sorry," he adds, softer now.

"Yeah," I murmur. "Me too."

Just then, something catches my eye. There's a blaze of summer heat, out of place in our drafty dining room. The scent of fresh-mown grass tickles my nostrils. And right in the center of Shane's chest, like a desert mirage, a distortion appears: a gnarled knot about the size of my thumb.

A block?

I blink and it's gone again, too quick for me to process.

"Will you tell me?" he asks. "If anything else happens?"

"Will you believe me?"

He doesn't answer. So neither do I.

Chapter Twelve

My week passes in a blur of paperwork. At least it keeps me shut in my office, far away from John Wood. Every time I use the bathroom or kitchenette, I make sure his door is shut first.

Home isn't much better. Shane tiptoes around me. *Let's watch whatever you want; no, you shower first.* Come Saturday, escape is less a desire than a requirement.

But I'm honest when Shane asks where I'm going. That's got to count for something.

The closer I get to town, the lighter my chest grows. En route, I stop for a box of Mrs. Brown's infamous puff pastries. Hopefully it's an appropriate sorry-for-freaking-out gift.

The bell above the entrance to Odds and Ends tinkles. A grumpy voice hollers from the back as I lean against the counter. "Oh, hello." The same tabby I met last time curls out from a bookshelf. He headbutts my ankles until I scratch his ear. "What's your name?" I examine the silver tag.

Chaucer

114 Main St.
Bea's Odds & Ends
NOT HUNGRY JUST A BRAT

"Sounds like you're a troublemaker, Chaucer."

"You have no idea." The beads draped across the back-room clatter.

I straighten, braced for a lecture.

Instead, Bea nods. "Wondered when you'd be by."

All my planned apologies melt together. "I'm sorry, I shouldn't have stormed off, I don't know why I—"

"Hey, your emotions are your own business."

I hold out the pastries. "Still, it was rude. I need to apologize."

"The only thing you need to apologize for is not bringing chocolate." Bea pulls the box from my grasp and inspects a cream-colored pastry. "The hell is this, vanilla?"

"Custard, I think."

Bea wrinkles her nose. Nonetheless, she pops the entire puff into her mouth. She chews noisily and shrugs at the cat. "Better than nothing." She claps her hands. "So. You're back and groveling. I assume you want to continue."

I didn't know how nervous I was until the relief hits. "Is… is that okay?"

"On one condition. Next time something trips your alarms, don't go running up a mountain in the pitch-dark?"

I manage a smile. "Fair enough." Then I take a deep breath. "Something else happened." As succinctly as possible, I summarize what happened in John Wood's office.

By the time I finish, she's nodding. "Energy is like anything else. Not everyone who works with it has good intentions."

"But I saw those same blocks around him. Doesn't that mean he's hurt?"

"Pain and anger are linked. Everyone reacts differently to being wounded. The healthiest option is to face it and work through it. Some people repress the issue and wind up hurting themselves. Others get angry. They project their pain, taking it out on people around them instead."

"So John hurt me to make himself feel better?"

"It doesn't, of course. Not in the long run." Bea frowns.

I think about Henry and Tyrone. About the brief glimpse I got of Shane's energy the other night. "Do blocks always get worse?"

Bea leans against a shelf of crystals in every shape and color. "Not always. Blocks show up when we're struggling. Emotionally, physically, mentally. Most people don't perceive their energetic field, but it's like your body. You get the sniffles and your immune system does its job without any conscious effort. However, if we fixate—get stuck in harmful patterns like addiction or abuse—the blocks get worse. Or if you go through a sudden trauma, the wound might be so severe that your energetic body can't recover on its own. That's where healers come in."

Healers. The word ignites something. It's like being in elementary school, reading under the desk when the teacher calls my name. An automatic jolt to attention. *That's me.*

Bea grins. "Yes, Lexi. I do believe that's you."

Did I say that out loud?

Before I can be too impressed, Bea stuffs another pastry into her mouth. She chews while circling me. "Hmm. Something's different." She lifts a hand and traces the air above my collarbone.

An answering tickle starts at my uvula, like a suppressed cough.

"Have you been doing energy work? Air maybe?" Bea purses her lips.

"Not really." I frown, thinking. "I spent the week catching up at work. Well. And getting into a fight with my husband."

"Aha." Bea straightens. "Petty or productive?"

"I, uh…told him what I've been experiencing. And about studying with you. He's convinced you're taking advantage of me, by the way."

She smirks. "Yes, this was all a long con to get baked goods." She rounds the counter and disappears into the back. After a pause, she shouts, "You coming?"

Sidestepping a display case of wire-and-crystal jewelry, I trail after her. Unlike the front of the store, with its witchy-cottage core vibe, the back room resembles a hoarder's den. Shelves are haphazardly stacked with books, vintage tea sets, antique toys, and more cat litter than Chaucer could use in a year. The only furniture is a lumpy couch, two mismatched velvet poufs, and a table coated in wax. The wax heap is so big it's formed towers, like the drip sandcastles my brother taught me how to make at the lake as kids.

"Air energy is all about the mind," Bea says. "Thoughts, ideas, how you express yourself. Blocked air can manifest as trouble speaking our mind or opening up. It can also affect our creativity. It traps us in old thought patterns, stifles new ideas, that sort of thing. Your block was related to the memory in your meditation. I'm guessing the talk with your husband loosened its hold."

I replay the memory. MaryBeth's laughter, the sinking sensation in my gut.

I think of the years afterward too. I always tried to conform to everyone else's expectations. In high school it kept me shy, borderline paranoid. But in college, around new people, that same adaptability became my greatest strength. I could blend into any social situation—so I did. I went to football games that bored me, accepted invitations to student clubs I had no interest in, happy just to be included. I dragged myself through business class after econ lecture, running on the perpetual dream of someday.

I had a goal, after all. If I kept my eyes on the prize, it didn't matter if I enjoyed every aspect of the ride, because what mattered was the destination.

And Shane... My throat tightens. *I love Shane. I really do.* Still, when we first started dating, I did the same thing with him. I pretended to enjoy the horror movies he loved, and I ordered the same beer at bars, even though I preferred wine.

We had a lot in common. Just not quite as much as he thought.

Thinks.

I don't join him for horror premieres anymore, and I gave up beer years ago. But there are still times I conform. Pretend. *Isn't that what marriage is? Compromise?*

"How do you fix blocked air?" I ask.

"You've made a good start. The biggest challenge will be expressing yourself. Even—especially—when it's uncomfortable." Bea points at the sofa. "Have a seat."

I perch on the brink of a cushion.

She rolls her eyes. "Relax. This isn't your office."

Sinking back, I dislodge a flurry of cat hair and sneeze. But it is comfier.

Meanwhile, Bea roots through a filing cabinet. She pulls out a box of emergency tapers and fishes a lighter from a repurposed terrarium. She melts the bottom of the candle just enough to stick it on top of the waxy castle, then lights the wick. "Today, I want you to work on focus."

"Will that help me express myself?"

"It'll get you out of your head, for a start." Bea points at the flame. "Meditate on the candle. Put everything else out of your mind. Be present. That's your assignment." She reaches for another book. Different cover than last time— guess she finished the Scottish Highlander romance.

"So I just...sit here?"

She smirks. "Trust me, it's harder than it sounds. Remember: stay out of your head." With that, she steps through the curtain to the front.

Great. More meditation. My favorite.

I try not to think about how abysmal I am at yoga. Or how I freaked out in Chloe's sensory-deprivation tank. I try, too, not to dwell on my last meditation, which sent me fleeing down a mountain in the dark.

Be present.

I stare at the flame. The faint bluish lick around the wick. The white-hot tip. Every so often, a curl of black smoke peels from it. I exhale through my mouth and the flame dances. I breathe a little harder, watching it flicker. I catch myself swaying along, left to right. Then I stop and ball my fists on my knees. *Hold still.*

Of course, the minute I start trying, I become aware of every itch and twinge in my body. My pulse flutters at my clavicle, in my lower left ankle, behind my knee. My back throbs from the angle of the couch cushions, so I straighten and clench my navel.

All the while, the candle continues to burn. Wax slides off like tears, adding to the melted castle.

My mind drifts to Shane. *I thought you were practical,* he said. I try to be, most of the time. But the disconnect runs deeper—the Lexi in his head is missing pieces. Day-to-day experiences so mundane we don't bother to share. Others I choose not to, like previous partners or meaningless flirtations. To me, they're like mint-condition collectibles. Expose them to light and they'd lose their shine.

Everyone has a few secrets, right?

But maybe I lock away too much. If Shane doesn't know the real me, whose fault is it? Maybe I should focus less on the Lexi in Shane's head and more on the woman in mine.

Also, I need to pick up milk.

I squeeze my eyes shut. The candle's reverse image plays behind my eyelids. When I open them again, the taper is half-melted.

How long am I supposed to do this?

When my thighs start to cramp, I decide it's enough. I blow out the candle and go hunting for Bea, braced for a lecture on giving up.

She's out front, stacking bath bombs in a precarious tier. Without a word, she passes me an armful.

"Well, I suck at meditating. No surprise there."

Bea looks like she's trying not to laugh. "What exactly do you think meditation is?"

"Not thinking?" I lay out a pyramid of bath bombs, gold dust coating my palms. "I keep getting itchy or going over my grocery list. I can't turn my brain off."

"It's not a light switch. Even Zen masters don't plop down and automatically go blank. Meditation takes effort. Our brains are hardwired to flee predators, hunt prey, or plot our next meal."

"Okay. So if it's not a light switch, how do I turn it off?"

"You can't." She finishes her bath-bomb stack and pats her hair, leaving a streak of glitter. "Meditation is active. It's the practice of choosing stillness, again and again. Your brain will keep piping up like a toddler demanding attention. Your job is to acknowledge the thought, thank it, and tell it you're busy. Whatever it has to say can wait."

"What if it won't listen?"

"Then you try again. And again and again and...you get the gist." She stretches, yawning. "I'm closing up now, but there's your homework for the week. Keep meditating."

I can't decide if it sounds too easy or borderline impossible.

Chapter Thirteen

Monday night brings girls' night once more. I arrive at Murphy's breathless, a little jittery but otherwise in a decent mood. On Sunday, I practiced meditating. I holed up in the bedroom and lit one of the decorative candles we've owned for years yet never used. It didn't go any better than at Bea's.

Today, though, I locked myself in my office over lunch and played an ocean sounds video. I got so focused on matching my breath to the shush of waves that I didn't realize lunch had ended until Rita from Accounts Payable came knocking.

For the rest of the afternoon, I felt calmer, more relaxed. So relaxed it didn't even annoy me when John sent a company-wide memo titled *Keeping clients happy and response times swift*.

Inside Murphy's, the girls sit at our usual table. They're laughing as I enter. Chloe wears an unseasonable tank top, while Tanya's bundled in more layers than Shane's grandmother.

I only make it halfway to the table when my temples start to throb. Murphy's, like any self-respecting dive, keeps the lights dim. Yet my eyes burn as if I'm staring down a midday ski slope.

No, not again. The headache at Christmas was a one-off.

I thought it happened because I was picking up on Tyrone's energy, so why am I feeling it again now?

"Lexi!" Chloe spots me.

I gulp stale, beer-scented air as I weave over to the booth. "Hey." I muster a smile and slide in.

This time, it's more than a headache. Awareness spreads through my bloodstream, carrying with it new aches. In my low back, my kneecaps, at the joints of my elbows, and behind my sternum.

What's happening?

It reminds me of the time Shane and I went to a punk concert. We were in front dancing and got stuck in the mosh, bodies pressing against me from every direction, other people's sweat slicking my skin.

"Good, you can be our tiebreaker." Tanya slaps the table. "Wylan from *The Showdown.* Weirdly attractive or just weird?"

Shane and I watch the reality show religiously—I got him addicted after Chloe hooked Tanya and me. Yet even though we saw the most recent episode yesterday, it takes ages to dredge up a mental image of the old southern man Tanya's talking about. I shrug. "Weird-cute? I could see it."

"Ha!" Tanya crows.

Chloe shudders. "Nooo, he gives me creeper vibes. At least lust after one of the nice guys. There's Olly—"

"The British kid? He's, like, twelve." Tanya gestures to the server, then points at me. He gives a be-right-there nod.

My stomach recoils. I'm not sure I can drink right now. Or eat. Or talk. Does it always smell this bad in here?

"Ageist. He's twenty-three!" Chloe scoffs. "Okay, fine. What about Sandra, she's got the sexy cougar thing going."

"Now who's ageist? She's only forty." Finally, Tanya catches sight of my expression. "Lex?"

"Sorry. Headache." I force a laugh. My body is being pulled in ten directions at once. Toward Liang, the sixty-year-old mechanic who gives Shane a firefighter's discount on car repairs, currently perched at the bar. Toward Ryan, behind the bar, who knocks a drink or two off our bill every week. Toward a white woman I've never seen before, who keeps eyeing the door.

I don't understand what's happening until my hands begin to tremble. *Energy.* That's what I'm sensing. Waves upon waves, too much to parse. A blasting radio only I hear.

My friends' smiles melt into concern.

"Can we go somewhere else?" I blurt out. No way can I hold it together for a full hour in here.

Chloe and Tanya trade glances. "Right now?" Chloe asks at the same time Tanya says, "Where?"

"What about the Barn?" The quaint independent bookstore at the heart of town is as different from Murphy's bar as we'll get at this hour. The Barn's café stays open until seven, which gives us a couple hours.

"Um...okay." Chloe drawls out the last syllable, then downs her nearly full glass of red.

I grimace. The wine is bad enough when you sip it.

Tanya shrugs on her coat. "Is everything all right?"

"Little headache, that's all. It's too noisy here tonight."

My friends glance at each other, then around the room. I can practically hear what they're thinking. Besides our table, there are maybe a dozen people in the bar, staff included. This is as empty as Murphy's gets.

I'll explain later. For now, I surge toward the door. The moment fresh air hits my face, I gasp in relief.

Outside, streetlights illuminate the slush piles. This is the worst part of winter. In November, the snow is still fresh and invigorating. In December, it's magical, accented by holiday lights and anticipation. Even early January isn't too bad, with the smoke of New Year's fireworks lingering.

By now, though, late January? Resolutions are making everyone irritable. We're sick of darkness; we want the sun again. The pristine white snow has gone, replaced by gray-black heaps alongside the road. Those mountains will pile higher and higher until the spring thaw, when we'll discover if any forgotten garbage bags froze underneath.

For a moment, I consider retreating to Bea's. But Odds and Ends is dark, shuttered an hour early.

Tanya and Chloe arrive in puffs of steam. "Better?" Tanya links an elbow through mine.

"Much." We fall into step.

Chloe snags my other arm. "So is this some kind of Drynuary thing, or—oh shit, it's not morning sickness, is it?"

I nearly trip. *She doesn't know.* When I was pregnant, Shane and I decided not to tell anybody until the end of the first trimester. And then, when I wasn't anymore...telling my friends seemed pointless. Nothing they could say or do would fix it. Anyway, I had Shane to help me shoulder it.

Us against the world.

So I laugh, a little strangled. "Neither. Can't a girl want a night off without something being wrong?"

Tanya squeezes my wrist. "Of course."

Chloe studies my profile for a few paces. "Is anything wrong?"

How do you fix blocked air?

The biggest challenge will be expressing yourself.

"Actually..." We're nearing the town square, but the sidewalk remains empty. Anyone braving the cold this time of year drives, even if their destination is only a couple of blocks away. "Lately, I'm starting to...question some things."

Over my head, Chloe and Tanya trade looks. "Finally," Tanya says.

"For the record, if this is your bisexual awakening, Tanya owes me ten dollars." Chloe wriggles her fingers at Tanya.

I blink. "What?"

Chloe rolls her eyes. "We're your best friends, Lexi. We can tell when something's up. You've been acting weird for weeks."

"Sorry." I grimace.

"Don't apologize." Tanya swats Chloe's hand. "Whatever it is, you can talk to us."

"It's just…hard to put into words." We round a corner and the Barn comes into view. Its large windows, still festooned in Christmas garlands, spill golden light. Just then, fat flakes start to fall. They stick to our hair, our cheeks.

"Hold that thought." Tanya detaches to jog ahead. She yanks open the door. We burst inside, a flurry of snow on our heels.

Already, the pressure on my temples has eased. The Barn's atmosphere is far more relaxed. One middle-aged woman browses the bookshelves. The only other person here is the owner, who leans against the counter texting.

We take seats in the otherwise empty café.

My nose and fingertips tingle as warmth returns. I look at Tanya first, then Chloe. Both are wind chapped, expectant. *They'll understand.* "I'm studying energy healing."

A beat, during which hope swells in my chest. Then Chloe bursts into laughter. "Okay, you almost got me."

Even Tanya smirks. "Seriously, Lex, just tell us."

I watch them. Wait.

Tanya's penny drops first. "Oh."

Chloe's already pink cheeks darken. "Shit, I thought you were… You're serious? What, like casting spells on the full moon?"

"She said healing, not witchcraft," Tanya chides.

"Hey, witches can be healers. I met some pagans in Bali who—"

"It's not like that," I interrupt. "Or, I don't know, maybe there's crossover. I don't know anything about paganism. Bea's teaching me."

Chloe wrinkles her nose. "That judgmental old bat?"

"She's just prickly. Once you get to know her, she's actually nice."

"I tried to get her to do a collab with me." Chloe tucks her hair behind one studded ear. "Would've been totally free promo for her store. But she took one look at my page and went off about how I was 'abusing the aesthetics of spirituality for profit.'"

Tanya and I trade glances. "Well...were you?" I ask.

"Last time I checked, you can't copyright herbs or crystals."

"True," Tanya replies. "But some cultures have specific ways of using plants as medicine. When they're misused by people outside that culture, it's damaging."

Chloe's shoulders tense. "You're right. Appropriation is shitty, but I wasn't taking from anyone. General witchy-looking stuff is popular right now."

"But if you were inspired by other people's posts, and they're posting stuff they appropriated..." I say slowly. "It's possible to mess up without intending to."

Chloe opens her mouth. Closes it again. Grimaces. "Still, does Bea have to be so..."

"Abrasive?" I smirk. "Pretty sure that's a feature."

Chloe snorts. The owner comes over, and we pause to order hot chocolates all around. When she leaves, Chloe looks back at me, still a little sheepish. "What's studying with her like?"

"Also, how the heck did that start?" Tanya adds.

"Because of the gala, actually." Once I start talking, it's hard to stop. I tell them everything, all the way up to my last training session with Bea and why Murphy's overwhelmed me today.

By the time I finish, our hot chocolates have arrived. The silky heat warms my throat. They still haven't said anything, so beneath the table, I nudge Tanya's leg. "Well?"

She glances from me to Chloe and back. "If it makes you happy, then I'm happy for you," she says carefully.

"But?" Chloe prompts.

Tanya exhales. "I don't want to be pushy or anything. But, Lexi, are you sure what you experienced doesn't have another explanation?"

I shrug and take another sip of cocoa. "Shane thinks there's a rational explanation."

Chloe hums. "Maybe. But I've experienced weird stuff before too. This one time we used a Ouija board at an ayahuasca retreat in Costa Rica—"

"I'm not talking about secular explanations," Tanya interrupts. We've both heard Chlo's Ouija story a dozen times. "When was the last time you went to church?"

For a moment, I'm stunned quiet. Tanya hasn't asked me that in years. Not since I made it clear I have no interest in returning. Unlike plenty of the other practicing LDS members in town—coworkers, neighbors who show up on our doorstep with baked goods—Tanya's never pushed.

"I'm not trying to re-recruit you," Tanya adds quickly. "But while we're talking about culture and religion, the religion we're raised in is important. Maybe you shouldn't close off that avenue just yet. Especially as you're processing these new experiences."

"Sure, because organized religion loves women stepping into their own power," Chloe mutters.

"It's different for you, Chlo." Tanya still hasn't taken her eyes off me. "Lexi was raised LDS. That's not something you can undo; it's her past. It's part of her."

"Yes. It'll always be my past." I think about Frank at Christmas. His calm self-assuredness. *Never saw reason to question it.* No matter how much I respect him—envy him, even—that will never be me. "But I'm focusing on my future now. I never connected with the church. Even when I went regularly, I didn't belong. These experiences feel different, more like me." I don't realize how true those words are until I say them out loud.

"Okay." Tanya extends her hands, palms up. "I hope you don't mind. I had to ask."

I rest my hands in hers. "It's okay."

She squeezes, then releases me to scoop up her mug. "Am I allowed to ask how Shane took it? Since I covered for you the other day..."

"Take a wild guess." I rub my forehead. "Pretty sure he thinks I'm having a psychotic break."

"Makes you wonder how many women who got committed to asylums back in the day were just spiritually awakened," Chloe muses. "Or, y'know, not into sex with their husbands. Or too into sex with their husbands..."

"Being too smart. Don't forget that one." Tanya scowls.

They riff more asylum diagnoses while my gaze drifts to the window. The earlier flurries have coalesced. Snow piles along the sill and coats the grimy sidewalk like a fresh coat of paint. Cars, streetlamps, rooftops—everywhere is white, as far as the eye can see.

For a little while, Garden Vale glitters again.

Chapter Fourteen

I stop by Bea's twice over the next week. Both times, I expect more instructions. Something dramatic like our mountain trip. Instead, she sends me to the back room with a fresh candle. Occasionally Chaucer accompanies me, purring on my lap like a sneeze-inducing heater.

More often, I'm alone with my thoughts.

"I could do this at home," I complain on my third visit.

"So do it," Bea replies. She's pacing the store with a basket, slinging in various objects: a clear crystal, a packet of catnip, a bag of Himalayan sea salt.

"I want to learn something new. We covered air energy. What element comes next?"

Bea picks up a green candle carved in the shape of a penis. "You'll know when it happens."

She loves saying cryptic shit like that. An ugly little voice pipes up: *Maybe Shane's right.* Maybe she really is a fraud. The middle school memory could have been a fluke, or me projecting, seeing what I want.

I force the doubt aside. "What are you doing?"

Bea stacks a white penis candle on top of the green one. "Order for a friend. She runs a healing retreat center in South Dakota."

"They specialize in dick magic?" I joke.

She doesn't laugh. "They specialize in sexual trauma healing. Physical and emotional damage can injure your energetic body as well. Her center takes a holistic approach to recovery. They have physicians, psychiatrists, and therapists on staff, along with energetic healers like my friend."

"Oh." I had no idea places like that existed. It's hard to imagine. "And, the doctors—the real doctors, I mean—they believe in energy healing?"

Bea clicks her tongue. "I keep telling you. Science and energy work are not mutually exclusive." She finishes filling the basket and lugs it to the counter. "Some of her staff think energy work is just a placebo effect. But they all agree: patients show the greatest improvement with integrated treatment. That's what matters. Helping people."

I picture an idyllic farmhouse on some remote plot of land. One of those hippie-adjacent communities with solar panels and a wind farm, vegetable gardens and pet chickens. I try to imagine who would go to a center like that. Someone who already believes in energy? *Or someone desperate. Someone who's exhausted all other options.*

Goose bumps prick my arms. For a second, the past claws at me. *Stop it.* The story ends well. The patients get help.

Imagine if that were an option for everyone.

"Shouldn't you be practicing?" Bea says.

In the back room, it's harder than ever to shut off my brain. Statistics march across my eyelids. *One in five women.* Millions of men, too, who we always seem to forget. And that's assault. Harassment must be even higher. Every single woman I've ever spoken about it with has been harassed. In college we laughed it off. *It was just a catcall; he only followed me home once.*

Only. Just.

I leave Bea's early, afraid these thoughts will follow me home, where I've got enough to deal with. There, Shane and I playact normalcy. We work out together one evening; invite Paul and Tanya for dinner another. If we toss and turn more than usual at night, neither mentions it.

Shane still doesn't approve of my lessons with Bea. "I don't want it affecting our life."

"It won't," I promise, believing myself. I visit Odds and Ends only when Shane's on call at the station.

But I catch him watching me more than usual: during movies or while I'm reading and he's playing video games. Now and then, I mention Bea. I want to normalize my studies, not hide them. He listens, un-Shane-like, without asking follow-up questions.

It'll take time, I tell myself when Shane texts me a link to an interview with cult survivors. And again one morning as he tells me about José at the station, who resisted getting help for depression for years. "There's nothing shameful about seeking treatment."

"No," I agree. "There isn't." Then, a minute later. "You think I'm depressed?"

"I don't know, Lex. I'm not a doctor."

I wash my yogurt bowl in silence, thinking of Victorian-era asylums.

If home's bad, work is even worse. I feel drained before I even step out of the car each morning. The computer screen makes my eyes throb, while to-dos pile up. Tasks that normally take five minutes suddenly seem impossible, monumental.

I'm wading through a draft of a client listing I should've posted yesterday when someone knocks on my open door.

"All caught up from the holidays?" John says by way of greeting. "I noticed you left early yesterday."

My shoulders clench. "Last I checked, I don't report to you. But thanks for the concern."

He lingers, long enough to make the hairs on the nape of my neck itch. Finally, I drag my gaze up. He's staring over my head at the top-seller trophies. "There was a time I thought I could relax too. Coast on my laurels." He offers a toothless smile. "Then you came along."

With that, he finally leaves.

I wait until he's across the office before I shut the door and lock it. My nerve endings spark.

Back at my desk, I light the storm candle I smuggled into the office. I glare at it so hard, my whole field of vision fills with tiny flames.

The old Lexi would've taken his intrusion as a challenge. *He thinks he can beat me? I'll show him.* I've done it before. I could do it again: hustle on weekends, work after hours at home. Sprint the extra mile that I've spent my whole twenties running.

The thought alone exhausts me.

It's not just John Wood. It's writing the same paragraph of description for the same type of property ad nauseam. Walking the same couple in the same outfits through the same boring new build with the same white walls and laminate floors.

I don't want to do this anymore.

That terrifies me. Because I have to; this is my job. It's all I know how to do.

As Tanya puts it one lunch, eating sad desk salads in my office while I complain about John, "You've got it made at Medina. Even if John regains top seller—which, frankly, I can't see happening—you've proven your chops. Plus, people like you. Nobody talks to John unless they have to. Accounts Payable draw straws when they have to chase his invoices."

I spear a forkful of spinach and avocado, then drag it through a puddle of balsamic. "What does being likable have to do with anything?"

Tanya's grin shifts into conspiratorial mode. "There's a rumor Don will be retiring in five years. He'll start training his replacement any day now..."

The sad desk salad revolts at the idea of five more years at Medina.

But quitting comes with a host of problems. I haven't polished my résumé in years. I don't even know where people job hunt these days. Probably not on the same forums I used senior year of college.

Then there's the money. The renovations we did bumped up our property taxes, and we already had a high mortgage. Shane makes decent money, but without my income, we'd be forced to dip into our savings before long.

Not to mention, we always planned on being a two-income household. When we started trying for kids—a thought that curdles any remaining appetite I had—we factored day-care costs into everything.

How was that less than a year ago? Those plans already seem like another lifetime.

Regardless of all the reasons to stay, a week later in Don DeCamp's monthly all-hands meeting, my resolve finally cracks.

The big meeting room on the ground floor is the only one large enough to accommodate the in-office staff, which is unfortunate, because it smells like stale body odor and yesterday's pizza. Don's in the middle of a presentation about a new office park breaking ground next summer. It reminds me of an aircraft hangar crossed with the monolith from *2001: A Space Odyssey*.

Don drones on about square footage and which companies

have bought in. Tanya scribbles *Why, God, why* in her daily planner, then nudges it my way.

Across the meeting room, John tips his chair onto two legs. When he catches me watching, his smirk widens. Prickles race along my spine. A beat later, a wave of exhaustion travels up the soles of my feet and settles inside my rib cage.

Another energy attack. Last time, I ran, but this time, I want to fight.

Without preamble, I surge to my feet. The movement startles John. He almost loses his balance but catches his chair at the last second, bringing the front legs crashing to the floor just as Don halts the presentation.

"Lexi." Don does not sound amused. "Did you have a question?"

"Yes." I keep my eyes on John. "I was wondering whether your policy on intracompany competition is still in effect."

Whispers circle the room.

John's eyebrows rise a fraction. I can't decide if he looks surprised or impressed.

I don't care either way. "John poached a sale I spent a month working on. He also warned me not to complain to you, implying it would negatively impact my reputation at Medina."

Don's face turns a series of increasingly alarming shades. As the whispers grow louder, Tanya touches her knee to my shin in a silent gesture of support.

After what feels like an eternity, Don manages a smile. "Thank you for bringing the matter to my attention, Lexi. However, I'd prefer to handle something this delicate in private. There are two sides to every story, after all, and I would hate for someone's public reputation to suffer over a misunderstanding."

"I'll forward my email chain and records of my phone calls

with the clients. John, I'm sure, can provide his contract with the date he closed."

Don's Adam's apple bobs. He darts a nervous glance around the room. "I assure you, I will get to the bottom of this as soon as—"

"That won't be necessary." The energy that sent me surging to my feet isn't finished. It licks at my fingertips, roars in my chest. I no longer feel drowsy or drained. Whatever exhaustion John threw at me is long gone. In its place, fire rears its head.

All at once, I know what I need to do. If I'm being honest, I should've done it months ago, but the idea scared me too much. I kept worrying over what-ifs and worst-case scenarios. I should have realized: getting stuck is the worst-case scenario.

But I can change it.

"I'm sending my information as a courtesy to the next colleague he tries this with. It won't be me." The words burst like sugar on my tongue. "Because I quit."

"Lexi, be reasonable," Don says.

According to Tanya, the morning meeting devolved into chaos after I left. I wouldn't know. I spent the rest of the hour packing my office. Then Don came knocking.

In the doorway, he fidgets with his tie. "Even if what you're saying is true, it was one client. Give me a chance to fix this. There's no need for dramatics."

Dramatics. From his point of view, I can see how it looks that way. "I'm not quitting because of John."

Don's shoulders relax. "Thank goodness. Because you're our best agent, Lexi. I really think, today's outburst aside, you have the potential to be a leader at Medina."

"You misunderstand. I am quitting. Even if it weren't for *his* dramatics," I add, emphasis only a touch barbed, "it's the right decision."

Awkward silence falls. Into it, my office clock ticks. Slowly, Don's expression shifts from surprise through confusion, until he settles on anger. "I hope you've thought this through."

"I have. In fact—"

Don interrupts. "Because if this is some spur-of-the-moment whim, don't expect me to rehire you once you regret it."

I don't need my new energy-reading abilities to decipher his expression. Every woman I know could predict what he's thinking. *You're being illogical.* Or maybe hormonal. Men love to throw that adjective around.

Never mind that men are just as driven by emotions, especially anger.

Never mind that some illogical choices will spare you a lifetime of regret.

"Thank you, Don, but I understand how quitting a job works."

A vein at his temple pulses. "I'm being considerate here. Have you thought about the consequences?" Suddenly, his eyes spark. He leans forward. "If this is a matter of compensation—"

"It's not."

"You are within your rights to negotiate. I shouldn't be telling you this." He gives a little chuckle that sets my teeth on edge. "It's my job to bargain on behalf of the firm. But you're our top seller, and I know that—uh…" He catches himself. "Some people find it difficult to ask for bigger percentages."

"People," Don? Or women?

"I want to make this work. But your hardball approach isn't helping either of us. Let's talk numbers like civilized people."

Don thinks he has me all figured out. That he can solve any problem with enough money. Looking at him, all the pressure building in my chest for the past few weeks cracks, and I start to laugh.

"I hardly see what's funny about—"

"This isn't a negotiation, Don." I grab my purse and dig out my office key card. Then I point at the filing cabinet. "These are my in-progress deals. Whoever takes over, give them my cell if they have questions." Most likely John will poach the lion's share. I don't even mind. "Good luck."

"Shouldn't I be the one telling you that?" He chuckles, attempting to salvage any authority.

"No, thank you. I won't need it." With that, I scoop up the box and sail across the floor.

Coworkers pop up from cubicles like prairie dogs. Most wave. Some whisper. I catch the word pregnant and my stomach clenches. *Mind your own business!* I want to shout. Women have plenty of reasons to leave shitty work environments.

Before I crack, Tanya's there, hugging me. "This changes nothing." Her voice is muffled by my shirt. "We're still going to hang out constantly."

"You'd better keep me updated on the watercooler gossip."

She laughs. It sounds watery. We break apart and sure enough, her eyes glisten. "Feels like the end of an era."

"It is."

We both smile. And I keep smiling, all the way down the elevator. Outside, the wind stings my nose, reddens my face. But it's sunny, the wind carrying a whisper of a promise: spring will be here soon.

Chapter Fifteen

Second semester our sophomore year, Shane almost dropped out. The recession hit the family business hard—a lumber-yard Frank Cole inherited from his grandmother. Shane's earliest memories were playing hide-and-seek among the pallets of fresh-cut wood.

Unable to afford payroll for the two remaining employees, Frank debated closing. When Shane found out, he packed his dorm room, determined to keep the company afloat.

His parents ordered him to stay at school. They said the best way Shane could help was to get a degree and choose an easier future for himself.

Shane argued that his parents taught him the importance of sacrifice. Now it was his turn.

The night before tuition payments were due, Shane and I went on a long walk. By then we'd only been dating a couple of months, but it already broke my heart to picture campus without him.

He asked what I thought he should do. My first instinct was to agree with his parents and insist he was making a mistake.

But then I thought about how, growing up, the more my father pulled away, the tighter my mother clung to him.

When he left, I promised myself I would never act like her. (I would never act like him either.) I would love my future partner with a light touch, not a stranglehold.

So I suppressed my instincts and rested both hands on Shane's shoulders. "Whatever you choose, I support you. It's your life; you've got to decide how to live it."

He stayed. The lumberyard closed.

"My parents made so many sacrifices for us," he told me a few months later, once the dust had settled, and Frank had landed a new job. "I thought saving my dad's business was the way to pay him back, but he was too stubborn to admit he needed help." He grinned at me. "But then you told me you supported me, and I realized I was wrong. I was clinging to the yard because it was my past, and I was scared to lose it. But sometimes...it's braver to let go."

Now I face my brave husband across our spotless kitchen. The more difficult our conversations, the cleaner the house is by the end. Tonight, evidence suffuses the room: a sparkling mountain of dishes, immaculate counters, gleaming sink. We even polished the windows.

While we worked, I explained my decision.

Before he got home, I drew up last-minute calculations: monthly expenses, short-term savings, a proposed timeline. Six months. That's how long we can afford. If I don't figure out what I want by then, I'll accept anything. Part-time work, freelance, even waitressing. I did it in college; I can pick it up again. Whatever keeps us afloat.

"Say something," I whisper. He's gone uncharacteristically silent.

Shane runs a hand through his hair. A soap bubble clings to the foremost strand, and I resist the urge to pop it. "Are you sure, Lex?"

"Bit late for second-guessing." He doesn't laugh. I wet my

lips. "I know it seems sudden, but I haven't been happy at Medina in a long time. It's like...you know at the tail end of a cold, when you stop noticing your stuffy nose? Then suddenly one day it's gone and you're like, oh shit, I forgot how great breathing is."

Shane rinses the rag he used to dust the cabinets, then drapes it over the faucet. "Look, if you're happy, great, but first the nonsense with Bea, and now this? We said we didn't want to change our lives."

"No, you said that."

"And you agreed." He crosses his arms. "Or was that a lie?"

"I said Bea's training wouldn't impact us. I never promised to keep every aspect of my life in stasis. This has nothing to do with her." Even as the words leave my mouth, I realize they aren't true. The rush of energy I felt right before I quit—it was pure fire.

What element is next?

You'll know when it happens.

"I just wonder if now is the best time to make such a drastic decision." Shane steps closer. He rests both hands on my shoulders. "You're not acting like yourself, Lex."

"Maybe not like I did in the past." I reach up and fold my palms over his. "We can't stay the same forever."

"No." His grip tightens, just a little, like he wants to pin me down, stop me from running somewhere he can't follow. "But we're partners. We're supposed to talk through the big stuff."

I soften. "I didn't mean to decide without you. Listening to Don's same old bullshit today...I couldn't take it for another second. It just happened."

"Exactly!" He shakes me gently, the way I've seen Frank jostle the grandkids when he's teasing them. "You've always been a planner. Making such a huge decision spontaneously isn't like you; you never run from a challenge."

"There is no challenge." Grasping his wrists, I slide them off my shoulders and step back. To soften the blow, I cradle our hands between us instead. "That's the problem. I'm stagnating."

For a second, I smell icy rain and decaying leaves. The exact scent of our college campus in fall. In that moment, I realize what Shane is thinking.

"Look, if this is really what you want, we'll make it work. But make sure it's not fear or anything else driving you." He thinks if he makes the same concession I once did, I'll change my mind.

It's as close to acceptance as I'm going to get. "Deal."

He weaves his fingers through mine, and I breathe in his familiar scent. But just as I tilt toward him, he lets go. "I'll finish the floors." He pads to the utility closet.

Acting on instinct, I draw a deep breath. Meditation has taught me how to clear my thoughts and center my mind, so it only takes a couple of breaths before my vision coalesces.

Energy envelopes Shane, his auric field more vivid than any I've ever seen. Henry's and Tyrone's looked like gray fog or hazy rain, but my husband's energy is iridescent. Or maybe I'm just seeing the fields more clearly now that I know how.

Prismatic strands rise up through Shane's body and back down to earth all around him, a web of infinite raindrops. I get the sense that if I look closer, each individual drop will contain its own miniature rainbow.

Except...something's off. Not a block, or at least not one I can see, but rather a sense of imbalance. I feel as if I'm walking through a fun house with furniture on the ceiling, the whole world flipped on its head.

"Lexi?" Shane's voice ruptures my concentration.

I blink and he's Shane again. Normal, albeit concerned.

I did it. Up until now, I've only glimpsed auric fields by accident. This was on purpose—I reached for Shane's energy and found it. Those endless hours in Bea's back room are paying off after all.

"I asked what you want to do next," Shane says.

I didn't even hear him. My brow furrows. "Got a few ideas, I guess. Nothing concrete."

I think about Bea's friend's healing retreat. Or the customer who came into Odds and Ends the other day, gushing. "Bea cured my morning sickness. Nothing the doctors gave me touched it, but all she did was lay her hands on me and poof."

What is a healer, precisely? A job title? A hobby?

With one last searching look, Shane shrugs and goes to fill the mop bucket. "Well, when you decide, keep me in the loop."

My throat tightens. It's not regret—for once, I'm certain I made the right choice. Still, I wish it hadn't hurt him. "You'll be the first to know."

Chapter Sixteen

The next morning, I arrive at Bea's bright and early. **Too** early. The hours clearly state 9 a.m.–6 p.m. It's nine thirty, yet the lights are off, the grate rolled down.

Too antsy to wait, I walk to the nearest coffee shop. Yesterday was unseasonably hot for this time of year, and today looks on track to be the same, resulting in deep puddles all along the sidewalk. Despite this, there's a bounce in my step. My body vibrates, a coiled spring of energy.

The whole day belongs to me—no emails to parse, no listings to write or invoices to chase. My only job now is to decide what I want.

A few months ago, this level of freedom would have terrified me. Now it's intoxicating. Even when I land ankle-deep in a puddle, water spilling over my low-cut boots, nothing dims my excitement. I feel lit from within, on fire with potential.

By the time I return with an XL latte for me and a black coffee for Bea, the grate is up. I bound through the door. "Guess who?"

At the cash register, Bea squints over her reading glasses. "Ugh. Are you a morning person? Knew there was something off about you."

"Ha, ha." I plunk her coffee down. "Wasn't sure how you took it."

"Black, if you're already this hyper." Then she pauses. Studies me more intently. "Ahh. That explains it." Bea shrugs into her coat. "Let's talk in the car."

"Where are we going?" I ask, startled.

Bea's smile only widens. "You'll see."

I haven't been to the Little Sahara Sand Dunes since an elementary school trip. To my surprise, I recognize the thin strip of scrub grass that serves as a parking lot. We pull up beside an empty minibus surrounded by tire tracks—ATV tour group, probably.

Bea parks the same way she drives, like she's auditioning to be a Hollywood stunt driver. We screech to a halt, and I give silent thanks the trip is over. Out the windshield, a vast expanse of sand stretches to the horizon. Midday sun illuminates the dunes, which are so bright my eyes water.

"Let me guess. We're here for another unblocking meditation?" I ask.

"Not quite." Bea lowers her sunglasses. She shoots me the same look she's been giving me the whole car ride, while I babbled about quitting and my argument with Shane. "Blocks aren't the only way our energy gets tangled up. You've been repressing your fire energy for a while."

"But not anymore. Isn't that a good thing?"

Bea grabs her water bottle. "Have you ever opened a bottle of cold champagne on a hot day?" She taps the cap. "When you barely touch the cage and the cork goes flying? That's what happens when you bottle up your most explosive element. Fire governs passion, anger, and the creative spark. Too much fire and we act reckless. That's when we need to rebalance."

For a moment, my excitement dims. *You're not acting like yourself.* "If fire's making me impulsive, is Shane right? Was quitting a bad idea?"

"Stop looking to other people for answers." Bea pops open her door. "Me, your husband, your friends… None of us knows what's best for you."

Then who does?

We climb out of Bea's beat-up old sedan. She circles to the trunk and fishes out a pair of hiking boots, which do not at all match her flowy long-sleeved dress. Next, she whips out honest-to-God racing goggles.

"Very steampunk."

"I was aiming for vintage." Bea hands me a matching set, along with a scarf. "Tie it like this." She wraps her own scarf around her mouth and then grabs a knapsack. "You carry the sunscreen and water, Ms. Hyper."

I sling the pack over one shoulder.

A faint breeze kicks up. Particles of sand sneak between my teeth and along my lash line. I position the goggles, blinking hard to dislodge stray grains. Imitating Bea's expert scarf placement is more difficult.

"Ready?" Bea doesn't wait for an answer, just takes off into the sand.

I follow, still battling the scarf. The moment I hit sand, my ankle boots sink. Why didn't I bring combat boots or something? Clumpy sand pours into my socks, mingled here and there with half-melted snow. The dunes are experiencing the mini heat wave too, so despite the cold ground, the air itself feels summer-hot. Already, I wonder if the full camel of water on my back will be enough.

The farther we walk, the more I sweat, struggling to breathe through the scarf.

"Fire energy is all about physicality," Bea shouts over the

wind, as sand dances around our ankles. "Heat, sweat, exercise, dance...sex too."

"I have a perfectly active sex life, thank you." Although, it has been a few days. Wait. Weeks? Is that right? Thankfully the scarf hides my blush.

"Join the club. This isn't about sex with a partner. Or even the act itself."

Wait. Who is Bea hooking up with?

"Fire is best accessed through physical activity, like the so-called runner's high. I want you to get into that headspace today. It'll burn off the excess fire and force you to face yourself. Are you holding back? What do you believe?"

I almost trip over the next mound of sand. "I don't know! That's why I need you to teach me."

"Good teachers don't give you answers. They teach you how to find them yourself."

A pit forms in my stomach. "But I have no idea what I'm doing."

"You'll figure it out. I believe in you, Lexi."

Warmth settles behind my breastbone. *It's just the heat.* "Okay, Yoda."

"Believe in you, Yoda does too," Bea imitates, voice and all. I roll my eyes so hard that this time I do trip.

We trudge on in silence. At first, it's nice to stretch my legs. After a while, it gets stickier and more miserable. Sweat pools along my spine, under my breasts. Every so often, I stop to gulp water.

But the farther we walk, the less I think about my aching muscles or building thirst. My anxious thoughts quiet, and the distant hum of ATVs somewhere over the dunes fades to the background. The wind and sand sting my forehead, sticking to patches of sunscreen, but I hardly notice.

The only thing on my mind is movement. One leg in

front of the other, my soles sinking through sand. I breathe in, out, in again.

All of a sudden, Bea stops. I almost collide with her. "What is it?"

She points. We're at the foot of a dune. The peak looks so high that from this angle, it appears to touch the sun at its zenith.

I catch my breath. "We're not climbing that?"

"No." Bea's eyes crinkle with amusement. "You are."

Great. I don't bother arguing. This is my first big lesson since she took me to the mountain, and I messed the air meditation up so badly that I refuse to disappoint her again. "What do I do up there?"

"How should I know? This is your journey."

I groan.

Bea laughs. "Get out of your head and into your body. That's all."

Oh, is that all? Easy for her to say. She doesn't have a head full of anxiety. I reposition the day pack. It's just water and sunscreen, but already it drags on my shoulders.

Squaring my shoulders, I start to climb. At first, I walk upright, but then the incline grows steeper. Sand slides underfoot, trying to drag me back to earth. I give up on dignity and sink to all fours.

The sand sears my palms. I'm so drenched in sweat and discombobulated from the unseasonal weather that I can't tell if the burn feels cold or hot. Cursing, I shrug off my jacket and wrap the sleeves over my hands. Then I crawl. It feels silly for a few paces, but after a while it becomes more instinctive, almost primal. I'm a kid again, fists buried in lakeshore sandcastles.

Somewhere in the distance, I hear ululations. Four-wheelers cavort over an adjacent dune. From this height, they look like beetles.

This height. My breath catches.

Sand stretches as far as the eye can see. The dunes blaze white under the bluest sky I've ever seen.

It's beautiful.

The heat is sweltering, though whether it's from the sun or just my body after this workout, I'm not sure. When I close my eyes, they burn. I open them again, tears pooling inside my goggles.

Far below, a tiny stick figure of a person jumps up and down, waving. I laugh at Bea. Then I struggle upright to wave back. I use both arms, fling them up and wide. The motion feels good.

I squint at the peak. I'm still ten feet below it, but it's such a narrow point, I doubt it would support my weight. *Move,* a voice whispers.

I sway to one side and then the other. A small motion at first, almost a stretch. I get my arms into it, cartwheeling over my head. My muscles savor the sensation as my head tips back. Sun paints my face.

It's not enough. I want more. For a split second, I hesitate, my rational brain breaking through: *What if you get sand in your mouth, what if you get sunburn, what if—*

I tug off the scarf. It flutters at my fingertips. I twirl, leaning back, mouth open wide, the way I caught rain on my tongue as a kid. Today I catch sunrays. Swallow fire.

The wind sings. I swear I catch melodies in it, musical notes. When I laugh, the wind does too. I spin in a circle, the tail of my scarf fluttering. *Get into your body. It's about physicality.*

Rocking my hips, I sway to the wind's tune. It must look ridiculous, but for once, I don't care. I fling my hips into it, roll my shoulders and my neck. The sand dances with me, rising from the dune in cloudy puffs. Ribbons of it stretch into the wind like streamers to scatter across the desert.

One grain of sand isn't much. The most it's capable of is irritating your eye for a minute. But together? A few billion grains create whole mountains.

I kick the sand, raise bigger clouds. In one smooth motion, I bend in half, grab fistfuls of the earth, and launch upright, tossing it into the blue sky. The longer and the harder I dance up here, alone on my mountain, the less silly it seems, the more I understand.

There is energy here.

At the first tug, I skitter to a halt, arms akimbo for balance. I concentrate, try to pinpoint where it came from. But the energy vanishes again as quickly as I sensed it.

Get out of your head.

Instead of thinking, I dance. Wild, out-there movements. The kind of dancing I would never do in public, completely un-self-conscious. I throw shapes with my forearms, splay my fingers to the sun. I leap, spin, backbend, curve.

The energy rises once more, snakelike. Up my ankles, knees, thighs. It settles in my belly, a warm sun, and from there, it spreads down my arms, up into the crown of my head. It is both familiar and not: the same energy I've been feeling for days, except stronger, calmer. A bonfire that's been burning for hours, not one that just ignited, busy clawing to life.

I burn from the inside out. I am flame made manifest. Fire. Heat. Life.

Up in the sky, I am free from earthly constraints. I become my essential self, pared to skin muscle bone—no, not become, I remember. Because she has been here all along. She is me, and this me is hungry. She lusts in a way I rarely let myself.

What? I beg. Maybe out loud, I can't tell anymore. *What do I want?*

More, comes the answer, deep in my core.

I want more than the life I've settled for. More than the same day lived over and over on repeat. More than that office, the same battles for the same clients. Quitting was so laughably, obviously the right move.

But it is only the beginning. There's so much further to go.

On some level, it scares me. "More" is selfish, unspecific. I was raised to fear "more." *Don't covet, don't question, be grateful for whatever you're given.*

If I reach for more, there will be no training manual. No bosses, no rules or regulations, and no guidance, either, because Bea's right. No one else can say what my path ought to look like. It is a dark landscape, one that won't be illuminated until I enter and become a torch.

So far, I've lived life by a plan, with every detail painstakingly mapped. I've listened to advice, compared notes, contorted myself to fit into everyone else's boxes. I assumed I should want the same things as everybody around me.

It's terrifying to admit that I don't, but at the same time, I have never felt so alive. Following my path will be hard, probably harder than I grasp yet. But I can do it.

All I need to do is leap.

At that thought, I turn to examine the slope with fresh eyes. Is it really that steep? I climbed it, after all. From this height… Well. It's a risk, but so is everything.

With a wild whoop, I fling myself down the dune. I land sideways and roll over the sand like a kid on a lawn. I'm laughing until I catch a face full. Then I'm coughing and laughing at the same time, crying and whipping through the sand. I land in a tangle of limbs and sand and a hint of blood. I touch a finger to my lip, wince at the bitten spot.

Then Bea is there, offering me her water. "Are you crazy?" But she doesn't sound angry. If anything, she seems impressed.

"Maybe." I feel my legs, my torso. No other injuries. I stand and gulp water, the taste of copper on my tongue.

"Good." Bea squints at my lip. "It's healthy to lose your mind now and then."

I snort. "Easy for you to say."

"Who, Batty Bea?" She lowers her scarf to drink, and then wipes her mouth with the back of one hand. "You might call me an expert on the topic."

Despite her smile, I sober. "We shouldn't have called you that."

She gestures dismissively. "Bygones." She squints at me and pretends to shield her eyes, as if I'm the sun. "Damn. You accessed the fire all right. Any messages come through?"

"I think—"

She tsks. "No thinking. What do you feel?"

I shade my eyes and squint back up at the peak. From here, my ascending footprints are visible—a jagged line, weaving back and forth. Beside them runs the smooth plane I rolled down. In some places, it crosses over, erases the footsteps. In a few hours, the wind will bury the rest.

I lower my arm. "I made the right choice."

Chapter Seventeen

That night, I dream of the desert. It's lucid, which is rare for me. I'm climbing the dune again, only this time it's night. The sand feels cool as fresh sheets, the grains fine like silk. I'm nude, but not embarrassed. There's no one else here to see.

Even if there had been, so what? A body is a body. Clothes, I realize, are responsible for the illusions we cast—people look so much sexier partially dressed than we do naked. Completely bare, we are simply exposed, vulnerable... Honest.

When was the last time you were completely honest?

I am alone in the dream and aware it is a dream, yet... there's another presence. A nagging sense of more, just out of reach. I whip left to right, but no matter which direction I turn, whoever they are darts out of sight a heartbeat faster.

Why are you doing this?

I startle awake with the question on my lips.

Across the bed, Shane's alarm bleats. He pads out of the shower with his towel around his waist, awake before it as usual. "Sorry, sorry." He slaps the alarm off. "Go back to sleep."

Already the dream has begun to fragment. There was

sand, and a question, but what...? I rub sleep from my eyes, push the covers back. "It's fine. I'm awake."

In the bathroom, I wipe steam from the mirror. Over my shoulder, my husband pretends not to watch me. *Too much fire and we act reckless.* "Hey, Shane?"

He turns around.

"I should've talked to you before quitting. It was my decision, but...we are partners."

Some tension eases from his stance. He towels his hair, digests this for a moment. "Change is hard for me," he says eventually. "Especially change I don't understand."

"If it makes you feel any better, I don't understand it either."

"My wife quit her job and she doesn't know why. Oh yes, now I feel loads better." But he's grinning as he says it and moves closer.

I meet him halfway. He pulls me against his damp chest, wet patches spreading onto my nightshirt. "Honestly, it was worth it for the look on Don's face alone."

Shane laughs into my hair. "Wish I could've been there."

"He tried to lecture me on salary negotiation."

"Please. Like you're not an expert saleswoman."

"Pretty sure 'woman' and 'expert' are mutually exclusive in Don's book."

Shane brushes a finger under my chin, tilts my face up. "I'm glad you quit," he says, soft and sincere. "That place didn't deserve you."

The words warm me all the way through. I hook both arms around his neck. "Bonus, now I've got more time to spend with someone who does."

"Oh?" He bends to kiss my temple, my cheekbone, the corner of my jaw. "Who's the lucky bastard?"

I tip my head back, laughing. "I believe you've met."

Shane buries his face in the crook of my neck. "Hmm,

maybe." He grins, teeth grazing bare skin and drawing a shiver from me. "We are the same person, after all."

It surprises me how easily I fall into a new routine. Breakfasts with Shane, followed by mornings at the gym, where I work up a bigger sweat than I have in years. Depending on her mood, Bea rolls out of bed to open the shop anywhere between its advertised opening time of 9 a.m. and shortly before lunch. More often than not, by the time she arrives, I'm already there waiting with takeout. She only eats three foods: pizza, Thai, and baked goods. I don't mind. The last thing on my mind is food.

While Bea takes phone orders, helps customers, and runs healing sessions on the top floor—a floor I'm not allowed to visit yet—I practice meditation. Bea wants me doing an hour a day. Right now, I manage half on a good day.

In addition, she sets me seemingly random, impossible tasks. One day, she hands me a pincushion shaped like a tomato, dozens of pins stuck in it to form a cat face. "Tell me where this came from," she says. "Who owned it? How did they feel about it?"

Another day, as one of her regulars browses, Bea pulls me aside. "Find out why he's here." I start toward him, but Bea bars the aisle. "Without talking to him."

I feel like a contestant on a prank show. I keep waiting for hidden cameras to pop out, revealing an audience in hysterics over how gullible I am. *She actually thinks she can read minds.*

But one day, Bea hands me a silver brooch and I flinch so hard I drop it. Bea snatches it up with a knowing smile. "What do you sense?"

This time, I shut my eyes. She lowers it onto my palm again. Even though I brace for it, the wave of terror is overwhelming—every nerve in my body fires. I want to fling it away and run. "It feels...bad," I hear myself say. "Frightening. I smell blood. Someone's crying..."

"What else? Use more than your physical senses. There's energy in the object, the same energy as in you or me. You'll recognize it. Let go of your conscious mind."

The back of my tongue tastes metallic. I choke down air. *More than my senses.* "Somewhere cold, lonely..."

"That's it." Bea's voice sounds far away. "Tap into the emotion."

"I'm alone." My voice doesn't sound like mine anymore. "He left to get help. It's so cold. The fire went out; I can't restart it. Oh God, she's dead, isn't she?"

When I open my eyes again, Bea's expression has sobered. I practically fling the brooch at her.

She catches it. "Nineteen forty-three. Barb and Donald Riley went for a drive with her sister, Pat. It started snowing as they were coming over the mountains. Donald lost control and flipped the car. Pat was killed on impact. Barb lasted a few hours, but by the time Donald returned with a search party..." Bea tilts the brooch to the light. It's a bouquet of ruby-studded roses. "She was wearing this."

I shudder and rub my arms. "Why would you give that to me? Why do you even have it?"

"The heavier the emotion, the easier it is to pick up." She pockets the brooch. "They were my maternal grandparents."

Oh. "Shit. I'm sorry, I didn't—"

She shakes her head. "Before my time, obviously. Donald remarried and lived a long life. My mother didn't tell me that my grandmother wasn't her birth mother until I was twenty."

"That must've been hard." I know a little something about family secrets. How they fester.

She nods. "But that was good, Lexi. You're making progress."

She rewards me with a trip to the secondhand shop. Together, we paw through items. Most give me nothing. Then a black poodle skirt sets off a riot of butterflies. Holding it, I get flashes of rainbow lights, the taste of cheap vodka. Bea confers with the shop owner. The woman who sold him the dress only wore it once, to prom.

Over the weekend, Bea gives me homework: practice reading people.

I visit a café in the morning, the mall for lunch hour, and finally the library until it closes. In each location, I position myself in a remote corner and slow my breathing, clear my mind. When my vision blurs out of focus, I see it.

Energy.

Mostly auric fields. Cocoons of energy that engulf people. Some are different colors. A yellow haze surrounds a white man eating an egg-and-cheese sandwich at the café. Purple and green stripes encircle a Black woman studying at the library. But most people's auric fields resemble Tyrone's—an almost-clear desert-mirage shimmer I can barely make out.

Sometimes I spot blocks. Bea says with more experience, I'll learn which blocks are serious. I'm beginning to understand what she means. A man on crutches in the mall has a thick, gnarled block around the foot he favors. The energy near it moves sluggishly, if at all. But the block looks old, incorporated. Like when a tree trunk grows around a foreign object. If I released it, I doubt it would do anything but improve his mood.

Other blocks seem deceptively minor at first glance—an older woman at the café, a dozen tiny blocks swarming her like gnats. But the longer I look, the worse I feel. My head fills with a symphony of high-pitched whines.

"This is a latte," the woman yells, loud enough to hear across the café. "I ordered a cappuccino." And then, in response to the server's murmur. "No, it isn't! Unlike you, I know the difference. Where is your manager?"

Her energy reminds me of John Wood. The way he attacked me, possibly without even realizing what he was doing. I'm tempted to intervene. But before sending me "into the wild," Bea made me swear not to touch anyone else's energetic field.

"Why not?" I asked. Then, nervously, "Could I hurt them?"

"I'm more worried about you hurting yourself at this point."

So I just grimace apologetically at the server. Before I go, I stuff a twenty in the tip jar.

Monday rolls around. Remembering how claustrophobic I felt at Murphy's, I beg off girls' night. Bea's lessons tire me out. Fill you in next week, promise. I add a million hearts. Tanya says I'd better, because she has fresh office gossip. Chloe offers to threaten Bea for working me too hard.

But then next week rolls around and the bar still sounds like an exhausting prospect. Any chance I could get another rain check? I ask.

Okay seriously, is Bea holding you hostage? Chloe replies.

SOS emoji if you need rescued, Tanya adds.

What is she, the Titanic?

At least I beat Shane home every night.

"How go the magic tricks?" he's taken to asking when he gets in. Annoying, but an improvement on suggesting psych evaluations.

I stop telling him about the lessons. Instead, we text each other news clips. He sends an article about a famous medium failing a double-blind experiment. I send a research paper on psychic phenomena published by a respected science journal. He replies with the wiki entry on observer bias. I fire back an interview where a Nobel Prize-winning physicist says atheism is incompatible with the scientific method.

In person, we joke. It's playful and easier than broaching the truth. But sometimes it leaves a bitter aftertaste.

In bed, I listen to his breathing and consider my mother and father's relationship. Is falling into their pattern inevitable? Maybe one partner must always be rigid, the other bent over backward to accommodate them.

If so, I can't tell which I am.

The next Monday, I sit cross-legged on the Persian carpet in Bea's back room. A fresh candle drips sunny-yellow wax onto the growing tower. Upstairs, the floorboards creak—Bea's up there seeing a patient. I suppress my curiosity.

For the first few minutes, all I think about is the twinge in my lower back, the cramp in my calf. Eventually, my breath drowns it out, though. I focus on my lungs as they expand and contract, contract and expand.

My pulse slows.

Time passes. My vision slips from focus. The room warms as a long, hot waterfall of sensation cascades from the crown of my head. And then...

Energy. All around me, in every direction. It's like peering at the world from beneath a veil.

My auric field.

It's the first time I've seen my own, even though I've spent so long studying other people's.

My breath goes shallow so as not to disturb it. Wrapped inside the field, the individual strands of energy appear razor-thin. Like Shane's, up close my energy is not clear or any one color. It's multifaceted. Every color of the rainbow, as well as a few I have no name for.

When I raise my hand, the energy ripples like a pond surface disturbed—or, no, not a pond. It has the sheen of an oil slick, though none of the slimy undertones.

I can't touch it, exactly. It shifts whenever I do, goes where my body moves. Still, when I stretch my arms overhead, the energy changes. It speeds up, energized somehow by movement, which gives me an idea.

Bea said I shouldn't touch other people's energy yet, but she didn't say anything about my own.

I stretch my legs out. The cramp in my right calf is still there, and sure enough, the air above it pools too, a motionless clump. Careful not to touch my leg, I reach for the energy and smooth my palms through it. It stirs, but the moment I withdraw my hand, it quiets again.

So it can move, but it needs more momentum. *An object at rest will remain at rest...* Vague physics lessons threaten to break my concentration. *Stop thinking.*

I raise both hands overhead. Slowly, I bring them back down, palms cupped, to trace my body—not touching my skin, just dragging my fingers through the auric field itself.

A ripple of power moves with me, an ocean wave speeding toward the shore.

When it reaches my waist, I bend double, continuing to push it along my thigh, over my knee, and finally to my calf. The wave hits the block, and a sudden memory springs to mind.

The chalk-and-cheap-deodorant scent of my college physics classroom. The soft rustle of paper, a faint flavor of plastic and ink. Test day. I suck on my pen, struggling over a problem set. And then...

The warm press of skin against my calf. I know who it is, though I don't remember his name, all these years later. Every day, he inched his body closer to mine. Found excuses to touch me—a brush here, an "accidental" graze there. He was always ready with an excuse when I called him out.

Our professor, who I stopped after class to complain to, shrugged and told me to sit somewhere else.

Old anger ripples to the surface. I splay my fingers and push—past the calf, all the way to my toes. The energy rolls with me, over me. It floods through the memory in a torrent, freezing and burning at once. Finally, the ghost of his touch fades too, washed bare.

A tingle spreads in its wake, reminding me of muscles waking from a long sleep. The sensation makes me burst out laughing.

I feel incredible. Light and fresh as if I've just stepped out of my morning shower. And the cramp is completely gone. I stretch my calf, massage it. Nothing.

"Holy shit," I murmur.

The auric field vanishes as my concentration snaps. The rest of the world floods in—Chaucer purring next to me, Bea laughing with a customer out in the shop. Guess her healing session finished. Part of me wants to race up front and share what just happened.

Another part recalls Bea's warning and how she never lets me observe while she's healing customers. She keeps saying I'm not ready.

I don't want to spoil the excitement with her warnings yet, so I hug Chaucer instead. "I did it," I whisper in his ear.

He opens one hazel eye, unimpressed, and rolls away.

"Well. Same to you."

That night, still high on success, I go to bed early. Healing one tiny block felt so good that I'm eager to try more.

Alone in our bedroom, Shane's movie blasting downstairs, I light a candle and settle in. It takes longer to reach the right headspace here. My attention drifts to the door, head full of excuses in case Shane comes in.

Forget him. Concentrate.

After an eternity, my auric field reappears. I grin, pulse thrumming. Yet my smile fades as I look closer.

Earlier, the energy streamed past. Tonight, the whole auric field has slowed to the pace of eye floaters. It drifts lazily, almost stagnant in places.

What's wrong?

My vision goes blurry. It's hard to focus. So slow, slow, slow... I yawn.

I'm just tired. That must be why. I blow out the candle and shuffle under the covers, where I immediately fall into a sleep so deep I don't even hear Shane come in.

I don't think about it again until the next day. Two coffees deep, unable to focus to save my life, I abandon meditation practice to look for Bea.

She's perched at the counter, nose-deep in a new book.

"Can your energy slow down?" I ask. "Or, your auric field, I guess."

It takes her a second to drag her eyes from the page. She gets more immersed in novels than I do in meditation. "Well, everyone's energy flows at its own pace." She marks her page using the nearest object—in this case, a bundle of dried rosemary. "Your elemental constitution plays a factor. Air and fire are quick-moving, whereas earth and water are more sedate. And of course, blocks and imbalances can affect your field."

I worry at my lower lip. "What about in one day? Could someone's field flow quickly in the morning, then slower at night?"

"Sure, if something drained or altered their energy."

My shoulders relax. "So it's normal. Like getting sleepy."

"Not quite that normal. It shouldn't happen often." Bea squints at me, then lays her book aside. "Why do you ask?"

A little jolt of panic. My first instinct is to avoid the

question, but did I learn nothing from the air lesson? I need to speak up. Be more open. "Well...I, ah, tried something new yesterday."

Bea's gaze sharpens. "I warned you not to try to influence fields yet, Lexi."

"I didn't touch anyone else's! Just mine. And it worked! Or at least, it felt nice while I was doing it. But then later last night, I tried again, and my whole field seemed...sluggish."

Bea massages her temples.

When she doesn't say anything, I cross my arms. "You said to listen to my instincts and stop relying on everyone else's opinions."

"Yes, Lexi. But if you just learned how to jog a mile, you can't go out the next day and run a marathon. You tried too much too soon. You need to pace yourself."

None of us knows what's best for you. Bea said so herself. And she was right—I look everywhere but inward for guidance. I default to my parents, teachers, Shane, even to my shithead former CEO's advice. I'm finally listening to myself and Bea lectures me for it?

With effort, I swallow the irritation. *Be polite.* My mother's favorite mantra.

"I will."

"But hey." Bea touches my shoulder. "Congratulations. You touched your field for the first time; that's a huge step." She glances at the grandfather clock by the back entrance. "Celebratory bakery run?"

I force a smile. "Sure. I'll grab my purse."

Chapter Eighteen

Spring arrives in fits and starts: a thaw here, a wildflower there.
Then a late snow falls and sprinkles frozen petals throughout
the drifts. The last of it is still melting when Shane suggests a
drive to Salt Lake City. Eric and Tyrone will move east in two
weeks, so the family has planned a surprise send-off.

Considering we haven't seen the Coles since Christmas—
and I've barely seen anyone besides Bea and the occasional
customer—I'm excited. But I also don't want to fall behind
in my studies. The day before we leave, I stop by Odds and
Ends and ask what I should work on while I'm away.

Bea acts like I just asked for directions to Mars. "What do
you mean?"

"Well, I'll be gone all weekend. Should I go to cafés in
the city, try to read auric fields there? Or maybe find more
objects to practice reading, or...is there anything new I
should try?" My voice rises hopefully. It's been weeks since
Bea has given me any real lessons, as if she doesn't trust me
to know my limits anymore.

"You office workers all have grind complexes." She rolls
her eyes. "Take a break. Relax."

Does Bea know how frustrating she is? "That's my assignment. Relaxing."

"Your assignment is to get used to not having assignments. I swear, education these days…" She wanders off, grumbling about academia not preparing anybody for real life.

So the next day, bags packed and car windows rolled down, I try my best to follow orders and relax.

Shane blasts classic rock. We both sing along—him on key, me all over the place. Neither minds. I stick a hand out the window to let it drift on the currents. I've missed this.

By the time we reach Eric and Tyrone's apartment complex, Frank Cole's ancient Ford pickup is parked out front, Holly's vintage suitcase strapped in the bed.

Shane groans. "I keep telling her not to leave stuff sitting out. This isn't the country."

"I'd rather get taken advantage of than never trust a soul," I do my best impression of Holly's strong Utahn accent.

Laughing, Shane jumps into the truck to unstrap the luggage. We haul it up along with our own bags. Before we even reach Eric's floor, voices spill down the stairwell. Sure enough, his and Tyrone's apartment door hangs wide open, the place already crowded.

"What the heck," Shane shouts by way of hello. "We agreed to surprise them together."

Holly detaches from her stranglehold on Eric. "I couldn't wait any longer."

"Shane. Lexi." Red rims Eric's eyes, but he's smiling. "You didn't have to come all this way. We're not moving to the other side of the planet."

"Just the other side of the continent." Holly sniffs. "As far from me as you can get, huh?" She's teasing, but I sense an undercurrent of fear.

"Incoming." Frank points out the window. A minute later, a flock of kids stream inside. Shane's middle sisters, Becky and Hannah, arrive next, followed by Becky's husband and Hannah's life partner, staggering under various diaper bags.

I wade through them to the kitchen, where Tyrone brews coffee. "I'm sure this is exactly how you envisioned your last weekend at home."

Tyrone laughs. "To be honest, yeah." He surveys the room, and his gaze snags on Eric. "That smile is worth all the chaos."

Eric grins from ear to ear, with a niece and nephew clinging to each leg and a third braced on his hip. He's always been so close with his family.

"How's he doing?" I ask. "And you too?"

Tyrone sighs. "Honestly, I go back and forth. I'm excited to see my mom, don't get me wrong. And there's things in New York I've missed. The food, for a start. But…" He lowers his voice. "I'm worried about him. Ever since we decided, he's been really withdrawn."

My eyebrows rise. "Eric? Withdrawn?"

"I know, it's bad." He grimaces. "I get being nervous. This wasn't exactly either of our first choice. I just don't want him to resent me. Taking care of my mother is my responsibility, y'know? Not his."

"Partners share the good stuff and the hard crap." When he huffs, unconvinced, I nudge him. "Imagine the reverse. Would you resent Eric if you guys had to move to help Holly or Frank?"

He scrunches his forehead, considering. "Depends. In this scenario, are we taking care of the pets too? 'Cause the dogs are all right—except the purse-sized one, he peed in my shoe—but I'm pretty sure Holly's new cat wants to kill me. I woke up with it on my face last visit. Sir, I do not know where your ass has been."

I snort. "Okay, no pets. Would you resent him?"

"Of course not." Tyrone's features soften. "Hell, even with the damn pets, I'd be in. Long as Eric handles all poop-related concerns."

"There's your answer." We bump shoulders again.

Shane steps into the kitchen, nodding at the pot of coffee. "That still going?"

"Sure thing; grab a cup."

The guys talk apartments, neighborhoods. I've never been to New York, but Hannah went to NYU, and Shane visited her a couple of times. The place names all fly over my head, but Shane seems impressed by wherever Eric and Tyrone's new apartment is.

While they chat, I drift into the living room.

Becky's husband asks after my family, trying to be polite. I stammer a vague response. Aside from sending each other the occasional funny meme, my brother and I haven't spoken in months. I never even told him I quit my job. And Mom...

She hasn't called since Christmas. It's my turn to reach out, but I'm not ready yet.

"Lexi!" Frank rescues me, cell phone in hand. He's recently discovered selfies and taken to them with all the enthusiasm of a teen on his first social media platform. "Get in here." He's been dragging Eric around the room, snapping photos with everyone.

Obediently, I duck into the frame. Eric drapes an arm over one of my shoulders, while Frank takes the opposite.

"On the count of three." Frank grins. "Say 'ménage à trois.'"

Eric practically inhales his coffee. I double over. Shane's sister Becky, who's busy corralling the twins, jerks upright. "Dad. What do you think that means?"

"A group of three!"

For a while, I let the party sweep me up. Since I started studying energy, I've avoided big gatherings. Even at the café or the mall, whenever the crowd thickens, I leave. Too much energy all at once gives me sensory overload, like the one time I tried to visit Murphy's.

But being here, surrounded by people I love…it's almost the opposite. Everyone's energy buoys me and seems to replenish mine. There's something magical about coming together to honor a transformation. Eric and Tyrone's life is changing, so we gather to mourn the past and toast their future simultaneously.

Change is hard for me, Shane said. *Change is hard for everyone*, I wanted to tell him. Even good change is bittersweet. We must let go of the old to embrace the new.

As the party crescendos, however, a new feeling tugs at me. My eyes stray to Eric more and more. Over the course of the afternoon, his smile grows wooden and stiff.

I'm worried about him.

Dinner scents waft from the kitchen. Tyrone sidles up to Eric, murmuring something in his ear. Surreptitiously, I lean against the wall and slow my breath. Within moments, my gaze unfocuses.

Tyrone laughs, but Eric looks like he's forcing it. He kisses Tyrone's cheek just as Frank calls their names. They both look up and pose for a picture. As they do, the air around them both coagulates.

Tyrone's field catches my eye first. Like at Christmas, it shimmers, barely visible. A handful of small blocks dot it, no larger than my own block that I healed. But now, with Tyrone standing beside Eric, I pick up something else. Wispy strands extend from Tyrone's field, like thin ribbons of cloud. They all drift toward Eric, who…

I inhale sharply.

Blocks clump all over Eric's chest. Grayish fist-sized marks, so thick I can't make out his T-shirt underneath. They remind me of blood clots or tumors, the kind of thing that screams *wrong* the instant you see it.

Side by side with Tyrone, it's obvious Eric's whole auric field is moving at a crawl. As I stare, all his energy seems to pour into the growing cavity at his chest.

Shit. I've never seen an auric field like this. *No wonder Tyrone's worried.*

The guys separate. Tyrone shoots Eric one last glance before he follows Hannah into the living room. As he walks away, the wisps in his auric field grow longer, like invisible strings straining to reach Eric.

Can your partner affect your field?

I make a mental note to ask Bea later. In the back of my mind, she's saying, *Take a break. Relax.* But I'm also trying to listen to my gut, and right now, my gut screams: *Do something.*

Eric needs help.

Someone puts on music. The nieces and nephews dance, some more wildly than others. In the kitchen, Holly and a couple of the husbands bustle. Eric shuffles into the dining room and props himself against the wall near me. Every so often, his eyes stray to the cabinet where he hides their wine collection whenever his parents visit.

Once my vision clears, I join him. "Hey. You okay?"

He lets his head thunk against the wall. "Course. Got a new job; dunno if Shane mentioned."

"That's great!" I punch his bicep. "In New York?"

"Remote. But the headquarters are in Manhattan, in case I need to be there for meetings." He goes quiet again.

"Stop me if I'm prying, but...you don't look too excited."

"I am!" He attempts a smile. "Really, it'll be fun. Ty's mom is great. It'll be nice to get to know her better. Plus, a couple of our friends moved to North Jersey last year. Apparently that's not too far from Midtown. And, you know,

153

a paying job is always nice…" The longer Eric talks, the more his smile droops.

He glances at the kitchen, where Holly directs his brother-in-law at the stove. A niece darts by and Holly laughs.

Eric's jaw clenches.

I look to his chest. I can't see his energy anymore, but I still sense it, a sinking feeling in my gut.

Help him. But how do I explain without sounding like a complete weirdo? I'm only used to discussing this stuff with Bea, who already knows everything, or Shane, who's so dismissive I don't go into detail.

Then again, I'll never learn to heal if I can't talk about it. "Do you believe in energy?" I ask abruptly. *Too general, Lexi.* "Not like, electricity. Spiritual energy."

Eric blinks, thrown by the change of subject. "I guess? I mean, I think there's more to the world than just the physical. Why?"

"Well, uh…" I tug on a stray lock of hair. "Lately, I've had a few…experiences. It's made me question things."

Eric side-eyes me. "Please tell me you saw a ghost. I've always wanted to. Sometimes I take the long way home through this graveyard just in case—"

"No." I laugh weakly. "No ghosts. It's more like…occasionally, I look at a person—a living person—and there's this energy all around them. It's part of them, but it extends beyond their body too. Like a cloud. And when I see it, sometimes I know stuff about them. Things I can't explain."

Eric's expression melts into polite confusion.

I scrub my hands over my face. "Sorry, I'm not being very clear."

"No, I think I get it." He pauses thoughtfully. "There was this one time, when I was little. Probably my earliest memory. Shane and Becky went to the big playground, but

Dad said I was too little, so I had to stay in the yard. Only, Shane or Becks must've left the gate open by mistake. I got lost, wound up in the woods behind our neighbors', and I fell. Hit my head, twisted my ankle so bad I couldn't walk… They found out later I had a mild concussion."

"Ouch."

He nods. "Anyway, Mom was at work, but she said she felt a stabbing pain in her ankle. Suddenly she just knew that I was hurt, where I was, everything. She came racing home. Found me before Dad even noticed I'd gone missing."

My eyes widen. "Shane never told me that."

"Doubt he remembers. Hell, I haven't thought about it in years." He trails off, eyes finding his mother in the kitchen again. "But you're not the first psychic in this family."

I snort. "I'm hardly psychic. Anyone can do this stuff." Bea made that very clear in her early lessons. "But I have been studying it."

"Oh?" Eric's eyebrows inch higher. "What's Shane think about that?"

"Take a guess," I mumble, and he laughs.

"Don't worry." He claps a hand on my shoulder. "My brother's the designated family skeptic. He takes the job very seriously. But he's put up with the rest of us his whole life, so he's used to disagreement."

I nod, not reassured. Since we started dating, Shane's made it clear he values our similarities. He calls us the same person, two halves of one brain. He talks about how hard it was being the odd one out in his family and how meeting me changed all that. *Us against the world.*

I clear my throat, force the worry away. "Anyway, I mention it because I saw your energy just now."

"Let me guess, I'm dazzling." He tips his chin back and strikes a pose.

I don't answer.

"Oh." His face falls. "Not good news?"

"It's not necessarily bad," I hasten to say. "Your energy—my mentor calls it an auric field—looks a little blocked." *More than a little.* "Blocks happen when we're going through difficult times. Sometimes they clear on their own, but yours... Well. It seems pretty serious. A professional healer would know how to fix it, though."

"To be honest, I'm not sure I understand," he replies slowly. "I mean, I respect that you're into this stuff, but..."

"You don't have to understand it. Just visit me and Shane before your move. I'll take you to see my mentor. She's a healer. She'll be able to—"

"Lexi. Babe." He cuts me off with a gesture around the apartment. "There's no way we have time for an impromptu visit to Garden Vale. We haven't even started packing." He wrinkles his nose at the pile of cousins eating something red and sticky on his white couch. "Or cleaning."

"Right. Of course." I frown, thinking fast. "Let me talk to her. Maybe she could drive up here one day this week."

"Can't you do it?" Eric asks. "If it's so urgent."

"I..." *Shit.* Bea's warning echoes. *You need to pace yourself.* But my instincts are screaming the opposite. *Help him.* "I guess I could try?" *What are you doing, Lexi?* "But I've only been studying for a little while. And I've never tried to heal anyone else. There's a chance I might make it worse."

Eric waves off the protests. "I trust you." I can't tell whether he's only saying that because he doesn't believe any of this in the first place. "So what do we need?"

"Need for what?" Frank's familiar baritone interrupts. Too late, I realize he and Shane have drifted within earshot.

"Lexi's going to heal my... What did you call it? Auric field?"

I want to sink into the floor.

Shane laughs, a touch too loudly. "Don't mind her. Lexi's been on an alternative medicine kick since she quit her job."

Frank frowns. "Gotta be careful. Lot of dishonest people out there looking to take advantage."

"That's what I told her." Shane's eyes haven't left mine.

I cross my arms, shift so my right hand is in Shane's eyeline. Then I raise my middle finger. Today, it's not *us against the world*. Just the regular meaning.

The fine lines over Shane's forehead tighten.

Meanwhile, Eric shrugs at his father. "You buzzkills aren't invited, then." He links arms with me. "I, for one, can't wait to see what Lexi can do."

One hearty, home-cooked meal later, Eric and I stand on the empty rooftop of his apartment complex. A yoga mat sprawls at our feet, and a handful of pigeons squint curiously from their nests. Tyrone leans against the door to the roof, watching.

Much to Shane's dismay, Eric announced our plans to the entire family during dinner. Tyrone wanted to come. I don't know if Bea has a policy about partners attending healing sessions—whether it's a good idea or not—but Eric said he didn't mind, so...

Their apartment building faces the historic Marmalade district, on the edge of downtown. From up here, Temple Square and the Capitol building are visible. Flowering trees line the streets, with Victorian and Queen Anne houses nestled among them. Inhaling, I catch the scent of magnolias, even five stories up.

"Real talk, Lex. If we'd bought this place instead of renting, how much do you think we could've sold it for?" Eric leans over the roof's edge.

Tyrone looks like he's resisting the urge to haul Eric back to safety. "Nope, do not depress yourself. We never would've gotten a mortgage in our twenties anyway."

"I'm just curious!" Eric straightens back up.

Tyrone exhales in obvious relief. "Uh-huh. What's that do to cats again?"

I stifle a laugh. "Couldn't tell you anyway. I'm out of the real estate biz; dunno if you've heard."

"About time." Eric smirks. "Never struck me as the right place for you, Lex. It's all about sales and people-pleasing. You're too creative for that."

I roll my eyes, but I'm smiling. "Thanks."

"Change all around these days for Coles and company." Eric's mouth tightens into not quite a smile anymore. It's been happening all night, whenever he thinks nobody's looking.

"I'm gonna miss this view," Tyrone says softly.

"Me too," Eric murmurs.

"I'm sorry you have to leave." I watch them both, chest tight.

Eric shrugs. "It's fine."

"It's okay if it's not."

He shrugs again, then turns his back on the view. "So, energy healing. I don't have to eat eye of newt or anything weird, right?"

"No amphibian eating." I point to the yoga mat. "Just lie down and I'll do the rest." At least, I'll try.

My nerves flutter. I've only done this once before, on myself, and the block was nowhere near as complicated as Eric's.

While he gets settled in, I wet my lips. "Like I said, I'm new at this. I'll work slowly, but if anything feels off, tell me right away. The last thing I want to do is make it worse."

Tyrone stiffens. "Wait, what?"

Eric reclines on the yoga mat, arms pillowed under his head. "It'll be fine. Lexi knows what she's doing." He winks at me.

"Please don't accidentally curse my boyfriend," Tyrone says.

"I'll do my best. Hands at your sides, Eric." I wait for him to obey. "Okay. Now, we're going to start by focusing on our breath. I want you to inhale deeply." His chest rises. "And exhale. Good. Breathe in...and out."

After a few breaths, Tyrone pads to a folding chair someone abandoned up here. He perches on it, gaze fixed on Eric. My usual anxious thoughts kick in. *What's he thinking? How strange do I look?*

By now, though, I've had enough meditation practice to quiet my brain, or at least tune it out.

I breathe in the same rhythm as Eric. In, out. In, out. Eric's shoulders relax from around his ears and his legs rotate out, muscles going limp. At the same time, my mind sinks into the now-familiar rhythm.

With the scent of flowers in my nose, stars beginning to peek through the dimming night sky, the shift comes easier than ever. Between one breath and the next, Eric's auric field materializes.

Even braced for the sight, the block startles me. It's so obviously out of place—a dark wine stain on pristine white silk. The rest of Eric's energy is brilliant, the same multifaceted, iridescent hue as my field or Shane's. As anyone's field, I'm beginning to realize, if you look closely enough.

The healthy parts flow like ocean currents, but the block is a dam. Constricting and *wrong*.

On the next inhale, I bend to trace my hands just above his chest. Eric gasps and my whole body locks up in panic. "Are you all right?" I whisper.

"It tickles."

With effort, I relax again. From the corner of my eye, I catch Tyrone doing the same. "Remember. Anytime you want to stop, say the word."

I move slower this time, reaching in slow motion. Starting at the crown of his head, I lower both palms into his auric field. The skin of my palms tingles, a bit distracting, though not unpleasant.

It's different than touching my own field, like the scent of your home compared to a friend's. On the next inhale, my hands skate lower, across Eric's face, and then above his throat.

Just like at home, a wave of energy moves with me. This time, it's easier to direct. I cup the wave's edges, shape my fingers to direct the flow. Steeling myself, I pull the wave into the block.

The light, airy substance I've been touching thickens to molasses. Both of my arms sink wrist-deep, then grind to a halt. I grit my teeth and push, but everything's in slow motion now.

Behind my eyelids—when did I close them?—memories flicker.

I am a baby, cradled in my mother's arms. "Shh, shh." Her voice is familiar, though her face isn't visible. "I've got you."

Blink. I'm older, all gangly legs and elbows on a couch in an unfamiliar room. Grand piano, a stone fireplace… Wait. *The Coles' living room.* Only the decor is different, the furniture outdated. "I just know, okay?" The voice coming out of my mouth is higher-pitched than usual, yet still recognizable. Eric.

"Sweetie." The same voice as before. Now I place it— Holly Cole rubs my shoulder. "You're too young for all this. You're confused."

"I'm not confused." I shove off the couch, even as every

cell in my body screams to go back. *Beg if you have to, just make her understand.*

Blink. Another unfamiliar room. Brown benches, green carpet, white walls. *A chapel.* Someone mutters in the row behind me. I don't catch the words, but it doesn't matter. Holly's there, whipping around. "My son belongs here just as much as any of you. More so, if you only came to gossip."

Blink. I am wearing dark robes, rolled diploma in hand. Holly crushes me to her chest. "I'm so proud of you, sweetie." She pulls back, tears standing out along her lash line. "I know I haven't always been as supportive as I should have—"

"Don't." I hug her just as fiercely. "Don't you dare. You're perfect, Mom."

She laughs, but it sounds brittle. "I am far from perfect. Look at Clarissa."

"She's happy."

"Only far away from me. And Shane…"

"He's a few hours' drive, that's all."

"Everybody wants to leave."

My arms tighten. "Not me. Not ever."

Somewhere at the edge of my attention, I am aware of my own hands, poised in midair over Eric's chest. The block clumps between my fingers, a glutinous texture that makes me want to gag. Instead I knead my fingers deeper.

Someone's crying. Me or Eric, not sure which.

Blink. I am on the couch in this very apartment. Legs kicked up, head resting in a warm lap. Hands toy absently with my hair.

"Eric." When Tyrone speaks, the vibrations tickle my scalp.

He is reading something on his phone. No, not his phone—Eric's phone is the one covered in Formula One stickers. Ty's eyes dart across the screen.

I already know that no matter how many times he rereads the words, they won't change. "They'll pay me out through the end of the month."

Tyrone sets the phone down. He looks both older and more exhausted than I've ever seen. "Maybe it's time."

I am sinking, sinking, sinking.

Blink. I am back in the Coles' living room. This time it looks the way it does nowadays. It's still decked in Christmas decorations, in fact, the same ones that were up this year. I am on the floor, face buried in my hands.

"Sweetie, what is it?" Holly sounds torn between amusement and confusion.

Look at her. I owe her that much. *I owe her so much more.* "Ty and I have been talking. And we think, maybe the best move for us, at least for right now…"

The words drone. I am not listening. I am watching my mother. She's trying so hard not to cry. But I know her too well.

With a gasp, I jolt back to myself. At first, I don't know why. Then I feel Tyrone's arms wrapped around my shoulders. My legs have gone limp, splayed on the roof. He's holding me upright—he must have caught me before I fell.

"You okay?" he murmurs.

Eric stirs. "Hmm?"

"Shh, relax," I say. Straightening, I flash Tyrone a quick nod of thanks.

The wisps are back, more noticeable than before. They're made of energy too, connecting Eric and Tyrone. As I watch, energy funnels between them but only in one direction. It flows from Tyrone to Eric, almost like he's trying to hold Eric upright too, without even realizing.

It gives me an idea.

My hands still hover over the block, which remains

stubbornly in place. Rotating my fingers, I knead the energy like dough. At the same time, I reach for my own field. It rises up my navel and spools along my arms, a sight that reminds me of my air meditation. I think about all the emotions I bottled up. "Tell me how you're feeling, Eric."

He swallows, silent for a moment. "Weird."

Tyrone shoots me a worried look.

A few minutes ago, that would have terrified me too. Now, I'm more confident. The block softens under my ministrations. A few clumps slip through my fingers, melting back into the auric field. *It's working.*

"Weird is okay. Describe it. It doesn't have to make sense."

"Everything's so...heavy." His voice quivers. "My whole body, like I'm stuck." He screws up his face, fighting tears.

The block stiffens too. "Don't hold it in, Eric."

"But..." Now his voice really shakes. "But I shouldn't feel like this." A tear slips from one closed eyelid. He dashes it away. "I'm supposed to be excited. I want to be excited, for Ty, and for me. But I keep thinking about..." A faint sob. Then he grits his teeth, growls in frustration. "It's so stupid."

"It's not stupid. It's human."

"It is stupid. It's my fault." Another tear escapes. His chest jerks.

All the while, the block continues to melt. My energy pours into Eric, through him. Somewhere above and behind me, I sense Tyrone's energy doing the same. And all around us, something more joins. A breeze picks up, cool and invigorating. The stars glitter above, distant pinpricks of heat.

Sparks skitter over my palms as static shocks jolt from me to Eric. Tyrone inhales sharply, as if he senses it too.

A fistful of the block turns transparent. One squeeze and it glides away, defused and reabsorbed into the auric field.

Keeping my hands in place, I tilt sideways until my shoulder touches Tyrone's.

"It's my fault," Eric's saying, softer now. "I promised."

Tyrone shoots me a confused glance.

But I stretch into the guilt. Acknowledge it. "Holly's your mother. She wants you to be happy."

"Not like this. Not far away from her." He hiccups. "I'm supposed to be the one who stays. If I go, she'll think I still haven't forgiven her. She—" He breaks off in another hiccup. "She'll think she drove me away."

Beneath the guilt surges an undercurrent of fear, one I recall from childhood. Walking in on my mother sobbing on the couch. The gut-deep belief that I'd caused her pain. She would hurt forever, and it was all my fault.

"Maybe," I say. Tyrone elbows me sharply. Even Eric cracks an eyelid in surprise. "We can't control how other people feel. Sometimes our life choices make them sad. But…"

I place the heels of both palms over the remaining knot, a hard little ball of fear. Without even trying, calm flows from the sky, through me, into him. *I'm not removing anything*, I realize. Only rearranging it. Energy never dies; it changes form. This blocked terror is the same as Eric's healthy joy. It's the same energy in me, in the wind and moonlight and stars. I am transmuting, an agent of energy working upon itself.

For a brief instant, I embody the willpower of the universe.

"You can't protect your mother by hurting yourself. Holly wants you to be happy."

The fear twists. Writhes. "We should both be happy." Eric swallows thickly. "It's not fair."

"No," Tyrone says quietly. "It's not."

With that, every muscle in Eric's body goes limp.

The block dissolves.

As it does, the wisps of energy from Tyrone pull taut. The

connection isn't one way, I realize, nor is it stable. Eric's auric field draws on Tyrone's by habit now, draining him. More energy funnels away from Tyrone, but it's a simple matter for me to raise a hand. I slice through the wisps, snapping tendrils delicate as spiderwebs.

Both auric fields blink out of sight at once.

I sit back on my heels, watching Eric's chest rise and fall, the tears drying on his cheeks. "All done."

Eric doesn't seem to notice. He lies still for what feels like eternity. Long enough for my anxiety brain to switch on. What I did felt right. But was it? What if I made a mistake? Suddenly, Eric gasps, and both eyes fly open. "Holy shit. I think it worked."

I let out a breathy laugh. "Really?"

He sits up and whirls to face me. "I don't know what you did, Lexi, but I feel..." He gives his head an experimental shake. His broad grin reminds me of Shane. "It's like I had a sixty-pound weight on my chest and it's just...gone."

I can't help it. I start to smile too.

Tyrone huffs as he bends to kiss Eric. "Had me worried for a second there." He glances back at me. "Y'know, I could've sworn I felt some of that. Whatever you were doing."

I raise my hands. "Want to go next?"

He screws up his face. "I'll pass. But..." He glances at Eric once more. "Thanks."

"You're missing out," Eric says, smirking. "She's good with her hands." He starts to laugh. Softly at first, until I groan. Then he doubles over.

Before long, I join in. So does Ty, all three of us falling against one another, no idea what's so funny. There's a hum between us, though, a lingering connection.

In the warm afterglow, I think: *Maybe I can do this.* Maybe I can be a healer after all.

Chapter Nineteen

Prickly silence fills the car on our drive home. Outside, mountain vistas zip past. The views resemble computer screen savers, only spoiled by the multilane highway.

Last night, riding high on success, I failed to process the extent of Shane's irritation. We stayed up with Eric and Ty until well past midnight. At one point, Holly and Eric disappeared for almost an hour. They returned red-eyed and sniffling, hugging harder than ever. Over her shoulder, Eric mouthed *Thank you.*

"Your girl's kind of a miracle worker," Tyrone told my husband, but Shane didn't answer. I assumed he just hadn't heard.

Now, in the clear light of morning, it's obvious something's wrong. Shane hasn't said a word since we left. NPR drones in the background. When the exit for Garden Vale pulls into view, I can't take it any longer. "What was that back there?"

Shane glances in the rearview, as if I mean some roadside pit stop. "What was what?"

"You ignored me all night. You haven't said a word today. Hell, the last thing you said about me was 'Don't mind her.' Since when do we dismiss each other in public?"

EVERYTHING WE NEVER KNEW

"My family's not public." He adjusts his grip, leather steering wheel creaking. "And I wasn't dismissing you. Just this woo-woo stuff you're suddenly into."

I exhale through my nose. "I don't expect you to change your whole belief system just because I have. But I need you to stop belittling my experiences. Especially in front of other people."

"Okay, then can you maybe not bring it up with no warning in front of my relatives?"

"My bad. Didn't realize this was a secret too," I mutter.

"What do you mean, too?"

My throat constricts. I stare out the passenger window. "We've kept stuff from your family before."

At the exit ramp stop sign, he idles and lowers his voice. "If you're talking about last summer...I was following your lead. You didn't want to tell your friends, so I thought—"

"It's fine." The words dry up. There's so much I should say, but it all sounds trite. False. I don't have the right words yet. Maybe I never will. I take a deep breath and face him. "I didn't realize my 'woo-woo' stuff was on the same level, but they're your family. If you want to hide it, that's your choice."

"I never said you had to hide it. It's just..." He taps the wheel, a nervous rhythm. "My parents are traditional. They may seem open-minded about stuff nowadays, but when we were younger... Look, it took them years to cope with me leaving the church. They'll freak out if they know you actually believe this New Age bullshit."

"See? That, right there. You don't have to call it 'bullshit' just because you don't understand—"

"Fine, I won't call it what it is." At the next green light, he slams on the gas. "But not everyone is going to be okay with whatever you're exploring."

"What, my spirituality?" My voice goes tight, sarcastic.

"Healing? Helping people? Which part wouldn't they approve of?"

He grinds his jaw. Doesn't answer.

"You're the only one who's uncomfortable, Shane."

"So what if I am? I'm allowed to feel uncomfortable when my wife starts acting like a complete stranger." He takes the next turn a little too hard.

I grip the seat belt. "Excuse me for not living up to the Lexi in your head. I'm human; I change. So do you, for that matter."

"Can we just not talk about it? That's your usual go-to anyway." Another turn. We're almost home.

"You're the one always pushing me to open up!" I glare out the window. The streets blur. Or are my eyes watering?

"About real things, not these delusions."

"Well, maybe it's hard to get real when your partner judges everything you say."

The turn signal ticks. We've reached our street. "I'm not judging you," he says, quieter.

I scoff.

"Okay, maybe I sound judgmental sometimes. But it's because I don't understand, Lex. Everything we've been through, even the times when I could barely get two words out of you, I've always felt like we were on the same wavelength. Now…"

He pulls up the driveway and parks under the sycamore tree. The one we talked about building a tree house in, back when we expected to become three someday.

Steeling myself, I undo my belt and turn to meet my husband's eye. "I get that you don't understand what's happening to me. Hell, I barely do half the time. But the more I study this stuff, the more I learn about myself. If I can't share it with you, then I can't share me."

"So this is your entire life now?"

"You know that's not what I mean."

He drags a hand through his hair. "Do you remember our vows?"

I almost laugh.

We wrote our own, curled up in his dorm senior year. It was a joke, or so I thought at the time. A fun what-if. But Shane saved the notes. He read them at our wedding, a civil ceremony in his parents' town.

"Of course I remember." We both agreed "love, honor, and obey" wasn't our style. We nestled together on Shane's too-small bed and talked about what we wanted in a marriage.

Now he recites them again, from memory. "I promise to hold your hand when you need support and to ask for yours when I stumble. I am my own person, but with you, I'm stronger. I promise to trust you. I promise to choose you, every day. Neither of us knows what the future holds—"

"But I promise we'll face it together" I cut in, my voice a rough whisper. "I'm trying, Shane. You're the one shutting me out."

He closes his eyes. When he opens them again, his jaw is set. "You're forgetting. Why did we add the first line?"

In the dorm, Shane's broad hand wound through mine. His fingers were so thick that whenever we held hands for too long, the space between my ring and middle fingers ached. I don't remember the last time I noticed that. Maybe I've gotten used to it?

Or maybe we stopped holding hands.

Shane's window had a view over campus, looking out onto stick-figure trees covered in buds, a world on the precipice of spring. "What scares you the most about marriage?" Shane whispered.

"Becoming my parents."

He laughed. I didn't.

"I mean it. Their marriage was a complete disaster. Dad did whatever he wanted, whenever he wanted. Mom was so scared he'd leave that she never fought him. She took it out on us instead. And then, when he finally did leave…"

Back then, still fresh, my father's absence had carved a hole through the whole family. Ricky and I hated him for it. He never deserved to have that much power over us.

Shane rubbed my shoulder in slow, steadying circles. His touch, like always, called me back into my body.

"I don't want to be the kind of person who ignores what's right in front of them," I said. "Dad didn't believe in consequences—not for him, anyway. He thought he should be able to vanish for months on end without anyone getting angry. And Mom, her whole universe revolved around Dad. If he was home, she was great, attentive, over-the-top giddy. When he was gone, she blamed everyone but him. Me, Ricky… It's like she lived in another world. She couldn't acknowledge what was really going on. She still can't."

Shane reached for a notepad. He sat up, pen scratching. When I saw what he was writing, I froze.

Our Marriage Vows.

"Bit presumptuous." I wriggled my bare ring finger.

He winked. "Just covering my bases." He started to write again. *#1. I promise to hold your hand when you need support, and to ask for yours when I stumble.* He kept going. *And if I'm bull-headed enough to think I know best, I promise to believe my wife when she says so.*

I swatted his shoulder. "We can't say that in public."

His grin widened. "That'll be the quiet part. Just for me and you."

Now, in our silent car, I watch that scene play out behind his eyes. "I'm worried about you," he says. "I understand quitting a job that's not working out, and I get being curious about spirituality or whatever. But I can't help thinking about your mother—"

"No." My voice reverberates in the confines of the car. Suddenly, it's too cramped in here. "You don't get to play that fucking card, Shane."

"You told me how hard it was for you when she ignored reality."

"Not like this!" I snap.

"All I'm saying is maybe you should see the counselor again."

"I tried that."

"You went for a month and then quit. That's too soon to get any real benefit out of—"

"So you're a therapist now? Diagnosing me based on what, exactly? My interest in a topic you won't even discuss? Unbelievable." I grab my door handle and wrench it. But Shane left the locks on. I scramble to undo it, but he pushes the global unlock at the same time, and the door latches again. I let out a frustrated growl-scream.

"This is what I'm talking about!" Shane gestures.

I don't even recognize you.

I'm not sure if that was my thought or his. I finagle the lock, fling the door open so hard it hits the mailbox.

"Dammit, Lexi, just—"

I slam the door and storm toward the house. Behind me, Shane battles his seat belt, cursing. I don't slow, ignoring his plaintive shouts.

Inside, I bolt for the stairs. I know I'm acting like an angry kid, fleeing the scene. I'll need to face Shane eventually, talk this through. But right now I'm too deep in my head.

He kicked me right where he knew I hurt most.

I take the stairs two at a time and storm into our bedroom.

I rip the sheets from the bed, balling them under one arm and snatching the nearest T-shirt.

It's Shane's, which makes me irrationally furious. But I don't linger. I storm across the hallway and throw open the guest room door. I leave a trail of socks and underwear, tangled in our sheets for God knows how long. I fling the sheets onto the guest bed, lock the door, and open the window, spring chill be damned.

Somewhere downstairs, Shane calls my name. Up here, alone, I can finally breathe.

The guest room is sparse. We only make the bed when we have company. Otherwise, it's a makeshift storeroom. My old sewing machine stands in one corner, buried in Halloween decorations. On the opposite wall lurks Shane's exercise bike, hung with garment bags: a couple of dresses, the suit Shane wore to the Holiday Gala. My heart lurches. That seems so long ago. Someone else's life.

The hall floorboards creak. "Lexi?" Shane knocks.

I flop face-first onto the unmade bed, grab a spare pillow, and hold it over my ears.

"Let's talk, please." He knocks again. Jiggles the knob. "Be rational."

Rational. I want to scream. Instead I squeeze the pillow tighter and take a deep breath. I count backward from ten, then rinse, repeat.

By the fifth countdown, Shane finally walks away.

My mind always feels sharpest first thing in the morning. It's as if snow falls across it each night, erasing the footprints of the day before.

Today, however, my thoughts remain sluggish. Light burns my eyelids. Groaning, I reach for Shane, only to smack a wall.

Where am I? I crack an eyelid, disoriented. For a moment, I think we're back at Eric and Tyrone's. Everything's fine—or if not fine, at least unspoken.

Then I recognize the guest room ceiling. Yesterday floods in.

I can't help thinking about your mother.

With another moan, I curl under the covers. Shane knows all my weak spots. He's the only person I've shared every detail of my past with—the only one I trusted.

I never dreamed he would use it against me.

Maybe if I don't move, I'll fall back to sleep. If I wait long enough, Shane will be at work by the time I go downstairs. But after ten minutes, I realize it's pointless. With consciousness came all my usual racing thoughts, anxieties.

Out in the hallway, our bedroom door hangs open, the lights off. I see nothing inside but rumpled sheets. Relief floods my system, followed quickly by guilt. Avoiding my husband won't work forever. Still, I'm grateful for the time to get my emotions in order.

I brush my teeth, shower, and change. Instead of rehashing last night, I consider what to ask Bea. For example, what was the energetic connection I sensed between Tyrone and Eric? Were those wisps good? Bad? Neither?

Questions crowd my head as I jog downstairs. At the bottom, I run smack into Shane. "Morning!" He brandishes pancakes slathered in whipped cream and strawberries. "Made your favorite for breakfast."

My sleep-addled brain takes a moment to catch up. "Thanks, but I'm not really—"

"I called in sick. Thought we could spend the day together. Since you're not working right now, might as well take advantage, right? Hey, maybe we could go up to the lake."

"Shane."

His too-eager smile stiffens. "About yesterday…"

But I'm already backing up. "Can we talk later? I'm running late for Bea's." Shrugging into my coat, I grab the car keys.

"Look, I shouldn't have brought up your mom, but—"

"No. You shouldn't have." I can hardly bear to meet his gaze. The hangdog expression, the apology pancakes. Part of me worries I'm being immature.

Another part—a bigger part—is afraid of what we'll say if I stay.

The cinnamon rolls I bring to Odds and Ends aren't nearly as delicious as Shane's pancakes. Yet by the time I finish recounting what happened with Eric, I've devoured two.

Bea's still picking apart her first roll, uncharacteristically slow. "It sounds like it went well. I'm glad."

"But," I prompt. It's written all over her face.

"We agreed you would pace yourself. Then you leap from one practice session at home straight to messing around in someone else's energy."

"That's why I suggested he come to you first, and—"

She holds up a hand. "I understand why you did it. Doesn't make it any less risky." Her unrelenting stare makes me squirm. After a pause, however, she sighs. "Maybe it is time for more hands-on practice." Bea reaches for the illegible mess that serves as her appointment calendar. "One of my regulars will be in next Tuesday. I'll see if she's comfortable with you sitting in."

I keep my tone playful, afraid she'll change her mind. "Am I finally graduating to upstairs?"

"Consider it a trial run," Bea replies, faux-grumpy.

My heart sings anyway. *Bea trusts me.* First Eric, now this. I'm finally making real progress.

Chapter Twenty

An hour before closing, the shop bell jangles. Bea's in the back, so I go to help the pair of customers: one blond, one brunette.

Their faces resolve and my eyebrows fly up. "Chloe? Tanya?" Then I laugh, because Tanya's darting nervous glances at the shelves like she expects something to leap out and attack her. She hasn't set foot in this store since she was a teenager. "What are you doing here?"

"Search-and-rescue crew." Chloe pulls me into a brief, crushing hug.

Tanya joins her. "We haven't seen you in a month. I was starting to wonder if Bea locked you in a basement some-where." She's joking, but she checks over her shoulder as she says it.

I stifle a laugh. "No basements." Then I wince. "Has it really been that long?"

Tanya does her best irritated-mother impression. "It certainly has, young lady."

"We figured you were gonna skip today, too, so we'd better ambush you," Chloe adds.

It's Monday. I didn't even realize. The guilt twists, an increasingly familiar companion. "I'm sorry. Things have been so hectic, between the shop and home…days sort of blend without a work schedule."

Chloe nods. "Side effect of funemployment."

"Where's your boss?" Tanya squints at the checkout counter the way you might check a bathroom for poisonous spiders.

"She's not my boss."

Both Tanya and Chloe raise their eyebrows, unconvinced.

Rolling my eyes, I gesture at the poufs by the bookshelves. "She's packing mail orders. Have a seat. I'll be done in a—"

"We're not staying," Tanya interrupts. "We just came to ask if you're joining us."

I hesitate, torn. On the one hand, it would be great to catch up—and even better to avoid Shane for a couple more hours. On the other, Murphy's is the last place I want to be right now.

The longer I pause, the more Tanya's smile fades. Chloe fidgets with her rings, avoiding my gaze.

"Of course," I say, a little too late. "No, yeah, of course I'll come. I've missed you both. Sorry it's been so long."

"Don't mention it," Tanya replies, tone edging toward hard.

"We've all been there," Chloe agrees, even though we haven't. Not even when Chloe is at her most jet-setting do we go an entire month without catching up.

The guilt metastasizes as Tanya reaches for the door. "Shall we?"

"Oh, I…" I check the back. "Should probably wait until Bea's done."

Chloe looks dubious. "Please tell me she treats her employees better than her customers."

"For the last time, I'm not—"

A distant crash interrupts, followed by a curse. Beads rattle as Bea storms up front. "Lexi, have you seen the… Oh. It's you." Bea slams a box on the counter. She ignores both me and Tanya to scowl at Chloe.

Chlo wiggles her fingers. "Miss me?"

"Wondered why my blood pressure was so low." Bea gives us her spine and hoists the box onto the postal scale. "Let me guess: now you're selling organic snake oil."

Chloe shoots us a look behind Bea's back. Tanya pulls a sympathetic face. "Listen…" Chloe fidgets with her earrings. "I took down the posts you pointed out."

"Congratulations. Do you want a parade?"

"No, of course not." Chloe eyes me this time, her lips thin. "I'm trying to—"

"To what, give shitty advice to strangers on the internet? Must be nice to make a living that easily."

Chloe plants her hands on her hips. "Oh yes, so easy. How much engagement do you get on social? I could give you a few pointers."

"How generous. No thank you." If the disappointed-grandma glares Bea gives me are intimidating, they're nothing compared to what she throws at Chloe now.

"Fine. Suit yourself." Chloe plays it off with a laugh. But I know her too well—her nostrils are flared with fury. "Tanya, you ready? Meet us whenever you're done, Lex."

"Wait." For a second, I glance from them to Bea, torn. Her face reveals nothing. Is she upset? But so are my friends, and I've been neglecting them. "I'm coming." I grab my coat from the rack. "See you tomorrow, Bea."

She doesn't answer. Just stands there, radiating disappointment, until the door shuts between us.

"Seriously, what is her problem?" Ensconced in our usual table at Murphy's, Chloe lets her anger surface. "Beatrix O'Neill has been a condescending ass to me from day one. It's like she's mad I'm successful. Sorry I don't own a languishing brick-and-mortar nobody visits because the vibes are toxic as fuck. I don't understand how you put up with her, Lexi."

My name jerks me to attention.

The stifling atmosphere I sensed last time was no anomaly. We've been in the bar less than five minutes and my temples already throb. No matter how deeply I breathe, I can't get enough oxygen.

Everywhere I look, emotions claw for attention: anger, giddiness, despair.

Swallowing hard, I focus on Chloe. "Bea's not all bad. I mean, yes, she's blunt. And a little rude."

"More than a little," Tanya murmurs.

"But she's usually right, if you swallow your pride long enough to listen."

Chloe huffs in irritation.

"General you," I add quickly. "Not like, you you."

Tanya flags the server. He doesn't bother to stop by the table, just starts grabbing our usual: two glasses of red, a Diet Coke for Tanya.

"I was trying to apologize." Chloe flips her hair back from her face. "Then she insulted my entire industry."

"You know how people in her generation are about social media."

"Not all of them," Tanya points out.

Chloe studies me. "Whose side are you on, anyway?"

"Do there have to be sides?"

The server brings our tray. We each accept our drinks. Nobody proposes a toast. Tanya and Chloe take long sips, avoiding my gaze.

I set my wine aside unsampled. "It took me a while to figure Bea out. But once I gave her a chance—or, once she gave me a chance—I started to really like her."

Chloe sips again. "Pass."

Silence descends.

The headache spiderwebs across my forehead. The longer we sit here, the more intense it grows. From pressure to pain to nails drilling into my temples. I'm not focused—not even trying to meditate—and yet, from the corner of my eye, I glimpse energy.

The bartender's auric field hosts a whole constellation of blocks. A regular on the far end of the bar has such a dense field that I can't make out her features.

Closer to hand, Tanya's field appears bright as sunlight. Chloe's is harder to parse, quicksilver thin. A few small blocks stud it, reminiscent of her piercings.

I blink and it all vanishes. The room sways, off-kilter.

"Are you all right?" Tanya's eyes jump from me to the wine and back.

"Actually, no." The words are out before I consider them. "Um...I don't know why, but, there's something about Murphy's. The last time we were here, I got a terrible headache, and...I don't know if it's the crowd or the smells or the energy?" I flash a guilty, embarrassed look. "But being here is kind of overwhelming."

"You should've said!" Chloe twirls her glass, red liquid swirling. "There are other bars in town."

"Or we could go wild," Tanya says. "Check out someplace without alcohol."

Chloe wrinkles her nose. "Where's the fun in that?"

"There's a new spa by the library." Tanya's voice sounds like it's getting farther and farther away. "They've got hot baths, massages..."

Somehow, Tanya always knows what I need. "Oh God, yes. Are they still open?"

"Till eight. Chlo?"

Chloe makes a show of pouting, but the promise of hot

tubs does the trick. After a quick pit stop at Chloe's—since she not only lives nearby but owns enough bathing suits to fill an entire closet—we stride into Garden Vale's new, surprisingly swanky spa. It looks like it was lifted straight out of some European city. Plants dangle from the walls, and the central area features a series of interconnected pools beneath Moroccan-style arches, arranged so you can swim from room to room. Tucked in a side wing are the steam rooms and saunas, all circling an ice-cold plunge bath.

We choose the hottest bath, nestled in a quiet corner. Every so often, hidden nozzles in the ceiling release a delicious scent. According to the nearby sign, it's neroli, sea salt, and jasmine.

The moment the water closes over me, an involuntary sigh escapes. Heat sinks into my muscles, relaxing knots along my spine.

The headache receded as soon as we walked out of Murphy's, but the rest of my body didn't get the memo until now.

Tanya drifts over to me. "Is that why you've been avoiding us? Murphy's?"

Was I avoiding them? Tilting backward, I float. The bubbles tickle my spine. "I didn't want to ruin our tradition. And I figured the headache was a coincidence. But..." I think back to every time they've texted over the past few weeks. The way I kept deciding to skip, *just this once.* "Yeah. I'm afraid my Murphy days are done."

"Their wine is pretty shit," Chloe says. "I mean, nostalgic and all, but we can spring for someplace with more options than 'house red blend.'"

"Even for us nonpsychics, it's a bit depressing in there," Tanya adds.

I splash her gently. "I'm not a psychic."

"Then what are you studying?" Chloe lounges on the side of the hot tub. With her head tipped back, her hair spools out like fronds of seaweed.

I've never actually claimed it out loud, but now seems as good a time as any. "I'm studying to become a healer." Just saying it induces a giddy thrill.

Tanya scrunches her nose, dubious.

Chloe just seems confused. "I thought you were learning about that stuff you saw around people. What did you call them, fields?"

"Auric fields, yeah. They're our energetic bodies. Healers help people who have energetic wounds."

"This from the woman who used to make fun of me for reading horoscopes." Chloe sticks out her tongue.

"Sorry." My face flushes, not just from the heat of the water. "Back then I was so closed off."

"And now?" Tanya asks, carefully neutral.

I laugh. "Now all I know is how little I actually know about the world. But healing... It's always been part of me. It was dormant for a while, until—well, speaking of astrology, Bea told me about this thing called the Saturn return."

"The what?" Tanya looks at Chloe, who shrugs.

"Don't look at me. Things I know about astrology: I'm a Leo, end of list."

"It's when Saturn returns to the same place in the sky as when you were born," I say. "Kind of like a quarter-life crisis from the universe."

"Hard pass." Tanya frowns.

"Can you have more than one?" Chloe asks. "'Cause I'm pretty sure I've had like five life crises already."

We laugh.

"And you believe that's what happened to you?" Tanya still seems skeptical but not in an abrasive way—not like Shane.

"I guess?" I sink lower into the steaming water. "It would explain why I suddenly got fed up with work, and why I'm experiencing this stuff now. I've been sensing energy even more often since I started practicing."

"Practicing how?" Chloe sits up, interested.

After so long tiptoeing around this subject at home, it's a relief to let it all out. The lessons, the meditation, watching people's auric fields in the café. Healing myself and then Eric. By the time I finish talking, we're all beet red.

"We should probably migrate before we cook," Tanya says.

In the warm pool—which feels borderline cold after the boiling hot tub—we drift beneath bright tile ceilings. Moorish lamps flicker on the walls.

"It's a lot to take in," I admit. "It's okay if you don't believe me. God knows Shane doesn't."

"Of course we—" Chloe starts, but Tanya interrupts.

"Shane still doesn't approve?"

"Definitely not." I squeeze my eyes shut. "If anything, it's gotten worse. Anytime I even mention Bea, we fight. It's like he wants to fix me, turn me back the way I used to be."

"What an ass." Chloe huffs.

Tanya readjusts the high bun she's piled her curls into. "He's worried about you. I'd worry, too, if Paul was going through a quarter-life crisis."

"Worry I get. Insulting and belittling my experiences, not so much. He said I was acting like my mother."

Tanya glances at me. "Are you?"

My friends have gotten earfuls about my mother's guilt-trip calls and the long spans of silence between. They know pieces of our history: how she let Dad walk all over her, how she alternately leaned on and blamed me after he left, how she still relies on Ricky, who lives at home.

They don't know the bigger pieces, though. Only Shane

has heard the why, and look where sharing that got me. *I can't help thinking about your mother.*

The pause expands.

I tip backward to watch steam curl up past the tiles. "My mother ignores reality because she can't handle it. If anything, I'm doing the opposite. Healers help people work through their problems by addressing them."

"Like you're working through your fights with Shane?" Tanya says, a little too innocently.

I groan. "He refuses to believe anything I tell him. How do I work through that?"

"So prove it." Chloe shrugs. "Eric was able to sense when you healed him, right? Heal Shane and he'll have to admit you're right."

It's tempting. So many times during arguments, I've wished I could project ideas into Shane's head. Words get jumbled, but ideas are pure. When I first started with Bea, I didn't have enough control. Now, though? I'll bet I could do it.

Then I remember Bea's latest lecture. *We agreed you would pace yourself.*

"I can't." I let out a frustrated growl. "Bea says healing Eric was too big a risk."

"But it worked." Chloe scrunches her nose. "Bea is such a control freak; she's probably just jealous you healed someone without her."

Tanya tucks her knees to her chest. "Anyway, whose opinion matters more: Beatrix O'Neill's or your husband's?"

"You agree with Chloe?" I blink, surprised.

Tanya lifts one shoulder. Lets it sink again. "If it works, Shane will understand what you're going through. If not, maybe you'll see Shane's point that there could be other explanations." Tanya holds up a palm to stave off my protests.

"I'm not saying you're imagining everything. But Bea's ideas are so...out there. 'Spirituality'"—Tanya actually air-quotes—"isn't the only path."

"What's wrong with spirituality?" Chloe turns to her.

"I never said there was anything wrong with it. But Lexi would be better off discussing this with her own community."

"Oh, sure. 'Cause organized religion has no problems." Chloe snorts. She climbs to her feet, water cascading over her bikini.

"I trust the church more than someone who isolated Lexi for weeks." Tanya stands too, arms folded. "Bea's obviously driving a wedge between Lexi and her husband. Plus she's kept Lexi from seeing us—"

"Stop it!" My voice echoes, too loud. A couple floating nearby splash upright and glare at us. With a sheepish wave, I lower my voice. "It's not Bea's fault me and Shane are fighting. And she's not why I haven't seen you two either. I told you: I just don't want to go to the same bar and have the same conversation every. Single. Week."

Silence falls.

At least my friends have stopped glaring at each other. Now they're both scowling at me, though. "You're bored of us?" Chloe says.

"Not of you." My neck feels hotter than it did in the bath. "I was bored of me. My job, my life... Everything's changing. I'm still figuring out my priorities."

"I see." Chloe's deadpan is more dangerous than her bite.

"See what?" I move toward her, but she backs up, maintaining the distance between us.

"It's pretty clear where we are on the list."

"Chlo, come on. You're important to me. You both are." I look to Tanya for backup, but she doesn't meet my eye. She's watching Chloe instead, concerned.

"Well, you've got a funny way of showing it." Chloe squints at the nearest clock. "I'm starting to prune. Meet you at the lockers?" With that, she surges off through the pool, so fast that waves break in her wake.

Guilt churns in my gut. "Shit."

Tanya watches Chloe's backside. "She'll cool down."

On the far end of the pool, the couple has settled into an embrace that borders on NSFW. "I really am sorry it's been so long."

Tanya studies me for a moment. "You're not acting like yourself, Lexi."

"I know." What I want to say is *do I have to?* Is there some contract we sign at the start of a friendship? *From now on I pledge to color inside the lines of your expectations.* No deviations. No upsetting the balance.

Maybe there's a better question I should be asking. *Who am I?* Everyone but me seems confident of the answer.

"Where the hell have you been?" Shane demands the second I set foot inside the front door.

For an instant, I spiral into another house, another life. I'm walking into my mother's home an hour past curfew because I couldn't stand it there, couldn't breathe inside, ever since that night.

Where the hell have you been?

Out.

Out doing what?

I couldn't tell her the truth. I couldn't say *walking in circles because I have nowhere else to go.* So I bared my teeth.

Why bother asking? You won't believe me anyway.

Her shouts usually scared me. That night, I savored them. Her anger was proof I could still fight back.

Just not when it counted.

"Lexi?" Shane's voice ruptures the memory. He's on the steps, half in shadow.

It's all right. You're safe. I'm a lifetime away from that little girl. "Didn't you get my text?" Shrugging out of my coat, I set my keys down. "I went out with Tanya and Chlo."

"Where? You weren't at Murphy's."

It takes me a second to realize that wasn't a question. "You're following me now?"

"No. But since I took a whole day off for nothing, I met up with some guys from the station. Figured I'd see if you needed a lift home."

"We went to the spa. I didn't think alcohol was a good idea in my current headspace."

Slowly, he pushes off the stairs and descends. When the hallway lamp lights his face, my chest tightens. His eyes are red, bloodshot.

"Shane..." *How did I manage to fuck up every relationship in my life at once?* "Can we talk?"

"If you're finished avoiding me." He folds his arms.

Can't argue with that. "You're right. I have been. I'm sorry. But I didn't want to say something I'd regret."

"What's our rule?" is his only reply.

Apologies don't have qualifiers. We made the rule after our first big fight, a year and a half into marriage. It was the first fight we couldn't resolve before lights out, the first time we slept in separate rooms. Since then, it's only happened twice.

Until last night.

"I'm sorry," I repeat.

For a long moment, we watch each other. Finally, he nods. "Me too. I shouldn't have dragged your mother into it."

"You know I'm terrified of repeating her mistakes."

"Which is why I'm so worried. We pick up behaviors from our parents. It's easy to repeat a pattern without real- izing it or wanting to."

I will never become her. The words nip at my tongue, but I swallow them. Shane would hear a challenge, not a vow. He'd whip out articles about nature and nurture, studies on parenting. I'm not interested in having more debates. I want to prove my point.

Heal Shane and he'll have to admit you're right.

My conversation with Bea seems like eons ago. Besides, Chloe had a point: healing Eric worked. Why was Bea so upset? And, as Tanya pointed out, Shane is my life partner. My promises to him come first.

My body is still loose, relaxed from the spa. I channel the detachment into my voice. "What exactly are you afraid of, Shane?"

He grimaces at the ceiling, as if to seek guidance. "We've been over this."

"Not in detail. Spell it out for me."

He stiffens, like a soldier commanded to attention. "I'm afraid you're losing your grip on reality. Hallucinating or, I don't know, retreating into magical thinking, because you don't want to admit what happened."

That catches me off guard. "What happened?" I repeat, bewildered.

My confusion only etches the fear deeper onto his face. "Lexi. You lost a child."

The hit lands, direct to the gut. Not because he drew the connection, but because I didn't. Because it hasn't crossed my mind in days, maybe weeks. Because he said *what happened* and my mind did not immediately leap to the bathroom, the blood.

What kind of almost-mother am I?

"Traumatic events affect our minds," he's saying.

Because I'm still reeling, the knee-jerk reaction speaks for me. "Don't blame her."

Her.

I have never said that out loud. *The child, the baby, the potential, the almost.* They, or sometimes it, when I'm at my most detached. Never her. It was too early to be sure—and maybe none of us can be sure, even at birth, since we don't yet know the person our babies will grow into. Before we lost her, though, some sixth sense whispered: daughter.

I was so certain. I'd even planned to make a bet with Shane during the appointment where we'd confirm the sex. We never got there, so I never told him. Afterward, I locked those memories away.

Now I remember. I wish I could forget.

Shane goes blank, the same way he holds himself after a bad fire, whenever the flames remind him how little control he has. "I'm not blaming..." He can't say it. "Anyone. Terrible things happen; it's nobody's fault. But we have to face the pain or it fucks us up."

We're getting off track. "What if I prove it's not all in my head?"

"I'm trying to—" Shane grits his teeth. "Can we have one sane conversation please?"

"You heard Eric. When I worked on his energy, he felt it."

"My brother's also convinced those ghost-hunting shows are real."

"So what've you got to lose?" I tilt my head, size him up. Shane loves a debate. Occasionally our still-practicing LDS neighbors stop by with pie, hoping to chat. I usually politely decline, but Shane serves them coffee and runs logic circles around their convictions. More often than not, I have to rescue them.

"Fine." He spreads his arms and squeezes his eyes shut. "Go for it."

A nervous flutter kicks. *What if...?* I suppress it. *No. This will work.* "Not here," I tell him. "You need to lie down. Get comfortable."

We wind up in the living room, Shane stretched like a cat across the sofa. He's tall enough that his arms dangle over the armrest, his feet wedged against the far side. "Let me guess, now we say the magic words?"

I roll my eyes. Suppress the flutter before it grows to an anxiety storm. I know what I'm doing. "If you're uncomfortable, tell me to stop. Otherwise, close your eyes and relax."

He squeezes his eyes so tightly his entire face scrunches.

"I said relax. Breathe in, nice and deep." His chest rises. "Good. Now out."

He listens for two more breaths before his lip curls. "What about a wand? If there's no magic words."

"Behave," I murmur. Don't rise to the bait, don't lose focus. "Breathe in...and out."

His smirk lingers.

He's so certain this won't work, so confident he knows how the world works. Even if dozens of scientists published proof tomorrow—replicable hard data on the existence of this energy—Shane still would not buy it. What does that say about his mindset?

Or mine? I'm positive this is real, yet the only evidence I've seen is subjective and personal. A case study of one.

My mind keeps interrupting, tripping my focus. I get stuck on the first step. Over and over, I forget to sync my breathing with Shane's, unable to follow my own instructions.

Finally, Shane's breath slows. His smirk slips as he sinks into the couch, fingers twitching, on the brink of sleep.

Slowly, almost painfully so, his auric field appears. It's

dimmer than last time, the colors muted. Maybe because it's night? The living room lights are off, our only illumination the hallway overhead.

Careful not to make a sound, I kneel beside the couch.

There is no obvious wound. No gray clumps or big pulsing mass like Eric had. Yet his energy is barely moving. Any slower and it would be a still surface.

Still ponds fester.

Just like the first time I glimpsed Shane's field, I feel my center of gravity shifting. The sensation, like being flipped upside down, is so intense I clap a hand over my mouth, seasick.

What is this?

It must be a block, some injury I can't see. I breathe through my nose in hard little bursts. The scent of our lemon floor cleaner gags me. Beneath it, I catch Shane's scent, sharper than usual and adrenaline-sour.

There is something else.

Beyond his auric field, over his stomach, I glimpse an indistinct, curling shape that reminds me of smoke. Unlike smoke, the longer I stare, the thicker it grows.

It pulses, assuming form first, then color, an ugly, blood-clot red.

No. It's not beyond his field—it's attached. Thin tendrils snake out of the thing's base. They wind into and through Shane's energy, where it branches like tree roots or blood vessels. A dozen narrow points hover right above Shane's skin, stingers prepared to pierce. The whole system feels tumorous.

The room dims as I hold my breath. Is Shane holding his too? I can't hear him breathing.

Fuck winning the argument. Pure, animal instinct takes over. *Get it out of him.*

I grab the base of the thing, like an amorphous tree root or tentacle. My hands clench around the fattest part, a foot above Shane's navel, where they make a squelching sound, a sick, wet sensation leaking under my fingernails.

The thing sparks. At the same time, a dozen branches burst from it and all plunge into Shane's body at once.

A rush of images assaults me. Hard and fast, almost impossible to parse.

Frank holds my hand in the middle of a frozen pond. "Don't let go," begs a little boy who sounds just like Hannah's oldest son.

"I won't." Frank is so young. Almost the same age as Shane now. "I promise."

We are whirling, laughing. Then I trip and Frank teeters too. He lets go. The back of my head cracks on ice. Pain clouds my vision, but the injury is nothing compared to the betrayal.

Now a little girl, the spitting image of Clarissa's daughter, flings a model plane out the window. I spent hours building it. It crashes into bushes, and I scream, "I hate you!"

When she bursts into tears, I realize I hate myself even more.

A pretty girl cradles my hand. She's young, baby-faced. *Were we ever this young?* We've never met but I recognize her from the profiles I stalked in the early, nervous-butterfly days of our courtship: Shane's high school girlfriend. "I'm sorry," she says. "I just don't think we have very much in common."

"Do we need to?" My voice is nearly Shane's now, albeit creaky with puberty.

She squeezes my hand, but it feels like she's reaching straight into my rib cage for a fistful of heart. "You deserve to be with someone who gets you."

Holly appears, younger and yet more harried than I've

191

ever seen her. "When you have your own house, sin all you want. While you're under our roof, you live by our values. Understand?"

"I understand." My hands are shaking. "I understand a fucking fantasy is more important to you than your own child."

"Language."

I'm crouched on a landing above the Coles' living room. Snatches of conversation filter upstairs. "Don't know what to...academic probation."

"The boarding school...some discipline..."

A creak. *Eric.* He's twelve or thirteen, gangly limbs already predicting his future height. "Please," he whispers, "don't leave me alone with them."

Guilt. Love. Fear. "I won't. I promise." But I already know it's a lie, because the decision is out of my hands. It's a wish, not a promise.

I am back on the ice, clinging to Frank's hand. My head cracks, my vision spots...

"*Lexi.*"

I gasp. My eyes fly open as I fall backward, onto the ice. My head hits the ground, but this time it's softer, cushioned somehow.

Someone is shouting. I ignore them. I need to concentrate. Figure out what's happening, how to fix it. I need to...

Rough fingers grip my chin. One pries my eyelid open, but I shove the hands away and struggle free.

"Lexi." Shane kneels beside me. I'm sprawled on the living room carpet, the back of my head throbbing. "What happened?"

There's water in my ears. He sounds far away, vague. "What do you mean?" I sound the same way, like I'm shouting down a long tunnel.

"You fell. I think you hit your head."

"I'm fine." It throbs in disagreement. "Did you feel that?"

His frown deepens. "Feel what?"

"When I touched your field." Or, I guess not his field. What the hell was that thing? "I saw you skating on a lake with your dad, and…was it Clarissa? She dropped your toy airplane out the window."

A long pause. "No. I didn't feel anything."

My head pounds. All the relaxation from the spa has evaporated. I force myself upright, leaning heavily on the couch. "Let me try again. I was so close."

He shoves to his feet and turns away but not quickly enough. I glimpse bared teeth, a furrowed brow. Guilt. Love. Fear. *I promise.* "You need some ice. I'll be right back."

For a split second, a ghost lingers at his waist. The thing I saw earlier, only smoke-thin now, barely visible. Most of its tendrils have burrowed into Shane's body. The sight turns my stomach. Yet a single one moves in the opposite direction. A shadow arm, a phantom tree branch. Hungry and yearning, it reaches for me.

Chapter Twenty-One

Bea is the last person on earth without a cell phone, so I write her an email. Locked in the bathroom, shower blasting, I type: Something is wrong with Shane.

As succinctly as possible, I describe the tumorous thing, the upside-down nausea, the snatches of memory. The only detail I omit is the fact that I tried to heal him. Bea doesn't need to know I ignored her advice again.

By the time I crawl into bed, Shane is already there. He pretends to be asleep. I let him.

In the morning, I wake to an empty bed and a frantic honking. Groggy, I stumble from bed. Did Shane forget his keys? We have a perfectly functional doorbell. Why…?

At the window, I rub away sleep. Then I straighten, suddenly wide awake.

The car in our driveway isn't Shane's SUV but Bea's Honda. A pair of fuzzy dice sway from the mirror. As I stare, Bea leans out the window. She's wearing a winter jacket and loose bell bottoms over what appears to be a one-piece bathing suit. She waves, mouths something, then honks again.

She's going to wake up half the neighborhood. I press a finger to my lips, frantic. Grabbing a bathrobe, I race downstairs. By the time I get there, Bea's on the stoop. She hands me a beach bag. "Get dressed," she barks by way of hello. "Bring a towel and a suit. I want to get there while it's still sunny."

"While it's...what?" I yawn, glancing at the clock. Just after six. My stomach tenses. What time did Shane leave? Did he sleep at all?

"Swimsuit, sunscreen, change of clothes. Go." Bea claps her hands.

Too tired to protest, I head back upstairs. Fifteen minutes and a large cup of coffee later, I'm perched beside her in the rattling sedan. "Are you going to explain?" I shout over the blasting classic rock.

"Your training," Bea shouts back. "It's time to work on the next element."

She floors it to weave through what passes for rush hour in Garden Vale. It makes me nauseous, which brings last night flooding back.

The alien rooted in Shane's field. The nausea. My failure to help the person I care about most.

He'll never believe me now.

But that's the least of my problems. "Did you get my email?"

"Why do you think I dragged my ancient ass out of bed at this ungodly hour?" Bea turns up the volume. "No more questions till we get there."

I rest my cheek on the window, suppressing a pang of guilt. Bea warned me to slow down. She told me not to meddle with anyone else's energy. I didn't listen, so now Shane's suffering. *What if I made it worse?*

Lake Powell is man-made, though you'd never guess it from the view. Turquoise water snakes under arched red rocks—what used to be Glen Canyon.

Tanya and I came here one Fourth of July with Shane, Paul, and a few of the other guys from the station. Our plan was to rent a boat and sail for the day, but the lake was mobbed. We wound up watching the tourists party from shore instead.

Today, Lake Powell couldn't be more different. Aside from the man who rented us the canoe, there's nobody else here. Then again, it is a weekday and cold enough to wear jackets over our suits.

For a second, I picture where I'd be if I hadn't quit my job. Shane and I wouldn't be fighting. Tanya and Chloe wouldn't be upset. I'd be at my desk, slogging through paperwork or maybe out hyping up a mediocre house to a prospective neighbor.

On the weekends, I'd sleep half the day to recover from the week. On Mondays, I'd convince myself I was enjoying the bottom-shelf wine and claustrophobic bar.

I was miserable. Yet it seemed fine at the time. Not too bad, anyway. Could always be worse.

I had no idea how much I hated my life until I stepped outside of it.

The canoe rocks. "You gonna paddle or is it my job?" Bea swats my paddle. I give her a playful splash before putting my back into it.

"Can I ask questions yet?" I call over my shoulder.

"Clearly you can, since that was one."

The sun plays across the water. Above it, striations in the rocks make me wonder how old this canyon is. What dramas played out here, long before humans were a blip on the universe's radar.

"What's wrong with him?"

Bea sighs. "You're always so fixated on right and wrong."

"You weren't there." I shudder. "You didn't feel that...thing."

"No. So I can't say for certain. It could be any number of issues. You felt off-balance, which could indicate energy imbalance. It could also be an unusual block, such as an entanglement from an outside source or someone draining his energy... Without being there, it's hard to guess."

My oars rise. Fall. Rise again. "Could you fix it?"

"Not every problem has a solution. And not every solution is quick or easy to define."

"But we're healers."

"Healing isn't linear. And we can't help someone unless they initiate the process. They're the ones who will need to sustain it, long after we've done our part."

I growl in frustration. "Then what's the point?"

"I'll pretend you didn't ask something so obvious."

We paddle on in prickly silence.

After a while, Bea sighs. "This lesson will be harder than air or fire, at least for you. Today we're concentrating on water."

"No, really?" I mutter, immediately feeling childish.

Thankfully, Bea ignores me. "You don't have much water in your elemental constitution. Water governs emotions, the subconscious, and dreams. Like fire, water also helps us change, but it's a gentler, more fluid change. Not burning the world down to start again, but patiently reshaping it."

The striated canyon walls glow red.

We lost a child, Shane whispers. Guilt floods the canyons in my chest. "If I don't have much water, and water governs emotion... Am I a heartless robot?"

"You've got emotions," Bea says. "Everyone does. You just have difficulty accessing them. You repress, rather than express, which bottles your emotions up. They'll explode if you aren't careful."

We have to face the pain. Fuck. Shane's right.

197

We drift beneath a high arch of rock, and the lake throws glitter onto its alternating red and brown bands. With my back turned to Bea, it's easier to be honest. "What if I don't express emotions the right way?"

Bea clears her throat pointedly.

"Okay, 'right' is the wrong word. But a lot of the time I don't even know what I'm feeling. Or why. Like, I'll be angry, but not about anything logical. If I go off, I might hurt someone or make a situation worse."

Like Shane. Did I make his problem worse? I can't ask Bea without admitting I broke my promise.

"Some emotions need to be voiced in order to be understood." Bea stills her oars. "I'm not suggesting you pick fights all over town. But working through your feelings in private, with someone you trust..."

"Is a good way to piss off all your friends and your spouse at once," I finish.

Bea starts to paddle again. "Expressing yourself may cause tension. But when you bottle it up, the tension's still there. Instead of briefly frustrating other people, you start a war inside yourself. The longer you hold everything in, the worse it gets, until minor frustrations become huge problems."

"So the options are hurt myself or hurt the people I care about?"

"Pain isn't always bad. Touching a hot stove hurts so that you learn to move your hand."

Suddenly, I have to laugh. I'm back on a rooftop in Salt Lake City, telling Eric he can't protect his mother by hurting himself. For a healer, I'm bad at taking my own advice. "I see your point."

"Good. Now"—Bea swings both oars up, as beads of water trail off the paddles—"tell me everything you associate with water."

"Life, I guess. We need it to live." I study my oars. They break the surface, the splash violent and disruptive. Yet in an instant, it's absorbed again. "The ability to weather changes."

"Better." I hear a smile in Bea's voice. "What else?"

My gaze flits to the horizon. The moon peeks over it, near full and about to rise. "The tides. Rising and falling, high and low periods... Um. Menstruation?"

"The womb is a powerful water symbol. It's where we all come from, the place we felt safest. Maternal, nurturing energy is an aspect of water too."

My pulse skips. *Maternal energy. Repressed emotions. Facing pain.*

I know why I'm here. What I need to unlock. I've needed to address it for almost a year. It looms on the horizon—the worst kind of anniversary, an antiversary, a date I wish I could forget.

The oars stop. My body locks up. I don't want to go there. *I'm over it*, I want to shout. Except that would sound like the complete denial it is. I'm not over it. I never will be.

"What else?" Bea prompts. She doesn't comment on my stillness. She only paddles harder, for both of us.

"Motherhood." The word sticks to the roof of my mouth. "Childbirth." The splash of her oars is deafening. "Loss and grief and longing."

"When we talk about emotions, we don't just mean the happy ones," Bea says.

We approach another outcropping. It is larger than the last, deeper. A dark hollow carved into the cliff. We drift closer, and I realize it's a cave. The water continues into the cavern, but all we see from here is darkness. A void.

The fine hairs on my arms stand on end. Caves make me nervous, especially ones in water. So much could go wrong.

Tides could rise to trap you, rock slides could block you inside, all sorts of unexpected slithering creatures might lurk, concealed in the shadow.

Yet now, the shape and the darkness tugs at my core. Calls my name until I understand: the face I'm most afraid of seeing in there is my own.

I fear myself, I realize. *But I don't want to anymore.* I point at the cave mouth. "Can we…?"

Bea slows the canoe. "No." I'm about to protest when she adds, "You go alone."

I understand. I don't like it, but I understand. It's the same reason I climbed the sand dune alone—if there had been someone up there with me, I never would have let myself go so freely.

Drawing my oars up, I lay them in the canoe. Then I stand, hips swaying for balance. I shrug out of my jacket and sweater, peel off my jeans. Goose bumps speckle my torso and bare limbs, even though I haven't even touched the water yet.

Bea's expression is resolute. "You've got this, Lexi."

I believe her.

Balanced on the prow, the water blazes turquoise, clear all the way to the bottom, at least twenty feet down. At the mouth of the cave, however, the turquoise turns to pitch.

I stare straight at the darkness and jump.

Water closes over me, so cold it steals my breath. Gasping, I break the surface. My hair streams across my face. I push it aside, wheezing again. My lungs are fists, my toes snowdrifts. *I should have kept my clothes on.* But they would drag me down, extra weight I can't afford.

"If you need me, shout." Bea drags a hat over her forehead and reclines in the canoe.

Leaving her to nap, I gulp one last breath of sunlight and

swim for the cave. Dark swallows my vision. Still, I keep swimming. Strong, determined strokes. When the last of the sun's afterimage fades, I slow.

Behind me, all I make out of the entrance is a halo, blinding to look at. I turn my back on it and embrace the shadow.

Water below, earth above. A womb. *Earth Mother's womb.*

My toes ice into solid lumps. My fingers tingle, ready to join them. I am shivering so hard it's difficult to tread water. Is it the cold? Or something more?

Confront it.

The analytical brain rears up. What are we doing here? Grief cannot be unleashed, cannot be set free. Grief must be mastered. It is dangerous, weak to surrender.

But I recognize the voice now. I keep mistaking anxiety for rationality. My brain evolved for savannas, to detect threats on high alert and survive horrible challenges by sheer force of denial.

My body remembers what my mind strives to erase.

Splashes echo in the cave. As my eyes adjust, I discern its shape: a dome overhead, pierced by a tiny pinprick of light. Water laps at the curved walls. There is nobody here but us—me and the water. No need to perform; let down the walls, take off the masks.

Stop pretending.

I sink up to my chin.

Stop pretending you didn't know she was a girl. Stop pretending you didn't plan everything—colors for the nursery; the exact date to announce it to everyone, plus exactly how you wanted to do it; the baby books you read; the tiny impractical shoes you bought on pre-order.

Water covers my lips.

You knew the first trimester was the riskiest. You'd both

read the data. You thought you were prepared. You told yourself, told each other: *We won't get attached. Not yet. Not until it's safe.*

You lied.

It was never safe. It would never have been safe, even if things hadn't ended so abruptly. It was too late. You already loved her.

Before she was even real, you loved her, and you fear that's why you lost her. Because you weren't careful. You didn't keep your distance. You got too attached too soon, you couldn't control yourself, and so look what happened.

I inhale deep, breathing into every crevice.

Grief wraps icy fingers around my ankles. She drags me under, just as my eyes fly open. They burn, underwater. But the longer I stare, the more the darkness resolves. It grows form, weight, meaning. Assumes body and persona, until I am gazing into her eyes.

The woman drifting in the waves across from me is younger, though you wouldn't guess it to look at her. Deep-purple bruises ring her eyes. Her parted lips are chapped, and she has not slept soundly in a week. Still, I would trade places with her in a heartbeat. Because she doesn't know yet. Her dream remains intact.

She is still a mother.

I watch myself, a little less than a year ago, stumble toward doom. My feet graze rock, and for a split second, I glimpse watery light far above, take note of the suffocating, frigid dark all around me.

Then the rocks underfoot resolve into linoleum. She's in the bathroom, breathing hard. *No*, she is thinking. But the pain is so terribly, obviously familiar. *No, please no.*

Already practiced at denial, she stumbles to the toilet. Sits down, mouthing prayers. Some she remembers from childhood, others she makes up on the spot. She grabs toilet paper, wads it up. When it comes back red, she cries out.

So do I.

Bubbles flood the surface.

I am no longer an observer. I share her pain. A searing fire in my chest; empty lungs; primal thirst. *Air, need air.*

I kick for the surface. Or at least, I try to. But the pinprick of light gets farther away by the second. It morphs until it is the single overhead bulb in our bathroom, hazily visible through waves. I might as well try to swim up the bathroom wall. My arms aren't strong enough; my legs won't kick off the linoleum.

On the toilet next to me, she is sinking too. At first, she props her head in her palms. But her elbows slip from her knees, her forehead drops to her kneecaps, then between. She goes boneless, oozes to the floor.

It is the day I first drowned. Today's a mere repeat.

She screams, but water muffles the sound. Not good enough. She deserves to be heard. I kick off the tile-rock floor-ground. This time, the water does not constrain me. A hot, angry current surges from nowhere, sweeping me up. I whirl and tumble, lose all sense of direction, all sense of body. The world narrows to a pinprick.

Only one sense remains: the pressure. My lungs are seconds from bursting.

Without warning, I shatter the surface. *Air.* I sputter, choke, suck it down. Shudders rock my frame. I take ragged, desperate inhales as sensation trickles back into my limbs.

Then I'm screaming. Raw fury, pain, despair—it all pours out.

The cave screams too. Amplified and twisted, until I don't recognize the voice. It's the water, the rocks crying with me.

The earth recognizes this pain. She is a mother, too, and she will outlive all her children.

She understands.

The screams melt into gut-deep sobs. Wrenching, whole-body tears. My head almost dips back under water, but right as I'm about to sink, my hand brushes stone. The current must have pushed me into one of the walls. I cling to it while the rest of my body folds. Then I lose myself and let the grief wash ashore.

With it comes everything I've tried to forget. How she might've looked. What her voice would have sounded like. What passions she'd harbor, whose heart she would inherit. Would she be fiery like me or have Shane's cool detachment in an emergency?

I cry for her, because she never got the chance. She never tasted chocolate, never swam in the ocean, never kissed.

I cry because I have kept her secret, as if she were shameful. She deserved better. I deserve better.

I love you, my daughter. I'll miss you. I need to let you go.

All of those are true at once.

I feel wrung out, emptied. Yet lighter too. Not relief, but perhaps its cousin. That feeling when everything has gone horribly wrong and you've cried yourself dry and all the problems still exist, but you're different. You hate the new shape of the world, but you accept it anyway.

What are wombs, but cycles? Purge and rebirth. You must brave the dark to reach the light.

I scrub glacial fingers over my cheeks, taking stock. Somehow, I'm at the back of the cave, the entrance impossibly far away. My legs feel bloated, my arms limp. I won't make it. I'm barely strong enough to cling to the wall, let alone swim all the way back to the boat.

Out of nowhere, a warm current wraps around me.

This time, less overwhelmed by the vision, I understand what it is. Energy. Calm, patient, impossible to resist. It scrapes me from the wall, even as I scrabble to hang on. But the current doesn't drag me under. It cradles me at the surface, the warmth renewing my tired limbs.

Suddenly, I have more than enough strength to start kicking again.

The current works with me. Every stroke propels me faster and cleaner than I'm capable of swimming. In no time at all, the entrance nears. Just as I reach it, the current peters out. The cold returns, the lake's surface still once more.

I pause, treading water, half in shadow.

"Thank you," I whisper. Maybe it's my imagination. But I swear the cave repeats it, in tongues old as stone. *Thank you, thank you...*

Yes. I should thank me too, for finally facing this.

Chapter Twenty-Two

There's a man on the curb in front of Odds and Ends. Blue jeans, leather jacket. He's slumped over, splayed fingers cupping his neck.

Bea wrenches the car into park. "Good luck."

I'm confused, until the man lifts his head. Shane studies Bea's sedan with bleak composure.

Fresh from the cave, my emotions hover right at the surface. The overthinking's still there—*he's following me, he doesn't trust me, why won't he give me space*—but it's buried under an avalanche of longing. My desire is pure, immediate. I know what I want, more clearly than I have in months.

I want to hold my husband.

You lost a child, he said last night. I want to wrap my arms around him and say, *We lost a child*. I found a release in the caves, but he needs it too. Why didn't I notice?

Shane stands while I undo my seat belt.

As I fling open the passenger door, he hurries across the street. Reading my mind, like always. But then he passes me. He circles to the driver's side, where he bars Bea's path.

"Did you have a nice day, Ms. O'Neill?" His voice starts loud and grows from there. "Have fun feeding my wife more fairy-tale bullshit?"

I freeze halfway out of the car, shocked motionless.

"What I can't figure out is why. Is she paying you, or do you mess with people's heads for the thrill?" He's shouting now.

I'm not the only one staring. It's a sunny spring weekday, just after five in the afternoon—Main Street is as busy as it gets outside of tourist season.

"Maybe you get off on destroying other people's relationships. Is that it?" His lip curls. "You're bitter and alone, so you have to make everyone else suffer."

The man I married would never act like this. A slithering afterthought hits me: *Doesn't he say the same about you, these days?*

Bea is uncharacteristically silent, frozen in place.

That triggers it. For a split second, I'm elsewhere. The star-studded quilt, a refuge turned trap. My whole body a rictus, throat choking on protests. And the touch. Impossible to escape.

Then I gag, here again. "*Shane.*" I storm around the car.

He ignores me. "I don't blame Lexi; she needs help. But you? You're feeding her delusions."

Finally, I reach them. I plant myself in front of Bea, flatten my hands on Shane's chest. "Leave her alone. This is between you and me."

He grasps my wrists. Pries my hands off.

As he does, emotion crashes into me: fury. So intense my ears ring, my fists balling without permission. I absorb it, helpless to prevent the bleedover.

"Do you even care?" he yells over me, around me. "Lexi fell doing some bullshit ritual you taught her last night. She hit her head. She could've—"

"Stop." My voice is a thunderclap. "Stop telling me I'm crazy."

At last, he looks at me. "You're not." For a moment, I glimpse my Shane. Tender and worried. "You're just confused." Then the anger slams back into place. "It's her fault. She's manipulating you, putting ideas in your head."

"You're one to talk." I raise my chin. This anger isn't mine, but that doesn't matter. There's too much. It has to come out. "You know everything, right? If your wife disagrees with you, something must be wrong with her brain."

"That's not what I'm saying!"

Across the street, curious patrons pop out of Murphy's like groundhogs.

Shane startles, glancing over. Far too late, he lowers his voice. "Last night scared me, Lex. I touched your shoulder and you didn't even react. It was like you were gone."

"That's no excuse to harass an innocent woman. Bea's helping me—"

"We never had any problems until she started helping." He gestures furiously behind me.

Bea has crossed the street. I didn't even notice. She holds out a clove cigarette, and a flannel-shirted Murphy's patron offers her a light.

Touching a hot stove hurts so that you learn to move your hand.

"We did," I say, turning back. "The problems have been here. If she brought them to the surface, good. We needed the push."

He scoffs. "Unbelievable." Then, before I reply, "I don't want you to study with her anymore."

The gawking bystanders melt. I forget the storefronts, the blue sky, the birdsong. It's just us, two feet apart. Might as well be a canyon.

"We don't give each other orders. 'I am my own person,' remember?" He threw our wedding vows at me first. Turnabout is fair.

"It's not an order." A glimpse of hurt beneath the anger. "I'm asking. Please, for me. Just…stop."

Just stop. Like it's easy. Like I can simply regress into the woman I was months ago.

I could agree. Stop taking lessons, stop coming to the shop. But it would be a lie. I can't unknow what I've learned. The canyon separating us becomes a gulf, a chasm.

"I can't."

Across the chasm, I watch my husband's heart break.

Despite the disaster of our last hangout, Tanya answers on the first ring. "My marriage might be over," I say.

She doesn't miss a beat. "Come here."

Ten minutes later, I'm wading through a sea of board books and drawings. "Rico's in his artistic phase." Tanya snatches up random clothes strewn about the living room. In the kitchen, Paul is at the stove, baby Rosa balanced on one hip, his Afro haloed by the overhead light.

"Say 'Hi, Lexi!'" He lifts Rosa's chubby arm.

In spite of everything, I smile. Tanya catches my eye, tips her head. *Upstairs?* I shake my head. For just a while, I want to playact normal.

She pulls out salad ingredients.

"No Chloe tonight?" Paul asks, jovial and oblivious.

I dart a guilty look at Tanya.

"She's busy," Tanya says. "But I'm sure we'll see her soon." The latter is directed at me, barbed. Such a mom.

I nod. *I'll talk to her.*

Tanya holds out an extra knife and I join her at the cutting board. While we dice vegetables, Paul updates us on work, as well as his plans around the house. Once I finish the tomatoes, he passes me Rosa. She's happy, babbling while she toys with my hair. I blow raspberries on her tummy, and her squeals punctuate Paul's story.

Rico pops in to show off his artwork. He preens at our compliments.

Tanya updates me on the office. Who took my old clients (John), who pissed off the entire accounts team (also John).

After dinner, Paul takes Rico to bed, protesting the whole way. Tanya and I tuck Rosa in. She must be exhausted. She's asleep before we even finish her favorite bedtime book.

Once her breathing evens, Tanya and I sprawl on the nursery floor. Bright-yellow sunflowers crowd the ceiling. Just a few years ago, it was a tableau of green dinosaurs for Rico. Before that, it was Tanya's craft room.

"Do you still make those macramé plant hangers?" I whisper. Rosa's white-noise machine babbles in the background.

Tanya rolls to face me, cheek pillowed in the crook of her elbow. "Not lately. Maybe when the kids get older."

"What's it like? Raising them."

Her gaze drifts to the mobile over the crib, little wooden planets Paul whittled himself. "Terrifying."

We laugh in breathy gusts, careful not to wake the baby.

She bites her lip. "I'm so scared I'll mess them up. But maybe that's inevitable. Maybe all parents mess you up. Mine sure did."

I'm quiet for a moment. "There are degrees to it, though. And we learn from our parents, right? Even if only how not to do it."

"True." She stretches. "Besides, I can't imagine life without them. Time changes when you have kids. Every day's a little eternity—one minute you're dead on your feet, the next you're having a laughing fit over how they pronounced 'broccoli.' Then you blink and they're four and they've become this entire person somehow. And you realize you'll spend a whole lifetime getting to know them, but you'll never quite learn everything..." She goes quiet. Probably because my vision's swimming.

I swipe at my eyes. Beside me, Tanya waits, patient as a still lake. The words that always stuck in my throat rise easily now. "I had a miscarriage."

"Oh, honey..." Tanya opens her arms. I fold myself into her. She wraps her arms around my waist, tucks her chin onto the crown of my head.

The tears keep coming, but I'm not embarrassed. It seems ridiculous I ever tried to hide this.

Tanya tightens her grip. She sways gently, side to side, until I stop shivering. Only then does she release me, just long enough to grab a spare blanket and sling it over us both. "When?"

"Last spring." Dried tears stiffen my cheeks. I scratch them with a corner of the blanket.

"Oh no, Lexi." Tanya blanches. "I kept badgering you about kids—"

"You didn't know." I shift onto my back. Honeybees weave among the ceiling sunflowers, dotted lines tracing the bees' curlicue flight paths. "At the time, I just wanted to forget. Except I couldn't, and then...I don't know. The longer I waited to say anything, the more it felt like I shouldn't still be hung up."

"Grief is grief. There's no timeline." Tanya toys with the hem of the blanket. "I had one, you know. Between Rico and Rosa."

My stomach sinks. "God, Tanya..." I had no idea.

"I was only seven weeks. Probably wouldn't have even noticed, except we were trying, so I was peeing on a stick every five minutes." She laughs breathily. "The doctor warned us they're common, but I still never..." She swallows. "Anyway. I felt weird talking about it too. Like it'd be... I don't know. Attention seeking, or something."

"Never."

A soft cooing sound makes us both freeze. We hold our breaths and listen to Rosa shuffle. After a minute, her breathing slows.

Trading guilty smiles, we wriggle out from under the blanket. I fold it over the rocking chair while Tanya scoops up the baby monitor. Together, we tiptoe into the hall. Tanya eases the door shut.

"Do you want to stay here tonight?" she murmurs.

I'm picturing Shane, crouched on the sidewalk. How badly I wanted to hold him. How much I still do.

But I am also thinking of his anger today. His heartbreak.

"Only if it's no trouble," I whisper.

She gives me her best don't-be-ridiculous face.

Downstairs, we make the pullout, then sprawl on it. Tanya procures chocolate ice cream while I recount the fight. "It's like he can't process me disagreeing with him. He needs an outsider to blame."

Tanya licks her spoon thoughtfully. "You could let him."

"Doesn't matter who he blames. I'm not the woman he married anymore. That's the real problem. He won't accept this version of me."

"Give him time to adjust." She passes me the pint.

The chocolate tastes darker than usual. Bitter. I hear Shane again, begging. *Please. For me.* I picture the thing in his auric field, its roots digging into him.

"Not sure we have time."

"Buy some, then." Tanya shrugs. "Stay away from Bea's shop. Doesn't have to be forever. Just for a little."

"If Paul asked you to quit something you loved, would you?"

She licks the curve of her spoon. "Depends. I'd at least consider it. Marriage is compromise." And then, at my expression. "Not obedience, before you get started. If he's asking you to give it up because he's jealous or trying to control you, then no, I don't think you should. But if he genuinely believes Bea is unsafe..."

I spear another scoop. "You're only saying that because Chlo hates her too."

Tanya taps my nose with her spoon. "Hey, I'm not taking sides. Maybe this isn't something you can compromise on. In that case, fair enough. All I'm saying is, it never hurts to consider all the options."

Chapter Twenty-Three

A scream wakes me at dawn. I bolt upright, pulse racing. But it's only Rico, scream-laughing from his parents' room. A minute later, baby Rosa starts to wail.

Pulling the blanket over my head, I check my texts. Notifications from Shane flood in. No doubt replies to my lone message last night: **Staying at Tanya's.** The number alone—*ten messages, really?*—floods me with dread.

I tap on Chloe's name instead. **Can we talk?**

It flips to Read immediately. I wait, pulse in my throat. No typing dots appear. After a minute, I shut the phone off and drag myself from bed. *From couch*, my aching lumbar corrects.

All through breakfast, dread piles up. It's bad enough fighting with Shane and Chloe at the same time. But what if Bea blames me for Shane's outburst? What if she refuses to teach me anymore?

Not to mention, I still don't know what's wrong with Shane. I can't heal him alone.

Like my first day all over again, I show up at Odds and Ends way too early. Instead of waiting, I pace the street. Crocuses have sprung up in patches of scrubby grass. Along with them come memories.

There's the vintage shop Shane and I visited on our first trip to Garden Vale. Here's the pothole where we blew a tire two years ago. And the empty store—this used to be a bank, remember? We opened our first joint account here, and we joked it was a bigger commitment than marriage.

Eventually, I perch on the curb, where Shane waited for us yesterday. Swallowing my nerves, I open his texts.

10:45 p.m. Are you seriously not coming home?
10:51 p.m. I shouldn't have yelled at that woman. But I don't trust her. She's not good for you.

The later the time stamps get, the more his regret bleeds through.

11:36 p.m. I've hardly seen you in weeks. I got scared, okay?
12:21 a.m. I don't think you're crazy. I never have.
12:24 a.m. Talk to me.
12:39 a.m. Please.

The last one breaks me.

5:04 a.m. Although it is not my preference, I understand if you would like more space to process. Let me know how you want to proceed.

It's so formal. Not like Shane at all. He must have asked someone for advice. One of the guys from the station? No. They'd've told him to show up at Tanya's with flowers. Maybe Holly, or one of his sisters? I picture him calling for help, waking someone in the middle of the night. Drafting and redrafting this text, alone in our bed. Finally hitting Send, then burying his phone under the pillows in panic.

Part of me yearns to go to him. But another part warns—
I'm not thinking straight yet. I'm upset from yesterday, angry
and afraid and raw. If we talk now, I'll only make things worse.

It takes several breaths until I'm steady enough to respond.
I'd like some space.

Like my text to Chloe, it flicks to Read at once. Unlike
Chloe, Shane begins typing right away. I watch the dots for
what feels like eternity. When his reply comes, though, all it
says is OK.

Bea finds me on the sidewalk a few minutes later. "Didn't
think I'd see you again." She unlocks the grate and rolls it
up to a chorus of meows. Street cats appear from nowhere
to circle her ankles. Bea empties two whole treat bags, then
shimmies past while they're distracted.

I follow. "My husband was completely out of line. I don't
know what got into him."

Inside, more howls. Chaucer paws at Bea's leggings, irate.

The longer she remains silent, the more my worry builds.
"I'll talk to him," I say. "It won't happen again."

"He's not my concern." She reaches down to scratch the
cat's ear. Chaucer only protests louder. *Food, not pets.* "You
tried to heal him, didn't you?"

I avoid her eye. Chaucer glares at me too, every inch as
disapproving as his mom. "I had to do something. He was
suffering."

"What part of 'Pace yourself' was unclear?"

"I just thought—"

"No," Bea interrupts. "You didn't." She straightens. Walks
into the back. Chaucer follows, near hysteria. She returns
with an open can and sets it right on the floor. He scarfs bites
so big I worry he'll choke.

216

Watching the cat, I exhale slowly. "You're right. I wasn't using my head. But he's my husband."

"All the more reason you shouldn't push his boundaries. Even if you were ready for work this complex, we need other people's permission to access their energy."

"He gave me permission."

Bea skewers me with a look. "Permission means nothing if he doesn't understand what he's agreeing to. Did you explain what you were doing? The potential risks?"

"But—"

"No, no but. Be honest with yourself. Why did you interfere? For his sake or yours?"

I lick suddenly too-dry lips. *She's right.* The only reason I looked at Shane's field in the first place was to win an argument.

"You feel like Shane isn't giving you space to grow," Bea says. "He can't accept your differences. That's understandable. But then you turned around and forced your lessons onto him."

"But it's my fault he's in pain." The words claw free.

Bea's shoulders slump. For a quiet moment, we both watch Chaucer eat. When she speaks again, Bea's tone is softer. "It's not your fault Shane developed an anxious attachment style. He has to do his own work, same as everyone. In his case, he needs to learn how to respect the boundaries of the people he loves." She pauses. "Actually, in both your cases."

Heat climbs my neck. "Did I make it worse? When I tried to heal him."

"Hard to say. I didn't see his field before."

"But you saw it yesterday?"

She nods.

"Okay." I force a deep breath. *Calm down.* We'll figure it out. "So what's wrong? Is it an imbalance or—"

She cuts me off. "I don't know."

"What?" I'm so used to her having all the answers. "You said if you saw his field, you'd know what was happening."

"No, I said I could guess. Everyone's energy is unique. Just like we all have different elemental constitutions, blocks don't behave the same way either, from one person to the next."

Chaucer tongues his can of food under a bookshelf, then flops onto his side, pawing irritably.

I kneel to pull it out. "So I can't help him."

"That's not what I said." Bea fixes me with her most grandmotherly glower yet. "Healing is about more than our energetic field. That's one aspect, but there are other ways to connect. Sharing what we've experienced, listening to other people's stories. Teaching the basic principles, like you and I have gone over—"

"Oh sure, Shane would love that," I grumble.

"Have you considered why he's so triggered by this?" When I don't respond, she sighs. "Your journey and his are linked. Romantic partners, especially long-term ones, share a bond. When one person changes, it alters the bond and affects you both."

Finished with breakfast, Chaucer starts to wash his face.

"I understand Shane is hurting. So are you. Your session at the caves was a start, but one powerful moment of resonance won't change your life. You need to process the experience and integrate the lessons you learned. You can't do that if you're running around solving your husband's problems instead."

"What's my problem? That I'm bad at being sad? I hate arguing with my partner?"

"I can't answer that for you." Bea scratches under Chaucer's chin. "Stink-breath here might have an idea, though," she coos. "What's that? Avoidance, you say? Yes, what is our friend Lexi avoiding…"

I groan. "Hint taken."

Bea smirks, far too pleased with herself. "On an unrelated note, I accept apologies in doughnut form."

Then I'm smiling too. Just a little. "Chocolate, I presume."

"Naturally."

What am I avoiding?

At home, I find an empty garage and a voicemail on the home phone. Strange. Nobody calls that number except...

Hi, Lexi. It's me, Holly. I stifle a smile. She always introduces herself, as if we won't recognize her voice. *I wanted to let you know that Shane drove up today. I'm not sure what happened; he won't say. But I didn't want you worrying. If you need to talk, call anytime. Love you.*

The voicemail beeps and I collapse onto a kitchen stool.

Well. I did ask for space.

Now that I've got it, the house feels too quiet. Cavernous, in fact. To clear my head, I start cleaning. Guest bathroom, master bathroom, downstairs powder room. Once I've scrubbed my arms sore, I pad through the house collecting towels and stray socks. I toss in loads of laundry, blast music, drown the quiet any way possible.

What am I avoiding?

With the basics out of the way, I move on to the seasonal chore list. The Christmas decor in the guest room goes into the attic. Then I weed through spring clothes, starting one bag for donations and another for trash. I sort the junk mail. Alphabetize the bookshelf in Shane's study.

What am I avoiding?

My cell buzzes and I leap on it.

Chloe. Still annoyed, but T told me what happened. Damn. You and Shane are my OTP. Rooting for you. Followed by a million hearts.

Hugging the phone, I roll backward onto the carpet.

What am I avoiding? Well, I avoided my friends for a month because I didn't want to explain that our hangout spot gave me the energetic equivalent of a migraine.

What am I avoiding? Tough conversations. Negative emotions. Grief.

I picture Lake Powell. Azure sky, turquoise waves, tiger-stripe sandstone. The scent of the breeze, the fine mist off the water. The cave. The dark. The screams.

I avoided that for so long. In the end, facing it felt… Well. Not good. But freeing.

Except, the grief swells again just thinking about it. *It's not gone.* It will never fully disappear. I'll have to keep purging, keep living with these feelings. The pain will continue to catch me off guard in the future, lashing out when I least expect, over and over.

That's the hardest part to accept. *I'm not fixed.*

Suddenly I'm laughing anyway. "Bea's right," I tell the ceiling fan. "I leap straight to fixing."

We can't fix grief. But maybe if I acknowledge it, we'll learn to coexist. And then the answer hits me. Or rather, the correct question.

What am I avoiding?

Not what. Who. I lever myself off the ground, grab an overnight bag, and start packing.

Chapter Twenty-Four

Holly meets me on the stoop. Her hug is so tight it crushes the air from my lungs. "Whatever's going on, just know I love you like my own," she whispers.

Unexpected emotion wells up. "Love you too." I try to wipe my eyes surreptitiously, but Holly fishes a tissue from her pocket anyway. "God, sorry; I'm a mess."

"Don't you dare apologize." She ushers me inside. Dogs swarm around our feet. "Shane's upstairs. Fair warning, I haven't seen him like this since he was a teenager."

Ominous.

"Thanks, Holly."

Bass music thumps overhead. I follow it up two flights to Shane's childhood bedroom. A mug of tea and a plate of cookies wait by the closed door. From Holly, no doubt, the tea long since gone cold.

I knock.

The volume drops. "I said I'm not hungry."

"It's me," I reply.

The sound cuts entirely. I hold my breath. There's a rustle from the other side. Footsteps approach the door. "Thought you wanted space."

I wait. He doesn't open it, so I lean my forehead against

the doorframe. "I thought so too. Then I realized I've had a lot of space lately."

"Just lately?" His voice sounds so close.

"Okay, avoidance might be my go-to." I study the white-paneled wood and picture every familiar line of his face. "I'm working on it." I'm close enough to hear his breathing. Or is that mine? "You really scared me," I say, softer now. "Shouting at my friend, accusing her of hurting me. It's not okay."

No, it's definitely his breathing, because it hitches. "Yesterday I wasn't...myself. Not that that's an excuse. There isn't one. But I..."

Squeezing my eyes shut, I reach for him. Even with the door between us, I catch flashes. Little Shane reaching for his father. Shane yesterday, crouched on the curb. A ragged hollow in his chest, and then *she can't be here, she came for me.* The sensation is drowning falling wanting all at once. *I have to get her out of here, have to save her, have to—*

He swears under his breath.

I snap to, fingers splayed on the door. "What's wrong?"

"No." The floorboards creak as he retreats. "We're not doing this. You asked for space; you're getting space."

"Shane, wait."

"See how you like being ignored for once." The music roars to life, drowning out the world.

How do I like it? I don't.

Slumped in the Coles' living room, one dog for a pillow and another burrowed under my knees, I scowl at the chandelier. The fine glass crystals shiver in tune to the distant bass.

Holly bustles in with a steaming mug of chai. She follows my gaze and tsks. "What did I tell you? High school all over again."

"You put up with that for four years?" I struggle upright. The pillow dog whines and army-crawls into my lap as Holly passes me the mug of tea. We narrowly dodge a spill.

"This is nothing." Holly settles onto a neighboring armchair. "You should've heard the music he listened to then." She flips her hair into her face and imitates a screamo rocker.

We grin. Slowly, mine melts.

"I won't pry," Holly murmurs. "But if you want to talk..."

I contemplate the mug. Almond milk swirls around the tea bag. "It's hard to explain."

"Try me."

The chai is so spicy, my nose tingles. I sip and trace its warmth down my throat. "Remember at Eric's going-away, when we went up on the roof?"

"To heal Eric's energy?" Holly seems nonplussed. "Of course. He and I had a long talk afterward. He said you really helped him."

The words warm me even faster than any tea. *At least I did one thing right.* Amidst the general mess I've been making for weeks.

"Something similar is happening to Shane. Only way more complicated. I tried to heal him too, but my intentions were all wrong, so I'm pretty sure I made it worse. Now he won't even talk to me."

Holly glances from me to the ceiling and frowns. "What does energy feel like? I mean, how do you... Do you see it?"

"Sometimes." I shrug. "Other times it's more like impressions. A taste, a smell, a fragment of memory that isn't mine."

"Like a dream, only you're awake."

I look over, startled.

She cradles her own mug, fixated by the steam. "First time it happened to me was the day Eric got lost."

I'd forgotten. "Eric said you sensed his injury?"

She nods. "I watched him fall. Then I kept getting images, impressions that led me to him." She takes a sip, then replaces the mug with a clink. "It scared me, though. I prayed I'd never experience it again. And I didn't. Not for years." She takes a deep breath. "Until this week."

Carefully, I place my mug on the side table, fingers trembling. "What happened?"

"Well, at first, I assumed it was my imagination." She flattens her lips. "That or a stroke. I was reading in the sitting room and I smelled smoke. I ran into the kitchen and shouted for Frank. Nothing was burning, though." She pauses to shuffle yet another dog onto the couch.

"Then, the next morning, it happened again. Only this time, I went downstairs and saw flames everywhere. The walls, the ceiling, even the grouting. I would've screamed, but I couldn't move. All of a sudden...it wasn't my kitchen anymore. Different furniture, different layout."

She buries one hand in the dog's ruff and closes her eyes. "There was a little girl. Curled up on the tile by my foot. Well, not my foot—this big black-and-yellow boot."

"The kind firemen wear?" I murmur, already guessing, dreading the answer.

Holly nods. "She couldn't've been older than five. Blond curly hair, just like Becky's used to be. Jeans and this sweet purple top..."

"Oh God."

Shane's first death.

The firehouse where he'd volunteered in college had lost people, but never someone he found. This was his fourth big call in Garden Vale, and his first time being first on the scene.

He said she didn't even look injured. Like she'd lain down for a nap. He fitted the oxygen mask, carried her out. He thought she was okay, but she never woke up. Her lungs were too damaged.

She passed away at the hospital. Smoke inhalation.

Holly's cup rattles. She sets it aside. "I woke up in bed. Figured it was a dream. I've heard the story; it was easy to imagine details. But it felt so real."

"That must have been terrible."

"Of course. But I understood my son a little better after. He's always been such a realist. Nothing wrong with that, but he struggles to process things that don't make logical sense. The messy, unpredictable parts of life."

In the weeks after Shane learned about the girl's death, he moved through the house like a ghost. He drifted room to room. Watched TV, straight-faced and silent, no matter what was on: comedy, horror. The only time he reacted was to the news. They showed a segment about the fire, and he called them vultures, stormed out.

I found him in the backyard strangling a tea towel.

"What is the fucking point?" He gestured at the yard, but I knew what he meant. "If that can happen to anyone, to a kid...why fucking bother?"

Because good things happen too? But he didn't need platitudes. I rested my chin on his shoulder, and he leaned back against me. I held him up, arms around his hips.

"It's fucked up." I studied the yard. The kind of backyard I'd dreamed of having as a little girl—a big oak tree, the perfect size for tire swings, with a broad lawn, a white picket fence, plenty of space for toys. "We feel like we're in control, but so much could go wrong at any second."

His breath hitched. When he finally turned, though, a different kind of heat lit his eyes. Then he kissed me, hard. Suddenly we were both desperate. Hands everywhere, in search of the real, the tangible. A belief we could touch.

At the time, it reassured me—Shane would never let me go. We were our own everything: religion, belief system, support. Now, I wonder. *Us against the world.* Did that limit us?

"He got harder after the fire." Holly's voice draws me back here and now. "More cynical."

"More realistic, according to him," I reply.

"Is it realism, though? Or is it a shield?" Holly shakes her head sadly. "Shane never clicked with the church. He hated going, even as a boy. Then, after Eric came out..." Her frown deepens. "I'll freely admit I made mistakes. A whole heap. I won't blame my kids if they never forgive me."

I think of Eric and his fears about moving. "They already have, Holly."

She flashes a quick, grateful smile. "I don't know. Shane... I tried to force him back to church. You know how forcing that boy into anything goes."

"Like arguing with a tree?"

She grins. It doesn't last long, though. "I think I tried so hard because he and I used to talk so much. We'd have these long conversations about all the big-picture stuff when he was little. I loved listening to his ideas. He was so eager, so excited by possibility." She readjusts the current dog in her lap. "Y'know, my kids were all different. From Frank and me, and from each other. But we each had our way of connecting. Those chats were mine and Shane's, which is probably why I took it to heart when we wound up with such different beliefs. I guess I just couldn't understand how my open-minded little boy became so rigid. Or why."

The story reminds me of the Shane I met in college, who curled up in a tiny dorm bed to daydream about our future. The one who confessed secrets in the dark and told me if the world had any purpose at all—which he doubted—then it must be to teach us about each other.

His mission had always been to help others, in whatever form that took.

I try to remember the last time we spoke like that. Surely not since the fire. Maybe not even before it. Since college, maybe?

Recently, I've changed. But maybe the change started earlier than I realized. Maybe we've both been transforming, all this time, and we're only now noticing.

Holly clears her throat. "Anyway. The dream. I must be imagining things."

She sounds so much like me that a lump forms in my throat. Half sympathy, half relief. *I'm not the only one.* I know exactly what she needs to hear. "No, Holly. I wasn't imagining things, and neither are you."

Chapter Twenty-Five

Over Holly's vehement protests, I rent a hotel room. I asked for space and Shane gave it to me. If he wants the same, it's only fair.

But I'm not going home yet.

Healing is about more than our energetic field. There are other ways to connect. Shane isn't ready, and that's okay. Someone else here is.

Holly meets me in a scenic neighborhood park, where we walk to a bench beneath a budding maple. In the distance, a preschool class runs wild, pursued by teachers. Laughter and shouts punctuate the otherwise quiet morning.

"So, you sensed Eric injure himself once," I say. "Then you had the vision of the fire... Anything else unusual?"

Holly hums under her breath. "Nothing visual."

"What about other sensations? A scent, a taste, a feeling in your body."

She chuckles. "My girls say I have a sixth sense. I always call right as they're texting me. Does that count?"

"Definitely."

"Oh, well in that case, there's plenty. A few days ago, I thought of my friend Cindy out of the blue, so I called her and she'd just gotten stuck on the freeway near our house.

Flat tire. Frank and I ran her a spare before the tow truck even got there. Or Mr. Cooper from church." Her smile droops. "He wasn't doing very well. He'd just turned ninety, and what with the dementia... One day, out in the garden, I smelled his cologne, and I could've sworn I heard his laugh—he had one of those big, booming laughs. His son called the next morning to tell us he'd gone."

I reach for her hand. She lets me take it and squeezes tight. Nearby, one of the preschoolers shrieks with joy. For a minute, we just watch them play.

"It's funny," Holly says. "When I was a little girl, stuff like this happened all the time. As I got older, it stopped. Well, except for the incident with Eric, of course, but that one seemed obvious to me. God led me to him."

God. I hesitate, Shane's voice in my head: *My parents are traditional. Not everyone is going to be okay with whatever you're exploring.*

Holly must notice my sudden discomfort, because she swats my knee. "Relax. I know you're not active in the church anymore. My beliefs are mine, and yours are yours. I learned the hard way: you can't guilt people into faith."

"Never dreamed you would. It's just..." I grimace in apology. "Shane didn't want me to tell you I'm studying energy work. He said you wouldn't approve."

"The mother he grew up with wouldn't have." Holly heaves a sigh. "But everybody changes, right?"

"That's what I keep telling him." I glance at her sidelong, startled to be having my least judgmental conversation in a long time with my religious mother-in-law. Life is stranger than I expected but sometimes more beautiful, too.

"Energy work. That's what it's called?"

I shrug. "There are lots of terms. Energy healing, auric field study, elemental work. Probably dozens more I don't know. The name's not important. Just like it doesn't matter if we agree on where it comes from—whether it's from God or the human spirit, or, heck, maybe someday we'll be able to explain it with science."

She nods thoughtfully. "And you're studying to do what, exactly?"

"Right now, I'm learning to sense and read energy. With more practice, I'll be able to use it to heal people, like Eric."

On the playground, a boy hesitates at the top of the slide. As we watch, another boy leaps past him and whizzes down the sleek metal incline, fearless.

"Could you teach me too?" Holly asks.

I never considered teaching anyone. I'm still a student myself. "I guess I can try? Or at least cover the basics."

"All right." Holly claps her hands. "Hit me."

"Now?" I can't help but laugh.

"Why not? It's a beautiful day, and I've got nowhere to be."

"Why not," I echo, as I try to remember my first real lesson. "Well, my teacher says there are five elements: earth, air, fire, water, and aether, which is the other four combined. We all have different amounts of each element in our constitution, which helps determine our personalities."

Holly plasters on a polite what-are-you-talking-about smile.

Okay, start over. "Would you mind if I tap into your auric field? It will give me a clearer picture of where to begin."

"Of course. Should I shut my eyes?"

"If you like. Whatever feels more relaxing. Then breathe in, nice and slow—that's it—and release…"

The distant shouts from the playground fade. As our breaths sync, my muscles soften. A tingle starts in the tip of my fingers and spreads up my arms, into my chest.

Holly's auric field winks into view, and I gasp.

Holly's shoulders tense, though she keeps her eyes shut. "What's wrong?"

"No, nothing. Don't worry." I'm grinning from ear to ear. Holly's energy is beautiful: a shining torrent of color, like nobody else's I've seen. Bea's comes the closest, her field a lighthouse beacon in a storm. But Holly's is the rainbow after the storm.

It took me a long time to perceive my own field—hours of meditation and concentration. But Holly isn't me. She's not antsy or unable to sit still. Maybe...

"Holly," I murmur, suddenly sure in a way I almost never am. "Open your eyes."

She does, and then she gasps too, her eyes going wide with delight. "Oh." She skims a hand through her field and ripples branch off in her wake.

"It's your auric field," I say softly. "This energy always flows through you. It's part of your body; you just usually don't see it."

"It's incredible."

From this headspace, it's easy to pick apart the colors and sensations. After the meditation on the mountain, the dance atop the dunes, and my swim in the cave, each disparate thread around Holly seems familiar. I recognize the elements and trace their energy patterns.

A branch of fiery heat wraps around her heart. "You love fiercely," I say. "You'll do anything for your family. But fire isn't your primary source of power."

Holly nods, still toying with her field. "I could've told you that."

"Your air is subdued too." Only a faint highlight around her forehead. "You don't overthink everything." *What must that be like?*

"That's Frank's department." She chuckles.

On the other hand... "Wow." Calm, cool waves coat her torso, her shoulders. "You have a lot of water. You're very in touch with your feelings, and you're good at expressing yourself."

The longer I study the water, the more my awareness shifts. I sense dozens of energetic strands branching from her. Nothing gnarled or frightening like the thing attached to Shane or even the wispy worry I sensed from Tyrone.

Instead, shining cords extend from Holly in all directions. Somehow, I know without asking where each one leads: one toward Clarissa and her family in California, another for Becky, Hannah, and their partners, plus all the grandkids. A pair reaches to Eric and Tyrone in New York. Frank, near Holly's core, seems to have the most secure branch. And, of course, there's one for Shane.

A final strand pours from Holly's navel straight into my chest. Hesitantly, I reach up to brush the spot. It feels cool to the touch, reminiscent of a brook on a spring morning.

Shaking myself, I turn back to Holly's field. "The fourth element, I'm not as familiar with." But even though I don't have any personal experience with the element that makes up the bulk of Holly's energy, it's so strong that I sense it anyway.

Her bedrock is earth. Its roots burrow into the ground beneath her. There's a solidness to her field, a physical presence most people don't have, as if she's a touch more here than the rest of us.

"Earth is your primary element," I say. She is grounded—a woman who grew up in the same town where she settled down, with no desire to stray. "You love your routine and the simple pleasures in life. You know where you belong, and you're genuinely content. Do you know how rare that is?"

"Oh, stop." Holly sniffs, hard. Then she laughs, touching a hand to her cheek. "You can really see all that?"

And more.

Holly lives in the home she dreamed of as a child—the house her parents built, on the land where they grew old. It is all she has ever wanted: connection to her family, solid roots. I suddenly understand why she struggles so much when her children move away. There's an old, sour note from Clarissa's departure in her field, as well as fresh, bright sorrow over Eric. I even sense concern for Shane and me, although we're relatively close.

Wound into those threads is a hefty amount of guilt, because she doesn't want to feel this way. She wants to be happy for her children, yet the resentment lingers. We cannot will away unpleasant emotions. Her children are different from her, and Holly regrets it.

In a single, breathless moment, I understand something about myself too.

I thought I was like Holly. As a girl, I dreamed about having a loving husband, children of our own, and the house with the white picket fence. I wanted it—or so I thought. But now, looking at Holly's deepest wishes, I realize...I don't. At least, not in the same way as Holly.

Everyone around me wanted to get married, have kids, settle down. I thought you needed to want the same thing. Isn't that adulthood?

No. There's another reason I craved stability and normalcy. I never had it.

Now I understand, I've been chasing a craving, not a goal. To be honest, I am happier now—arguing and confronting myself and messing up all over the place—than I ever was in my supposedly ideal old life. I'm finally moving in the right direction. And while I like this direction right now, I'll probably want to change it someday too.

Holly lives for routine and comfort. I admire that, envy

her. But even if I found that stability, it wouldn't bring me the same comfort. It's not how I'm wired.

I am not a rooted creature. I am built to chase the wind and burn like the sun.

How have I never realized this before?

Holly's asking a question, but I'm a million miles away. Seeing me, she extends a hand. Her energy reaches with her, and solid, steady earth scoops me into its arms. *I am me and you are you. The world needs all kinds to thrive.*

Holly asked me to teach her. Instead, she's the one teaching me.

I wonder if it's always like this. Does Bea ever learn from me? We are all mirrors, after all, none of us quite real in solitude. Together, we comprehend ourselves.

Slowly, the world drips back in. The spring breeze raises goose bumps on my arms, the sun warming the crown of my head. Holly's holding me, rocking side to side. I release her with a breathy laugh.

"You all right?" She peers at me.

I touch my cheek, surprised to find it damp. In the past, crying would've embarrassed me, because it felt weak or even shameful. But vulnerability is strength.

"I am." For the first time in a while, I really mean that.

"Good." She pats my shoulder. "So earth, huh? Makes sense. I love my garden. Frank always says I'd grow roots if I could, plant myself among the rosebushes."

"It's funny. Earth's the element I have the least of."

She winks. "Maybe that's why God sent you to me."

Chapter Twenty-Six

After Holly leaves, I meander the park's paths, stepping aside for the occasional jogger. Each time, I wonder about these passersby's stories. Are they happy? Chasing their dreams? Or are any of them like I was until recently, running on autopilot without even realizing what they want?

Maybe that's why God sent you to me.

I don't believe in the same version of God as Holly, but the idea of a collective unconscious has always captivated me. Stories, inspiration, and ideas all seem to have common threads—like scientists who discover the same breakthrough simultaneously, or movies that debut the same week with near-identical plots.

Maybe God is to aether what the other elements are to humanity: a combination of all of us, made up of and greater than its parts. God as mankind, each of us learning from our own multifaceted reflections: that, I could believe.

Something drew me to Holly, after all. Something's been giving me nudges all along.

Another jogger passes, so I step off the path. My shoes sink into the spongy ground, but it feels comfier than the pavement. I walk on it instead, keeping parallel to the path at first. Pretty soon, I branch away and wander beneath the trees.

The air under the canopy smells clean. I walk until I can

no longer see the jogging path, and then I pick the biggest tree, leaning against its rough bark to slide to the ground. Cross-legged among the gnarled roots, I meditate for the first time in days. No auric fields to study, no agenda.

I let go.

Time passes. On the fringe of my awareness, fragments of an idea gather. On a rooftop in Salt Lake City, wispy fronds of energy drift to Eric from his partner. In our dim living room, something ugly writhes above my husband, claws at me.

What is our friend Lexi avoiding?

Shane trips backward on the ice. The cord of energy stretches between Holly and me. My hand reaches for the back door just as a larger hand closes over it.

Your journey and his are linked.

Stiff muscles. Hot blanket, suffocation. No sound. No sight. Only sensation. I am frozen, immobile. *Stop it. Stop stop stop.*

I jolt awake. For a second I'm still there, still trapped, and my chest heaves. Then sunlight pierces the vision. Shading my eyes, I squint at my surroundings. I lie sprawled on the ground—I must have fallen asleep. How long have I been here? I was in shade when I first sat down.

I check my phone. Two missed calls and a text from Shane. My heart climbs into my throat. **Dinner?**

I brush my hair back from my face and check my reflection in the cell phone camera. Definitely need a pit stop at the hotel. But... **Yes.**

Shane makes a reservation in town. I beat him there, dawdling in the parking lot. The Cole family group text lights up while I wait—Eric sent a photo of himself and Ty in a coffee shop, posing beside another couple. **Met the next-door neighbors, p sure they're our new besties.**

236

The phone dings again. Tyrone. **Please never use the word bestie again.** Followed by a kiss emoji.

Holly replies next, a long string of heart eyes, and then some more difficult-to-decipher emojis.

Clarissa sidebars the Sibs & Co group chat instead. **Oh god, what does Mom think the wet emoji means??**

It's raining in the background? suggests Becky. She translates Holly best.

Grinning, I repocket my phone just as Shane sweeps into the restaurant.

He looks good, dressed in a button-down with the sleeves rolled, plus fitted jeans, his hair worn loose. He has his cell phone out too, but he puts it away when he spots me. "My family is so embarrassing," he says upon reaching the table. He hesitates, and I realize he's debating whether to go for a kiss.

He takes a seat without.

"Present company included?" I arch my eyebrows.

"This side of the table, definitely." He gestures to himself.

The waiter intervenes. We order waters and a starter. Even after he leaves, I keep the menu open, my eyes glazing over the words, not really processing anything.

"So—"

"Should we—"

We both speak at the same time. Laugh. Then we both wave each other on. Neither of us says a word. But we're looking at each other, at least.

Now that I've started, I can't stop.

From afar, Shane seems put together, but up close, he looks wrecked. Deep shadows circle his eyes, which are rimmed in red. Considering how little I've slept lately, I can't appear much better.

"This feels like the world's most awkward first date," he finally says.

We snort. I rest my chin in my hand and debate. There are a million things I want to say, and a million others I'm scared to. "I don't know where to start."

"I'll go first. I shouldn't have ambushed your..." He pauses just long enough to get my hackles up. "Friend. It was uncalled for."

"Uncalled for," I repeat.

"More than uncalled for?"

"You screamed at her," I say. "You accused her of... I don't even know. Brainwashing me? Tell me you don't still believe that."

The waiter returns with our waters. To judge by the speed with which he jogs off again, we can't be the only ones who sense the tension.

Shane gulps half of his glass's contents in one go, avoiding my eye. "No, I don't think she's causing whatever is happening to you. But she isn't helping."

"How would you know?" I scoff. "You barely listen when I talk about this stuff."

"'Cause it's all nonsense!"

"If it's all nonsense, why do you care so much whether I believe it?" I pick up my water, then put it down again, too tense to actually drink it. "Why can't you just be happy that I'm happy?"

He exhales through flared nostrils. "Okay. Why does it matter so much to you that I don't believe it?"

I remind myself that I didn't come here to fight. "You don't have to believe it, Shane. But you belittle me every time I bring it up."

"I'm not belittling you. We've been through a lot this year, and yes, okay, it worries me that a veritable stranger suddenly appeared, claiming to have answers about stuff only you can see—"

"Not only me," I interrupt. "Your mother sees it too."

"My mother." He frowns.

"She's experienced a lot of the same things. We started talking yesterday, and—"

"Didn't I specifically ask you not to? My family is not okay with this shit. I don't want them worrying."

"She's not worried," I say. And then, "Well, she is, because obviously we're a mess. But my beliefs weren't a concern."

It doesn't take much to nudge myself into the right head-space. It hasn't for weeks now. In a blink, Shane's auric field appears.

The block, or whatever it is, has grown. Barely any of his energy is flowing. It all pools around his waist, feeding the growth, which in turn has gone a deep, furious red. It pulsates, as bright as the fire coral we saw when Shane took me snorkeling in Cozumel.

The thickest branch of coral reaches for me.

I work to keep my voice even and my focus on Shane, not the thing. "Shane, something's really wrong. Your energy field has some kind of damage—"

"Do you even hear yourself?" He laughs, but it's a strangled, bitter sound. "Good job, you've noticed I'm upset. That doesn't take psychic powers, Lexi."

"Your mom senses it too. Ask her."

"Great. Now you're dragging my mother into your delusions."

Anger flares, fast and hot as the fire energy at the dunes. "*Delusions.*"

He tips his head back. "Okay, that came out harsh. Your, I don't know. Fantasies. Whatever you want to call them. My point is, you shouldn't encourage each other."

"Yes, that would be terrible," I deadpan. "If we do, we might realize neither of us is crazy."

Normally this is the point in the argument where I'd storm off. Let the flames die down so we can discuss things logically later. But tonight, I don't move a muscle. We stare each other down.

Gazing into Shane's eyes, I witness the moment the shift happens. He's himself, and then, in a blink, someone else—some*thing* else—slides into his face. Like an actor trading masks in a play. "Oh, I get it." I barely recognize his voice, which is suddenly low and terrible. "You're jealous."

"Jealous of what?" There's a reflection in his pupils. A speck of red, the exact same hue as the thing clawing from his waist…

"My family."

I freeze.

Freeze is always your go-to. Pathetic. The self-rebuke is old, a shadow from a past I never excavate, which only Shane knows enough to touch.

"I'm not jealous." Is that really true?

My husband smiles. It doesn't reach his eyes. "For the longest time, I figured family dynamics were just hard for you to grasp. But now I get it—you resent how close we are."

My hands quiver. *This isn't Shane talking.*

"You're mad because I have something you never will."

I reach for the calm of meditation, but all those hours of practice elude me. "I understand family dynamics better than someone who grew up with no actual problems."

"Oh, we have plenty of problems." He gestures between us. Layered over us like a second skin is the other aspect of this fight. Shane's energy, all but motionless a minute ago, churns now, boiling like a kettle close to overflow. As I watch, the fire coral protrusion at his waist moves too, growing solid and barbed. Without warning, it doubles in length.

Your journey and his are linked.

Just as I raise my hands, the branch plunges into my chest.

I flinch, even though I don't actually feel anything. The only clue it's there is a faint ringing in my ears. But when I look down, energy weeps from the wound, red clumps sloughing off to be reabsorbed into my field.

It's growing. Horrified, I grab the root, right where it enters my auric field.

Memories assault me. Nothing visual—only words, emotions. Shane's despair. *Dad, please, you can't really believe it's unnatural.* His betrayal. *Am I even part of this family anymore?* His dual convictions: *I know what's real.* But: *Nobody believes me.*

The impossible, cursed-Cassandra frustration of trying to change the ones you love. Beating yourself bloody against the logic barriers. You remain convinced that if only you could find the right words, you could win the argument once and for all, put all disagreements behind you.

Do we even live in the same world?

I release the branch with a gasp.

"Lexi?" Shane stands over me, expression torn between worry and frustration, but at least he's himself. "You blacked out again. How often does that happen?"

"It's not a blackout." I push the chair back and stand.

Shane catches my elbow. "Well, it's not normal."

His touch electrifies my entire body. Memories resurface. *How can you support this? You can't really believe—*

"Don't." I wrench free. "Don't touch me."

Shane raises his hands. "Okay, okay. At least make sure you're all right before you—"

"I'm fine." I grab my purse. *Get out of here.* That thing in Shane's field feels like a twisted version of the cord binding me to Holly. Whatever it is, the thought of it attacking anew overwhelms me. "This was a bad idea." With that, I shoulder past him and go out the door.

Chapter Twenty-Seven

You're jealous.

I have something you never will.

On the way back to Garden Vale, I drive worse than Bea—startling at every on-ramp, checking the mirrors so often I resemble the bobblehead dolls truckers glue to their dashboards.

Over and over, I replay our conversation at the restaurant. Aloud, I recite everything I wish I'd said, the million other ways our conversation could have gone.

Which version of our selves is truer: the calm, controlled ones or the monsters who surface when we're angry?

At home, the house is both freezing and stuffy. I fling open windows, doors. I was only gone a couple of days, but something rotted in the kitchen trash. While I'm taking it out, my phone vibrates. My heart leaps, both fearing and hoping it's Shane.

Mom.

I think of Holly, calling her daughters right as they're about to text her. I think of the ties binding people—of roots.

What am I really avoiding?

I answer a split second too late. Voicemail already picked

up, so I swipe to my contacts, then pause. Before calling back, I go to messages. There's a two-word text from my brother, sent five minutes ago. **Watch out.**

The phone buzzes. New voicemail. I don't even have time to open it before the phone vibrates again. Incoming call: Mom.

She only does this in her worst headspace. I know what to expect if I answer; we've done this dance a thousand times. My brother warned me for a reason.

Still, there is the unavoidable, impossible-to-ignore worry. *What if something bad happened? What if you ignore her the one time she really needs you?*

I pick up. "Mom."

"Finally. Are you screening my calls again?"

"I didn't get to the phone in time."

"Uh-huh. What about every other time I've tried you this week?"

Because I always second-guess myself, even when I'm positive, I double-check my call history. But there are no missed calls. No texts or other voicemails either. "I didn't get any calls this week."

"Last week, then. You always split hairs."

There are no calls last week either. None since Christmas. I take a deep breath. Hold it. Exhale. "I didn't realize you wanted to talk."

"You're my daughter. Of course I want to talk to you." The words warm my chest, until, "You're the one who makes it difficult. But I'll go on loving you, even though you hate me."

"I don't hate you."

"You've got a funny way of showing it."

This conversation is a trap. No matter what I say, I can never change the script. Just like with Shane—neither of us wanted to fight, yet we blundered into it anyway, actors in a play reciting lines we hate.

"Does there have to be a national holiday for me to speak to my daughter? Far be it from me to ask how you're doing after months without a word."

Your journey and his are linked.

Earth's the element I have the least of.

Maybe that's why God sent you to me.

Suddenly, I know what I'm really avoiding. "Mom," I interrupt. "Can I come for a visit?"

Bea and I kneel in the scrubby patch of grass behind the shop. It's not so much a backyard as no-man's-land, too small for either Bea or the jewelry store behind Odds and Ends to utilize. The narrow strip consists of two broken flagstones, half a dozen cigarette butts, and an old beer bottle filled with rain.

There are also long fronds of overgrown grass, a sprinkling of crocuses, and a veritable riot of buttercups.

I pick one and hold it beneath my chin. If I close my eyes, I can picture Ricky teaching me the trick. "If you turn yellow—look, see my chin?—you love butter."

I remember laughing. "Who doesn't love butter?"

"Right." Bea squints at me. "Earth energy. Are you sure you're ready?"

My thoughts leap straight to Holly. "Yes." She opens her mouth to argue, but I get there first. "I know you're worried I'm moving too fast—and I have, at times—but this is important."

"Your speed wasn't the problem." Bea examines me closely. "I was worried because you focus all your energy on other people's journeys, instead of your own. But this is definitely your lesson. Just make sure you're ready, because I suspect it'll be the hardest one."

"Oh." I can't decide whether having Bea's blessing makes me more or less nervous.

"You don't have much earth in your constitution, which means it's difficult for you to connect with earth energy. Often, our most complicated lessons stem from our roots." Bea rips up a clump of grass. Dirt rains into her lap, which she ignores. "Earth is our foundation, the ground into which we plant everything else. Without a stable foundation, what happens?" She sets the grass back on the ground, where it falls onto its side.

Flecks of dirt dust my calf. I brush them off. "Will it be like water energy?" The cave. The screams. "Things I've been avoiding?" It's warm in the sun, but I shiver anyway.

"Avoidance does seem to be your go-to framework, which implies that you learned it somewhere."

"Probably from my deadbeat father." I make sure there's no trash behind me, then sprawl on the grass. From this angle, the backyard isn't so bad. Blue sky, fluffy clouds...

"Could be," Bea says. "All I know is, you've been coming to my shop five days a week for months, and this is the first time you've mentioned your family in detail."

Grass tickles my cheek. "They're not a big part of my life." I've said the same sentence a dozen times, in college and after. Nobody questioned it until Bea.

"Why?"

Overhead, a cloud morphs from a castle into a coiling serpent. "Dad left and never looked back, so screw him. My brother... We keep in touch. But we're so different. We don't talk about anything real. And Mom is..." I wet my lips. "We don't get along."

Bea's quiet for a while.

"You said we need good foundations. Does that mean people who don't have a good childhood are screwed?"

"For better or worse, your past will always be part of you. For example, my childhood was obviously perfect, since I'm so wise."

I roll my eyes.

She grins. "But no, a bad childhood does not doom anyone to a bad life. We can always reprogram ourselves, break old cycles, and create a new framework. It just takes work."

"This is starting to sound like Corporate Speak Bingo," I mumble.

"Like what now?"

I roll over. "Lots of buzzwords. Dubious meaning."

Bea gives me an arch look. "All right, how's this: you can't recover from a wound until you look it in the eye."

My voice drops to a whisper. "What if I'm not strong enough?"

Bea clicks her tongue. "Lexi. You haven't even begun to grasp how strong you are."

Chapter Twenty-Eight

My hometown feels like another planet, but in reality, it's just a five-hour drive. Before leaving, I dial the only phone number I've got memorized. I have a recurring nightmare about being arrested and needing to make my one call here.

While it rings, I pray. *Not Mom, not Mom…*

On the fourth ring, a gruff voice says, "McKeen residence."

For a moment, impossible, wild hope surges in my chest. *Dad?* Then the dots connect, embarrassingly slow. "Ricky. Hey." My brother sounds older than the last time we spoke, at Christmas. Is that possible?

"She lives! To what do I owe this honor? Wait, should I not be joking? Nobody's dead, right?"

"All good news, promise." A guilty twinge—I hate that we only talk for holidays or emergencies. "Did Mom tell you I'm visiting?"

"Oh." The ellipsis is audible. "Kinda assumed she was, ah, misremembering."

I was afraid of that. I worry at my lower lip. "Is tonight still good?"

"Tonight." The next pause is longer, filled with a decade of unspoken rules. "Are you sure?"

"No." I laugh, breathless. "Mom said you're free, but if it's a bad time—"

"Of course not. Aside from the risk of giving Mom a heart attack, but that's inevitable."

I wind a strand of hair around one finger. "Will she be upset?"

"Are you kidding? She'll be fucking thrilled, Lex. We haven't seen you in, what, three years? Since the Salt Lake City trip?"

My mind whirs. "No, two. When you came to Garden Vale."

"Doesn't count," he says, and we both go quiet, remembering the disaster that visit became. He and Mom were supposed to stay for a week. They barely made it twelve hours. There's a not-insignificant risk of a repeat today, and we all know it. "I'll be there by seven. Need me to pick anything up?"

"You're bringing yourself. That's plenty."

Thankfully, we disconnect before I choke up. No backing out now. This is happening.

My mind tried to forget this place, but apparently my body didn't get the memo. At the exit, my subconscious takes over. I couldn't name a single street in my hometown from memory besides our own, and yet within minutes, sans GPS, I'm pulling up a familiar tree-lined cul-de-sac.

I park by the red mailbox with the scrape on the side. Ricky clipped it when he was learning to drive.

The house hasn't changed. Same weathered sideboards and clogged gutters. Same narrow porch chock-full of crap: worn-out shoes, rusty gardening equipment, cardboard boxes growing mold in the rain. Collections Mom will "get around to selling someday."

The front lawn looks decent because the neighborhood

association fines residents who neglect it. But even at night, the overgrown backyard is visible through the broken chain link fence.

Someone left the porch light on, at least.

Here goes everything.

I vault the front steps two at a time, afraid that if I slow down, I'll change my mind.

An old rake and what looks like a rabbit hutch block the door. The hutch still has hay in the bottom, gone to rot. It makes me wonder what happened to the rabbits.

The doorbell sounds tinny, so weak the heartbeat in my eardrums all but drowns it out.

Everywhere, I unearth half-forgotten memories: the porch swing, now buried in firewood, where Mom used to sit and wait for Dad's car after work. The pair of ice skates underneath, several sizes too small now, that I wore when Ricky taught me to skate at the pond.

But there are other memories too. Rotten ones.

This was a mistake. I almost retreat to the car, suddenly aware that I'm not safe here, so far from my comfort zone.

But home isn't comfortable anymore either. Nowhere is. And it's not because of Shane, or Bea, or my mother, or anyone else. At the end of the day, no matter how far I run, I'm still me.

I need to get comfortable in my own skin.

The door opens. "Lexi. Oh, my goodness." I barely register my mother's appearance—her new gray hairs and deeper crow's-feet, the same baby-blue eyes I inherited—before she flings herself at me.

We collide so hard I stagger. I hug her, more for balance than anything.

"It's been so long! Come in, come in. Dinner's all ready." She pulls me inside, giddy with excitement.

I feel five years old again, clinging to her hand. Why did I ever let go?

Then her grip tightens and the flashbacks intrude. Her hand, not on my arm but buried in my hair. My throat scraped raw from crying. *Stop, please.* Ricky trying to free me. *Mom, let her go.* My mother's voice, devoid of emotion. *Not till she learns her lesson.*

I wrench from her grasp.

For an instant, hurt flickers across her features, but she smooths it away. "How was the drive?"

"Not bad." I hug my waist and force a smile. "The house looks good." There are some new pieces of furniture and framed portraits on the walls, which help to disguise some of the old water stains. Religious tchotchkes cover every surface—statues of Jesus, Temples in miniature, pillows stitched with inspirational quotes.

Other things haven't changed. The photos of my mother and father on their wedding day. Honeymoon shots she never took down. Baby pictures, my brother's graduation, recent pictures from a beach I don't recognize. And...

I stop before a photo of me holding a Medina Property award. I recognize it—the first year I won, the *Garden Gazette* ran a feature on me. She must have printed this off the article. A strange mix of gratitude and regret hits me.

Mom doesn't notice. She's gesturing at a yellow splotch behind the photos, nose wrinkled. "Good? Please. Your brother has been promising to repaint since... Rick?" she shouts.

The stairs creak.

Then my brother descends, a huge smile on his face. It's the smile we both share with our father, the one Mom called his troublemaker. "If it isn't the prodigal sister."

"Big brother."

He takes the rest of the steps two at a time, then sweeps me straight off my feet. "You've gotten bigger," he grunts.

"I have not." I prod him until he drops me. "You've just gotten weaker in your old age."

He ruffles my hair and leans in, pitching his voice so Mom won't hear. "I'm glad you came."

My pulse flutters. Does he know?

No time to ask. Mom directs us to the kitchen. "Insult each other later; the food's getting cold."

The kitchen table is set for three—place mats, napkins, and all, the way Mom used to serve dinner before Dad left and she stopped caring. At first I take it as a good sign, but then I realize: I'm Dad now. She's trying to woo me home.

We hover as Mom fixes our plates.

"Sit, sit," she scolds. I glance at Ricky, noticing neither of us did until she asked.

You learned it somewhere. So many patterns we pick up without consciously realizing.

"So, how are you? How's Shane? How's work?" Mom finishes her own plate and grabs a fork, scooting her chair close to mine.

"Good," I start, but she bowls over me, breathless.

"You would not believe how hot it's been. And we barely got any snow this winter. Did you all get snow over your way? I mean, we had some at the start of the season, but hardly enough to count..."

Over her head, Ricky and I trade amused looks.

She notices, and her gaze darts to him. "Rick's picked up a few jobs at the Owens' farm, remember them? Oh, Johnny Owen used to have such a crush on you. It's too bad you went away to college. He's got four kids now, so we know he's certainly not shooting blanks!"

"*Mom.*" Ricky massages his temples.

"I'm just saying." She spreads her hands on the table, the picture of innocence. "You always wanted children, Lexi. Remember that life map they had you do in first grade?" She chuckles. "Gosh, you were so excited about yours. You planned to be married by twenty-one, because any older and you'd be an old maid. Then, what was it, you said you'd have your first baby at twenty-three, and you wanted five kids in all..."

I don't remember, though it sounds like me. I tense when she slaps my shoulder.

"What's the matter, did that husband of yours talk you into waiting?"

The pain still comes, but it's muted this time, easier to handle. "Actually, we had a miscarriage last summer."

Ricky's eyes go round. "I'm so sorry, Lex."

Mom reaches over to squeeze my hand. For a second, I think maybe... But then she clicks her tongue. "Oh, honey. You can't let that slow you down! Like me. I was so determined to have you. Your father, he wanted to stop after one, but I said, 'Not happening. I demand my baby girl.'"

Under the table, Ricky's leg touches mine.

Darting him a grateful look, I press back.

"Of course..." Mom lets me go to grab her fork. "I pictured my baby girl spending a lot more time with me than she does. Win some, lose some, I guess." Her laughter is high, false.

Shane said I act like my mother. Do I feign happiness this desperately too? I cast wildly for a change of subject. "How's work, Mom?"

For as long as I've been alive, she's worked at the town library. She used to bring Ricky and me, whenever Dad vanished into an affair. Some of my best memories are playing tag among the stacks or sprawling in the playroom while Ricky read me the fantasy epics he loved.

"Oh, fine. Doreen retired."

"No kidding. I thought she'd work till the day she dropped." I haven't seen Doreen in years, but I can still picture her graying bun and dark glasses. She seemed ancient back then, but she was probably only ten years older than Mom.

"We all did." Mom tuts. "Budget cuts. They offered a bonus to anyone who retired voluntarily." There's a fraught pause. She looks at Ricky.

I used to be able to translate all her expressions, but this one, I can't parse. I am suddenly and acutely aware of being on the outside of my own family, looking in.

"I took the deal too," Mom finally says. "Next month will be my last."

She could've said she's moving to Mars and I'd be less surprised. "Is that...something you want?"

Playing among the stacks wasn't the only reason I loved going to the library. At work, Mom was always on her best behavior. If Ricky or I frustrated her, we'd get a scolding, nothing more.

Not like at home.

"Had to happen sometime." Mom shrugs. "Besides, I'm needed here." Mom shoots another look at Ricky, and this one I recognize. Disapproval. "Someone has to maintain the place. Your brother's proven useless at all your father's old jobs."

"Oh sure, 'cause Dad did so much for us," Ricky mutters.

Mom's expression hardens. "Don't speak ill of your father. He had a difficult life." She always defends him, even now. Only she's allowed to criticize him.

Years of screaming matches well up, but I pour myself more water and choke them down. "I'm glad you'll have more time at home, Mom." Stay positive, avoid anything negative. Just like she taught us. I risk a smile. "Hey, we've got something in common. I quit my job at Medina."

JULIANNE HOUGH AND ELLEN GOODLETT

Now it's Ricky's turn to gape. "Seriously?"

"Wonderful." To my confusion, Mom beams. "I'm sure Shane will be happy to have his wife around more."

I exhale slowly. "That's not why I quit."

"Things would have gone differently between your father and me if I'd been home more." Her gaze drifts to the empty side of the table, wistful.

"Pretty sure the main issue was all the hookers, but okay." Ricky rolls his eyes.

"They weren't hookers," I reply. At least, I don't think they were. "Anyway, there's nothing wrong with sex work."

Mom snorts. "Your generation is so sensitive. Call a hooker a hooker! Call a—"

"Okay." Rick claps his hands. "We have a guest, remember?"

A guest. That's what I am to my own family. My face goes hot. "Ricky, it's fine."

"No, it isn't." He turns his scowl on our mother. "You promised to behave for one night."

In turn, she glowers at me. "I didn't start it."

It's ridiculous. We're grown adults. Is she like this when I'm not here? Or is it me? Maybe my presence regresses us all.

I breathe through my usual reflexive responses. It's a cycle, like Bea said. Cycles can be broken. Channeling every ounce of calm I don't feel, I fold my hands in my lap. "Mom. Genuine question. Are you trying to push my buttons, or is it an accident?"

"Good grief." Mom scoffs at Ricky. Bless him, he doesn't react. "You know, Lexi, maybe I am. Have you considered how it feels to have a daughter who never calls, never visits? And don't say I could visit you, because we both know you only invite me to look polite."

"Have I considered how it feels?" I meet her gaze. "Of course. I feel it too, Mom."

For a moment, she goes still. There's a tightness to her mouth, a shine along her lashes. I swear I'm getting through. Any second now, she'll break character and say something real, something true.

Then her mask slams back down. "So you torture me on purpose. You really are your father's daughter. First the running away, now this—"

"Stop it." Ricky skewers a potato. "Can't we have one meal together?"

"We could, if your sister showed a little respect under my roof."

"Oh, like you respect me?" I snap. She opens her mouth, but I hold up a hand. "I'm not finished. I told you I had a miscarriage and you blew right past it. That hurt, Mom."

Color rises to her cheeks. "It's not my fault you take everything so personally. You always have, ever since you were little. If I was late to pick you up at school, I was branded a bad mother. If your grades dropped, your teachers blamed me. I could never do anything right."

The walls shrink. No, I'm shrinking, reverting to the Lexi who cowered every time her mother raised her voice. The Lexi who felt guilty for every single thing—for existing.

"I never blamed you for any of that," I say slowly.

"You didn't need to." Mom scowls. "The teachers did your dirty work."

A hundred times, I've explained: I never told my teachers anything. It's standard protocol. They notify parents when a student's grades drop, and if a student's ride doesn't show up, they call home.

It's not my fault teachers noticed when I wore the same clothes for four days straight. It's not my fault there was no clean laundry. I was eight.

Suddenly, I stiffen, realizing. This is where the suppression started. Complaining to Mom either got me ignored or blamed, so I learned not to.

Mom glares at me, waiting for my riposte. We both know our lines. It would be so easy to fall into the same old play, but that's not why I came.

"I'm not going there with you," I say, voice calm and even. "Not today. Not ever."

Chapter Twenty-Nine

For a town this close to the desert, it sure is humid tonight.
There must be a storm brewing. The hairs on my arms stand
on end, though I don't smell rain yet.

The back door creaks open and shut.

Ricky finds me wading through the knee-high grass.
Occasionally I trip on old lawn equipment. "Looking for the
sandbox? It's over there." He points with an unlit cigarette.

I swallow my surprise. He never smoked before. Well,
aside from a little pot in high school. "Actually, I was trying
to find the dollhouse. The metal one?"

He lights his cigarette, takes a drag. "The one that looked
like something out of a horror movie?"

I laugh. It was hideous, half rust and half peeling stickers.
"It was the perfect size for the birds, though." I'd gotten the
idea after a robin's nest fell from our tree. The eggs shattered
on impact, tiny blue shells oozing acid yellow. My father
explained the circle of life. *The eggs will feed the grass will feed
the bugs will feed new birds.*

I wanted to keep the new birds safe, so I took my old
dollhouse and filled it with fabric scraps, paper—anything
I thought birds would like. By the time I finished, Dad was
gone, but I persuaded Ricky to nail it to the tree.

It's not on the nail anymore. I kick through the grass around the trunk.

"Mom threw it out a few years back." Ricky reaches my side. He extends the cigarette, but I shake my head, so he inhales again. "One of her cleaning sprees. Didn't last long, obviously." He grimaces at the yard. "I keep trying to throw shit away, but you know how she is. Unless it's her idea, she freaks out."

She clings to objects almost as tightly as to people.

I fold my arms around my waist. "Do you ever consider moving out?"

He shrugs, a quick, jerky gesture. It's the same way I shrug—tight against my body, trying not to take up space. "Moving out or running away?"

"Ouch, Big Brother."

"Hey, I get why you left. Mom can't handle her shit, so she takes it out on us. And Dad was the worst. But..." Smoke trails from his nostrils. "You kind of abandoned me too."

I want to deny it, but... "I know." A lump forms. "I never wanted to leave you. Hell, I didn't want to leave Mom either, I just... I didn't know how else to stay sane."

I look up to find him studying me, ash burned nearly to his fingertips. He drops the butt, grinds it under his heel. "New plan. Regardless of how you and Mom are doing, me and you keep in better touch." He sticks out a hand like we're going into business.

"Deal." I reach for it, forgetting too late about the trick he loved in middle school. He keeps one finger extended, dragging it along the inside of my wrist as we shake. Yelping, I yank my hand back and he dissolves into laughter. "Jerk."

The back of my neck prickles. From the thunderstorm? It feels like some kind of energy, at least. Then it brushes against me. Tentative, cool, unfamiliar. *Earth energy?*

Ricky straightens. A faint aurora haloes him, and I realize it's not my energy at all. This belongs to Ricky.

I study him from the corner of my eye. "Can I tell you something?"

"Anything," he answers. Zero hesitation.

"Sometimes I sense other people's emotions. Little snippets of memory, or how they're feeling. Ever since I quit Medina, I've been learning to channel it." He's quiet for so long that I let out an awkward laugh. "It sounds super weird, but—"

"Actually, I was thinking it sounds like you." In the distance, a flash lights up the horizon. Lightning. "You always knew when Mom was in a mood before she even raised her voice. And Dad... I don't know if you remember, but you used to warn me when he was about to leave. You'd sneak into my room—you were a bit creepy as a kid." He pokes my shoulder and I shove him back, playful. "You'd whisper, *Dad's doing it again.* You were like, five? You shouldn't have even known what an affair was, much less how to spot one before Mom."

"Or you," I point out. "Didn't Mom bribe you to steal his phone and check his text history?"

Ricky snorts. "Oh, God. And smell his coats for perfume. Was Jessica the one with the patchouli? That shit reeked."

"No no, the girl before Jessica. The one who worked at the tennis club. What was her name?"

His laugh transitions to a groan. "Then he tried to convince us he was taking tennis lessons..."

"We rented a whole court for his birthday, and he could barely serve."

"Mom figured it out halfway through the party and got so drunk on champagne we had to sneak her out the back so Grams wouldn't see..."

We both dissolve into hysterics. Somewhere far off, thunder rumbles, and I lean my head on Ricky's shoulder. "Thank you."

He's still chuckling. "For what, our fucked-up childhood?"

"For being the one I relied on."

He rests his cheek against the crown of my head. "I'm glad you got out," he murmurs. "I miss you, and I wish things were different, but if you needed to go, then…I'm happy for you."

"It was what I needed." I study the yard. Dew glitters in the moonlight. Dark clouds boil on the horizon, but they're not here yet. "Maybe it doesn't have to be all or nothing, though. Maybe we can try again?"

He drapes an arm around my shoulders. "I'd like that."

Rain patters on the windows. I'm curled up on the living room sofa, procrastinating. I'm not ready to go upstairs yet. The very idea ties my stomach in knots.

Just a couple more minutes. Then I'll face it.

Ricky went to bed half an hour ago. He gets up early for work, and since my visit was so last-minute, he didn't take the day off. I try not to worry about tomorrow or being alone with her. I've got more than enough to conquer before then.

Lightning flares. I count Mississippis. Five before the rumble. Is the storm five miles away? I can't remember the conversion.

The overhead goes out and I gasp.

"Sorry, sorry." It flicks on again—apparently we didn't lose power. Mom pads into the room. "Thought you went to bed."

In the dark window, my reflection is paler than usual. "Not yet."

She hesitates in the doorway. It's written all over her face: blatant, heartbroken yearning. "Honey…"

I turn around.

By the time I do, she's smiling, masked once more. "I'm glad you came." She crosses the room to offer a cheek.

My lips graze her skin, and I sense it again. Like the hint of my brother's energy in the backyard, but stronger. Cold dirt, stones under bare feet. The scent of fresh-cut grass, moist soil in the garden. And darkness, even more complete than what I faced in the cave. It is the pitch-black of earth that seedling roots claw through in the hopes their leaves might one day glimpse the sun.

It is every terrible memory coiled in one deadly seed. A past I can outgrow, so long as I stop giving it power over me.

"Mom." I look at her and glimpse a flash of fear, as if she's guessed what I'm about to say. "Do you understand why it's so hard for me to come back here?"

"You must be tired. All that driving…" Her fingertips flutter at her clavicle. It's the same nervous gesture she used to make whenever she was arguing with Dad.

Snippets of the past dart through my mind. Ricky and me crouched behind this very sofa, Ricky's palms clamped over my ears. Dad's yells, Mom's sobs.

"No," I say, "I'm not tired yet. I want to know if you remember why I left."

Outside, another flash, the thunderclap nearly simultaneous. The rain picks up, lashes the windowpanes.

Inside, silence reigns.

"Alexis, please." Mom extends her nails. She runs them over her collarbone, leaving faint red streaks. "I don't want to fight."

"Neither do I." I keep it simple, straightforward, with none of my usual fire. The calm is an unfamiliar sensation, especially here. I get the sense that if I'd come back any sooner, I'd have been just as panicked as ever, but now...

Roots stretch from the soles of my feet. My core solidifies, a tree trunk armored in bark.

I am stronger than I knew.

Mom still hasn't answered.

"If you don't remember," I say softly, "I'll tell you. It was the last real conversation we had before I left."

"You left to go to college—"

"Before that," I interrupt.

She doesn't reply. Maybe she can't.

I am tired of secrets. Unexposed to light, they curdle and rot. I'm finally ready to speak, even if it ruptures any remaining calm. I won't keep everyone else's peace at the expense of my own.

"Spring of my senior year of high school." My voice sounds like it's coming from someone else. Someone stronger and braver than I've ever been. "Uncle Chris came to live with us for a few months." Chris is my mother's brother, eight years younger. Their parents both worked multiple jobs, so Mom took care of Chris more often than not. He's her baby—more than Ricky or I ever were.

Her eyes are so wide they reflect the storm. She must remember. Too late, too slow, she laughs. It's high and breathy. "That was such a long time ago. Was it really your senior year? I could've sworn you were a junior."

Chris lost his job, got evicted from his apartment. He begged Mom to take him in, just till he got back on his feet.

Ricky was so excited. He loved Uncle Chris; he followed him everywhere whenever he visited. That spring, I could see it written all over Ricky's face—here at last was a replacement to fill the hole in our lives.

I was more cautious, suspicious even. Uncle Chris sensed

this and set about winning me over. He took us out for fast food, which Mom never allowed. On nights she worked late, he snuck us beers in the backyard. Over weekends, he taught us how to string a fishing line, how to pitch a tent.

By the end of spring, Ricky wasn't the only one who looked up to Chris—I trusted him too.

"He came into my room the night after graduation." At this, my tone finally quivers, but I remind myself it's not a weakness. Vulnerability is strength. "I woke up and he was lying in bed with me."

"Stop," Mom whispers.

I won't. Not again. "He said he wanted me." My throat burns. My eyes. My heart. "Do you know how that felt? I looked up to him, I loved him, I thought he cared about me." I grit my teeth and suck in air. "But I was just an object to him."

My mother swallows. "Maybe he meant—"

"He touched my thigh." I pretend she hasn't spoken. "He said he'd wanted me for so long, and now I was graduated, now I was grown. He said I must be asking for attention, wasn't I, wearing those pajamas. They were regular fucking pajamas."

My mother flinches at the curse. *Really?*

"I couldn't move." This is the worst part: the suffocation, the locked limbs, the rictus scream. All the proof of my pain was trapped inside. "I wanted to scream, I wanted to fight. But my body just. Wouldn't. Listen."

I froze and I spent years hating myself for it. I froze and then I convinced myself that if only I'd been stronger, better, less afraid, my uncle never would have touched me in the first place.

"Do you know what that feels like?" A tear spills over and I dash it furiously. "I prayed to God you would come in, or Ricky, anybody. But nobody came."

I shut my eyes and I'm there. In the memory I've fought so hard to avoid, beneath the comforter I picked out for my fourteenth birthday. Stars and planets, for the subject I planned to study in college. It was my refuge—where I hid whenever Mom got bad, breaking things or screaming.

My uncle turned that refuge into a prison. *I've seen you looking at me. Don't be shy...*

My chest heaves and I resurface. Tears swim in my mother's eyes. "The only reason he stopped is because I started to cry," I tell her. "I think he was afraid someone would hear."

After he left, I pushed my desk against the door. I spent the rest of the night wide awake, leaning against it, terrified he'd come back.

"Do you know what I did the next morning?" I ask, softer now, almost gentle. Because she does know.

Aside from Shane, my mother is the only other person who knows this story.

"As soon as I heard your voice, I ran downstairs and told you what happened. Do you remember what you said to me, Mom?"

She blinks once. Again. She turns to the window, daubing her eyes with the sleeve of her nightgown. "Honey, this was so long ago, I don't remember..."

"I do." My voice hardens. "You said: 'But he stopped, right?' That's all that mattered to you. Not that your brother cornered your daughter, or touched her, or said all kinds of shit a grown man should never say to a child. You only cared he didn't rape me."

My mother jumps at the word. "Of course I cared, Lexi."

"Not enough to make him leave." For another week— while I frantically applied for every cheap room for rent in or around my soon-to-be college campus—I had to live in the same house. I felt like a prey animal, scouting around every corner, barricading my bedroom door at night. I slept on the floor, covered in piles of clothing, unable to stomach my own bed or that fucking comforter.

Mornings and evenings, I went running. If I got home and Ricky or Mom weren't there, I walked straight back out. I'd wander the neighborhood for hours to avoid one minute alone with him.

The only other time he came close to touching me remains still seared in my brain.

I was walking toward the backyard, and I didn't see him in the kitchen. I reached for the doorknob and he reached for me.

I leaped away. He just laughed, holding the door for me. He enjoyed my fear.

"He was struggling, Alexis. He'd lost his livelihood and his home at the same time. I couldn't turn my own brother out on the street."

"You promised me you'd talk to him, but instead you went right back to life as usual. Do you have any idea how I felt?"

"I did talk to him!" Mom finally looks up. "I told him he could never do anything like that again. And he didn't, right?"

"Because I left!" I cry. "That's the week I moved out, Mom. You really never put it together?"

Her face crumples. "He's a good person. He has some self-control issues, that's all."

"Oh, is that all?" I scoff.

Mom bristles. "You're doing it again. Twisting my words."

"Because you don't listen to mine."

"I do listen. I'm sorry you're upset, but you can't hold this over my head forever." She stiffens and rearranges her nightgown. She's regaining her rhythm, gathering the shards of her broken denial.

I close my eyes. She's right about one thing. I am doing it again. Falling into old patterns. I didn't come here to fight.

Help me, I silently ask the earth.

The energy rises at once, stabilizing. It grounds me here and now, where the broken shards of the past cannot cut.

You always leap straight to fixing. Not every problem has a solution.

I did not come here to fix my family. No matter what I say, my mother is not going to suddenly understand what I went through. She will not stop dismissing my feelings or trying to make me second-guess my lived reality.

So why am I here?

For me. Because even if she won't listen, I needed to speak.

And I came to witness, to understand my roots, to face the pieces I've been avoiding. I reopen my eyes. Without moving a muscle, I open my other senses too.

My mother's auric field pulses deep blue, shot through with cracks and veins—a glass pane on the verge of shattering. The longer I stare, the brighter the cracks glow. Energy flows along the seams, as if she's battling to hold it all together.

Carefully, I raise a hand and let my auric field brush hers.

I am cradling a baby. It's late afternoon. I don't recognize the room. It must be the house Ricky talks about, where we lived until I turned four. Dad, Uncle Chris, and Ricky all hurry toward the door together.

"What are you all up to?" I call in my mother's singsong. It's a voice I've almost forgotten, the way she sounded before Dad left.

"Just guy stuff," Dad says. "You wouldn't like it."

So I pace the tiny living room, trying not to feel abandoned, shut out, left behind. I coo to the baby. "We're going to be best friends. You'll see."

The loneliness is enormous. Overhanging it all, something else looms: love and terror twisted so tightly I cannot tell them apart. *I don't know how to do this. I have to do this.*

"Why do you always have to pick a fight?" Mom is saying, in a voice as brittle as the cracks she's fighting. But I hear more than just the words. Touching her field, I catch echoes of the thoughts beneath. *Look what you did to your own daughter. No wonder she hates you.*

"You haven't seen us in years, you barely answer the phone when we call, and now you come home to complain about a decade-old mistake?"

You ruined her. Just like you ruin everything, Katrina.

"I'm sorry I'm not a perfect mother."

I'm sorry, I'm sorry, I'm sorry.

The scene is so familiar. I recognize her desperation to be closer, even as she pushes me away. She reaches, I run. It's our pattern. Hers and my father's too.

Running won't help. Fighting will only wound us both. I need to find another way.

Not apology—because none of this is my fault. I was the child. She was the parent. It is not my fault I exist. But it's obvious that she's suffering. She wants to be different; she just doesn't know how.

"I don't hate you," I say.

Her breath catches.

"I love you." So much it hurts. "I know you wish we saw each other more. Believe it or not, I want that too. I'd love for us to have a close relationship." Now for the hard part. The earth is still here, still supporting me. I draw on its strength. "But unless you're willing to face the mistakes you made—mistakes I cannot and will not forget—you will keep hurting me. As much as I love you, I need to protect my peace."

Her expression is hollow. Unreadable.

"If you're willing to put in the hard work, Mom, maybe someday we can be close." I let my walls down, let her see how much I want this. "But until then…I won't be coming back here."

For a long time, neither of us speaks. Finally, she whispers, "Hard work? Or impossible?"

Longing nearly pulls me under. I can't tell if it's mine or hers. Maybe both. We ache for a world where we can reconnect. One where the past doesn't loom over us both, and love vanquishes all the other emotions we share.

For now, we have only this world.

"Hard," I tell her. "Not impossible."

Leaving my mother to her shadows, I climb the stairs in search of my own.

For a place that has so long haunted me, my childhood bedroom proves anticlimactic. No memories assault me on entry. I perch on the bed to run my hands over the new white silk comforter. There are no ghosts here.

My uncle did not have the power to leave a permanent mark—not on this place, and not on me.

The only thing that surprises me is the size of the room. In my head, it was bigger. Turning sideways on the bed, I touch my toes to one wall and my fingertips to the other.

Mom has remade it into a guest room. The new bed has a sleek, modern headboard, a throw pillow stitched in block letters: Know Ye not that Ye Are in the Hands of God?

It could be a hotel room, if not for my high school diploma framed on one wall. Below it hangs a photo of me and my brother at a picnic thrown by the Young Women. Skimming the frame, I taste a fizz of soda, a burst of music, the sleepy-perfect tiredness of a full stomach and sunbaked skin.

I study this Lexi. Her eyes, her smile—some things don't change. We carry pieces of the past with us.

We don't have to drag the whole heavy load, though. We get to decide what we keep.

Lying down, I tug the comforter up to my chin and listen to the rain dancing on the roof.

There's no rush of energy. No tangible burst like on the dunes or in the cave. Alone in the dark, the only thing I feel is safe.

I sink into my bones while the house settles too. A creak here, a sigh there. My brother's faint snores up the hall—I'd forgotten how they sound. For the first time in what feels like forever, all the muscles in my body unclench.

That night, I dream of roots. Great gnarled trees burst through the kitchen linoleum; vines shroud the clapboard siding; sunflowers sprout from the roof tiles. I dream an entire forest, come to reclaim our house. I do not mourn. Not when roots shatter windows, nor when loamy earth swallows wallpaper and tile alike.

We are free now.

In the morning, I wake to find a single impossible buttercup growing straight out of the mattress beside me.

Chapter Thirty

A buzz sticks with me the whole drive home. Not happiness, exactly. My trip was hardly a joyful reunion. It takes miles to work out what the lightness in my chest is.

Hope.

For so long, I've been constrained by the past. Now, I'm finally looking forward.

Not to say that the future will be easy. I have habits to change, patterns to unravel, and about a million interpersonal problems to solve.

But at least I believe it's possible.

At the last rest stop before Garden Vale, I send four separate texts, all the same. Will you help me? A prayer and an incantation at once.

The house is dark when I pull up. No truck in the driveway, which means Shane must either be at work or still up at his parents' place. I experience a brief pang before reminding myself it's for the best.

What did Bea say? *You focus all your energy on other people's journeys.* Today is about my own.

The doorbell rings. To my surprise, Holly meets me on the stoop, dressed in bright florals.

"How did you get here so fast?" I ask. She pulls me into an embrace so tight I swear my bones creak.

She releases me with a sheepish smile. "You know, I woke up with the strangest urge to see you. I was a couple of exits away when I got your text."

Tanya's the next to arrive, Tupperware full of snacks in hand. "Mrs. Cole! Long time, no see."

"For the last time, it's Holly, dear. Mrs. Cole was my mother-in-law."

Tanya submits to a rib cage bruising, addressing me over Holly's shoulder. "I've got a showing at five, but I cleared my schedule till then. Will that be enough time?"

"If not, I'm in worse trouble than I thought," I joke, trying to quell my nerves. I'm not actually sure how long this will take, or if it will even work. I'm operating on pure instinct. Or… Well. Holly and Tanya might call it faith.

I glance at Tanya's empty passenger seat. "Did you hear anything from Chloe?"

She shakes her head. "I left her a voicemail, but…I don't think she's coming."

My chest tightens.

Tires squeal. All three of us startle as a rattling gray Honda whips around the corner. It fishtails into the driveway and screeches to a halt centimeters from Holly's bumper.

"Goodness," Holly murmurs. "Is she all right?"

"Oh, that's just Bea." I shade my eyes to watch Bea climb out of the driver's seat, combat boots first.

Holly surveys her with renewed interest. "Your teacher?"

Tanya, on the other hand, stiffens. She lowers her voice. "I didn't realize she was coming."

Even though Bea is too far away to have heard, she tromps in our direction, gaze fixed on Tanya. "Relax," she barks. "I saved all my hexes for your friend."

Tanya blanches, and Bea bursts into a cackle.

"You two are such easy marks." Bea nods back and forth between us.

"Generational thing, maybe," Holly muses. Then she opens her arms. "You must be Bea. I've heard so much about you!"

Bea barely has time to look startled before Holly's hugging the life out of her.

Suppressing a grin, I lead everyone inside. I can't help checking my phone one last time. My text to Chloe now says Read. Still no reply. I ignore a brief pang. *Figure yourself out first.* Then I'll address things with Chlo.

In the living room, I perch on the couch. Memories of my failed attempt to heal Shane well up. Today will be different. I have help.

"So... you all know my life's been changing lately," I say, while everyone settles in. Tanya sits on my right. She seems less on edge than when Bea first arrived, but I still catch her surreptitiously eyeing the older woman. I address Tanya first. "You might not understand everything I've told you, but you always listen to me."

My gaze shifts to Holly on my left. "And you're a constant support in my life, full of love and open to new ideas..."

Finally, I look to Bea, who leans against the fireplace. "You taught me how to trust myself again."

Bea grabs a fistful of skirt and executes a dramatic little curtsy. But I swear, for a second, her eyes go misty.

"But now..." I clear my throat, suddenly nervous. "Now I need your help." I lace my fingers in my lap. "Because you were right, Bea."

"My favorite sentence." She preens.

I roll my eyes, battling a grin. "I have to heal myself before I'll be able to help anyone else. And I can't do it alone."

Bea nods. "Just tell us what you need."

For a moment, I'm stunned quiet. All this time, Bea has guided me. If not through entire rituals, then at least to the starting point. I expected her to lead this, too, once I got the ball rolling. *Am I ready to take charge?*

But I recognize my second-guessing now. It's the same impostor syndrome I wrestled with at work, and in college beforehand. I always felt not quite good enough, always assumed everyone else knew what they were doing, while I faked it.

I'm more than qualified. In fact, I'm the only one who knows how to heal me.

Slowly, the pieces begin to click into place. A plan forms.

Before I can voice it, however, there's a knock at the door, so tentative I almost don't hear it. With a murmured excuse, I go to answer.

Chloe's on the stoop with a tray of coffees, shoulders tensed all the way up to her ears. "Sorry," she whispers, gaze darting from me to the cars in the driveway and finally to the quiet house. "Didn't want to interrupt if you'd already started. But in case I'm not too late...?" She raises the coffee tray like an offering.

Relief floods me. I shake my head. "You're just in time."

Back in the living room, Chloe sprawls on the carpet. She greeted everyone enthusiastically, even Bea—though I could tell by their gritted teeth that it cost them both.

I cradle the coffee Chloe brought, more for the heat than the caffeine. "When I visited my family yesterday, I recognized a pattern in my life. My father avoided attachment, while my mother chased it. And"—I dart a quick glance at Holly—"well, I avoid the hard stuff with Shane at

273

times." I dare a look at Chloe. "And occasionally with my friends too."

Chlo grins. We still haven't talked out what happened. We'll need to. But she's here—that means everything.

"I don't want to continue repeating the same pattern, and I think I know how to break it now. The last time I fought with Shane, there was something wrong with his energetic field." I shudder, remembering how it clawed into me at the restaurant. "I saw a cord connecting us—kind of like the one between us, Holly."

She nods.

"But the cords attached to your field looked healthy," I tell her. "To heal my energy, I think…" I catch myself. Always qualifying everything, even now. *I think.* I shake my head. "I need to cut my cords. All of them, so that new, healthy bonds can grow." I hesitate, in case Bea wants to interject.

She just watches, quiet and attentive.

"I wanted you all here for support. Some of you understand energy far better than me." I look at Bea and even Holly. "Some of you haven't experienced the same things—at least, not yet." I glance at Tanya and Chloe. "But I can only do so much of this work alone. My wounds are tied to other people, and so is the solution."

All my running, all my anxiety around letting people see the real, raw, imperfect me. I need to tear my walls down, or I'll be trapped inside them forever.

"Will you stay with me while I heal myself?" I ask.

One by one, Tanya, Chloe, and Holly each nod. Finally, I turn to Bea.

She holds out her hands. "We'll send you our energy," she says, with a glance at the others. "It's easy. Once she begins, simply envision channeling all your love for Lexi into her."

Tanya bites her lip. Chloe straightens eagerly. Holly lifts her chin, like a warrior preparing for battle.

"Thank you," I murmur. Then I have to clear my throat, because it's gone tight again. My emotions hang so close to the surface lately. Squaring my shoulders, I stand. "Okay. I'm ready."

Bea salutes. "You're the boss here."

"She really is," Chloe agrees. The two trade a borderline-friendly glance.

I lie down right in the middle of the hardwood floor. My friends surround me: Holly kneels by my head, Bea at my feet. Tanya and Chloe sit cross-legged on either side. The wood is cool against my back, hard yet bracing. It reminds me of earth energy.

"Bea, could you talk us through breathing?" I ask.

"Of course." She glances around. "Everyone relax into your posture. Start with a slow breath in, all the way to your belly..."

I let Bea's voice wash over me as I sink into this place—the home Shane and I designed ourselves filled with the people I love.

The only sound is Bea's murmur, accompanied by our soft breaths.

After a while, the room starts to breathe with us. The curtains flutter at the window, while the floorboards overhead creak and settle.

Bea's voice fades as our breaths synchronize. When I slow mine, everyone else follows.

The world shivers.

Earth reaches for me first. Warm and fortifying, it rises from the wooden floor, from the foundations of this house, my life. It is a hot meal in winter, a long hug from a friend.

Water surges in next. Too many emotions to parse: terror,

275

joy, excitement; the desire to hold onto everything and everyone I love mixed with the crushing knowledge that I'll never be able to hold on as long or as hard as I wish. One day, we'll lose everyone. In the meantime, we love hard enough to square that pain.

Fire hits me right in the chest. Passion, heat. Fury at the things I long to change; the burning belief that I'll be able to, that my life matters.

Finally, air gusts through our circle. With it comes a jumble of anxieties: rapid-fire thoughts, rational explanations for the inexplicable. It drives me crazy in the way only those I wildly love can drive me crazy.

Because, I realize, I wildly love myself. This woman I've become, the me I was always meant to find.

When I open my eyes, I see everyone's energy. Holly and Bea's auric fields are the brightest: Bea's a blinding white, Holly's a neon rainbow sheen. Tanya's is a deep, rich hue like gasoline; Chloe's transparent as a soap bubble. Each of my friends has her own strengths, her own weaknesses. None of us are without flaws—we all have imbalances and blocks among the dazzles of color.

We are beautiful, all the same.

To judge by the way Holly and Bea stare around the room—Holly bright-eyed and beaming, Bea looking satisfied, even a little proud—they see the energy too. Chloe has her eyes shut, forehead scrunched in concentration.

Tanya, on the other hand, winks at me. There's a serenity to her posture. She doesn't perceive things the way I do, but maybe she feels it nonetheless.

Finally, I turn my gaze to my own field.

Some sections glow bright, unimpeded. Small blocks cluster here and there—everyday struggles. The longer I study it, though, the more I perceive.

Before long, I glimpse the cords. Shining strands spiral out from my body in every direction, some with anchors near at hand—a silver thread dangles between me and Tanya; a flickering, uncertain line leads to Chloe; others stretch far away, to people in my past.

With my friends here, lending me strength, the biggest problems become obvious. A bruised gray-black cord near my hip attaches to a purpling wound, like a bruise in my auric field. There's also a fractured lightning-shaped line up my thigh, with a twisted yellow cord protruding from it.

All the problems I've repressed. Over the past few weeks, I've been excavating them, unburying layers of myself.

And then, of course, at the center of my chest—the fire coral. It burrows into my field, right where it hit me when I spoke to Shane last, directly over my heart. Webs and gnarls extend from its entry point, burrowing through my field.

Start small. Work your way up. The voice is both mine and not, a deep, instinctive knowledge.

I reach up with both hands to the crown of my head. Slowly, I draw energy into my palms. Then I reach for the first cord, at my temple.

It flickers: crouched in my father's closet, I was hunting for Christmas presents. Instead, I unearth a jewelry box. I open it to find a bracelet, engraved with a name that is not my mother's.

A rush of energy. This cannot hurt me now. The cord cuts, the flicker dies. The energy absorbs back into my field.

Another cord at my cheek: holding up a drawing. My father ruffles my hair without a glance. "That's pretty, hon." I am six years old but I know a dismissal when I hear one.

Another: I am sixteen. I hug my knees, perched in what used to be his favorite chair. In one hand, I cradle the cord-less house phone. In the other, my ancient Nokia, whose number I refuse to change, just in case. I will sit here all night. Neither will ring.

The early cords slice easily. The further I move—my hands reaching my throat, then my chest—the more difficult the blocks become.

Pounding on a bathroom door, begging my mother to open it. Ricky has a screwdriver, working at the hinges. I am terrified. Will we find a mother inside or a knife?

The door crashes inward. She's curled in the tub, the knife forgotten, her head lolled back. Asleep. Not gone.

This vision stops me cold. How can I walk away from her now? Just when I'm about to pull away—*Stop, I can't do this*— fresh energy floods me. A trickle at first, building to a rush.

Other memories overwhelm this one.

Chloe's imagining the first ski trip she and Tanya invited me on. I'd been work friends with Tanya, occasional lunch buddies, and then invited to drinks a few times, but this was our first group outing. I feel the powder in our hair, my stomach cramped with hysterical laughter at Chloe's jokes. I'd never met anyone as straightforward as her. It refreshed me.

Tanya is picturing the day she introduced me to baby Rosa. The look on my face as I cradled her—pure, unbridled joy.

Holly recalls my wedding day. Not the ceremony, but the hour before, in my dressing room. My mom had come, but that morning, she and I fought. She stormed out. Holly slipped inside instead and pinned the veil into my hair. Kissed my forehead. "You are the best daughter any mother could hope for," she murmured. At the time I'd felt torn, worried her affection was only pity. Now, I feel the bone-deep truth. She meant every word.

Tears shine on my cheeks.

They lend me the strength to keep going. I wrench the cord free and watch it melt into the ambient energy of the room.

Other blocks are embarrassing. The first time Shane brought me to meet the parents, I was jealous, watching his big family cavort on Holly's picture-perfect lawn. But embarrassment, like pain, is a clue. Where does it hurt? What needs to heal?

For now, I skip the wound at my heart, sensing I will need more power. I skim my hands along my sides until I brush the blue-black wound at my hip.

A hollow, where I longed for a child.

It is not hollow, I realize. Whether I can bear children or not, whether I choose to or don't, there is power here in the womb. Mother energy, nurturing energy—life, death, rebirth. There are so many paths to sharing that energy and building a family. Children are not the only way.

Part of my longing for a child is a longing for my own lost childhood. Part of the grief I carry here is for the girl I used to be.

Again, I falter, but my friends do not. Their love buoys me. It rushes into the space, pools between my thighs, behind my navel. I gasp, distantly aware that my spine is arching, my body moving on its own.

Tanya's eyes widen. She grips Holly's hand, instinctive, while Chloe takes Holly's other. Bea joins them, completing the circle just as lights in the living room flicker out. It doesn't matter. Wind pulls the curtains at the windows aside, sunlight flooding over the five of us.

I am lying on the floor, but I am also standing beside myself. Next to me is a girl I recognize. I take her into my arms and hold her close.

"I love you," I whisper into her hair.

A searing heat, and then the knot releases, the wound knitting its edges together. My body slumps on the wooden floor as the younger me vanishes. I lie, legs splayed, muscles limp, head spinning.

For a moment, I cannot move, cannot even raise my arms. But I have to. We are so close.

It takes all my energy to raise my head. The lightning crack on my thigh sparks like a gathering storm. Slowly, I peel my hands from the floor and aim them both at this mark. With difficulty, I grip the razor-sharp cord that protrudes from this block.

It is jagged, ice cold. Like grasping a blade. I'm almost surprised no blood wells up.

The memory bears my uncle's face, his heavy hand. I wrench at the knife, but it's slick with blood, burrowed too deep. I can't…

Someone's hand brushes mine. The touch is cool and gentle. I look over to Tanya, both hands wrapped around my own. She doesn't see the wound or the energy, only me, yet she knows what I need. She squeezes gently, reassuring.

Together, my gaze never leaving hers, we draw my hand down my thigh. I trace the same path he once did, in reverse. There's a suctioning sensation, a knife sinking into gristle. Behind my eyelids, winks of memories not my own: a strange man. A crowded dance hall, a corner, a shove. Tanya lashing out and kicking. My stomach churns, nausea climbing my throat. But I won't let go; I refuse to stop now.

Finally, with a soft hiss, the cord snaps.

Tanya releases me, tears in her eyes. I look at my thigh. No more lightning. My auric field is almost entirely clear. *Just one more.*

The pulsing red cord at my heart.

There's a reason Shane unconsciously bound himself to me. The same reason my mother clung to my father, the reason she tries to cling to me too—they fear losing me for good. But chokeholds are no way to love.

The answer is to face the fear. Let go. Trust I'll stay of my own accord.

Heat and light pour from the bodies of the women around me. It joins with my own heat, my light. Sparks dance over my skin. This will be the hardest fight, but I feel ready, calm in the face of it. I grasp the base of Shane's cord…right as he walks through the front door.

Chapter Thirty-One

"What are you doing?" His voice ruptures our sacred space.

Tanya sits back on her heels. "Shane, hi!" She tucks her hair behind her ears, radiating embarrassment.

At the same time, Chloe barks, "Little busy."

Only Bea and Holly maintain their concentration. I linger halfway, suddenly too aware of the material world. The hard wood bruises my spine, while sweat pricks at my temples. My auric field flickers, threatening to vanish.

In an attempt to hold on, I wrap both hands around the cord connecting me to Shane.

Mistake. It thickens, my energy flooding into it, feeding it. I try to pull away, but the cord swallows my hands to the wrists, trapping me in place.

Shane steps into the living room. His eyes dart to each of us in turn. "Mom? Lexi, what is this?" For a split second, I glimpse the real Shane: curious and concerned.

Then the cord pulls taut. I physically feel it, a hook behind my breastbone, sharp enough to make me gasp.

In that same instant, all the pain and denial and resentment slams back across Shane's features. His lip curls. "Where were you? I came home last night and you weren't here."

The hook digs deeper. I can hardly breathe for the pain.

All around us, the energy dims. One by one, auric fields disappear from view. First Tanya's, then Chloe's. Bea's flickers next. It's hard to stay in this space when Shane is around. I'm too aware of how ridiculous we look—me sprawled on the floor of our living room, my friends kneeling around, eyes closed. His doubt is contagious; it pokes holes in my willpower.

Why does it matter so much to you that I don't believe it? he asked.

But he stopped, right? my mother whispers.

Suddenly, I get it. Why Shane's doubt cuts so deep. It's not about disagreeing with my husband on one topic—it's a whole adult life spent second-guessing myself.

We need to be able to fight. To call each other out, question each other.

We are the same person, Shane always says. But it's not true. We need to be different.

I sit upright. My friends startle, shooting each other worried looks. Especially Bea. "Can we have a minute, ladies?"

They hesitate. Chloe tips her head in silent question, but I nod, resolute. They've already helped, more than they know. This part I need to face alone.

My friends file out. Holly's the last to go, her worry palpable from across the room. When we're alone, I rise to take a seat on the couch, patting the cushion beside me.

He sits, but he's coiled stiff, every muscle a drawn bowstring.

The effects of our healing session linger. I'm not in the headspace anymore, not fully, yet I still perceive a faint halo: Shane's auric field. No colors come through. It's like back at the very beginning of my training, when all I saw were hazy suggestions.

The cord, however, remains clear. A furious red scribble that binds our bodies.

"Shane." At the sound of my voice, he turns. There's a riot behind his eyes. Love, betrayal, hurt, guilt, desire, *desperation*. "You asked where I was last night. I went home."

Frustration turns to anger. "Don't lie to me. I was here, you—"

"No. *Home* home. To see my family."

Shock roots him in place.

I manage a weak half smile. "I know, right? Had some stuff to work out." My throat bobs. "Like why I've been avoiding you."

He doesn't move. Barely even breathes.

"I learned from an early age how to solve problems on my own. It's hard for me to ask for help. But...will you help me now?" My hands are shaking. I fold them to hide it.

But he's Shane, so of course, he notices. He peels them apart and grips my hands tight. "Of course. What do you need?"

"Just...be here with me? While I do this."

He hesitates. I can tell he wants to question me. Or worse, argue. The old patterns flare, eager to reengage.

"I'm not trying to magically solve everything," I say. "And I'll stop trying to force my worldview onto you. We can believe different things and still connect deeply. Look at your family: you all are so close, you love each other so much, but you stopped believing in the same faiths years ago." I squeeze his hands.

His jaw tightens. He doesn't squeeze back, but he doesn't pull away either.

"You're right about therapy. I'll try it again." *Healing is about more than our energetic field.* "First, though...will you let me try to heal us?"

He pauses for so long I forget to breathe. His eyes shine. Finally, he whispers, "I don't want to lose you."

"Then don't." The edge of my lip curls the tiniest bit.

Not taking his gaze from mine, he slides off of the couch and onto his knees. I follow, until we kneel face-to-face. His arms dangle at his sides, his chin raised. He's still tense because he doesn't believe in anything I'm about to do.

But he's not shutting me out. It's a start.

I take a steadying breath. Another. Slowly, my focus returns. Our auric fields shimmer to life. Mine looks strong and steady, brighter than ever. By contrast, Shane's still seems sluggish, all the energy draining into the cord at his core.

I take hold of it once more.

It is rough as tree bark, yet when I tighten my grip, my nails sink in.

Shane inhales sharply. I feel it too. Hooks in my chest, a clawing sensation. Pus leaks out of the cord and seeps into my nail beds, making my stomach roil.

At the same time, flickers of memory ignite.

Little Shane on the skating rink, reaching for his father. Teenage Shane watching his sisters and Eric tromp down the stairs, all dressed to the nines. Hannah, the oldest, pausing at the door. "You sure you don't want to come?"

"You go," he says. He knows he'd hate the social, but it still stings.

Shane reading in his bedroom when Clarissa bursts in. She grabs his hand, drags him downstairs to the kitchen, which is decked out in red, white, and blue streamers. Holly, Frank, and the other girls are already there, color-coordinated cupcakes in hand. "I'm going to France!" Clarissa squeals, waving the text notification with her mission call.

Staring at his sister, he wants to be happy for her. But all he can process are the arguments—is this right; is this ethical?—and underneath that, a burgeoning resentment: everyone else already knew.

Shane's emotions build. I still don't understand the

285

connections. We have to go deeper. I tighten my grip on our cord and pull.

Holly in the living room, wan and tired. A rare moment alone. Shane is passing on his way to bed when her voice stops him. "We never talk anymore."

The longing all but breaks his heart. But he cannot go there. The fights are too fresh.

The fights. They unspool rapid fire. Holly at the dinner table, tears streaming. "I don't understand what we did to deserve this."

Frank in the doorway to Shane's bedroom, stern. "While you live under our roof, you abide by our rules."

Holly and Frank in the living room, Shane poised on the balcony above, unseen. "I don't even recognize him. What happened to my sweet little boy?" Holly whispers, as Frank holds her.

Sparks of pain hit my chest, my stomach. Shane must feel it too, because he curses and sways on his knees.

And the cord... My eyes widen. It's beginning to tear free. But it's like uprooting a sapling—the more I pull, the more roots become visible, lodged in Shane's energetic field.

That's what I have to remove. The root. The core of this wound.

I send energy pouring up my arms. It folds around the red, writhing cord. At the same instant, faint pops sound. There's a patter on my shoulders, and I look up, distracted. My concentration flickers.

Every light bulb in the living room has shattered. Glass shards rain onto our shoulders, our hair.

Shane doesn't seem to notice. He's bent backward, arched almost in half, rigid with pain.

Finish it.

I lean back and pull harder. Removing the cord reminds

me of peeling glue from grout. The roots cling to Shane, the whole central mass stretching to try and remain attached.

Another memory, sharper now.

Shane perched on the living room sofa. Outside, the entire family is laughing, playing: Hannah and Becky in their usual duo, Clarissa stuck like glue to Eric. Frank and Holly have each other. It's only Shane inside, watching the rest. He props a book open in his lap, pretending to read. In his chest, loneliness yawns. Grows teeth.

He is alone. Things will never be the same again.

But then...

Then there is a college campus. A familiar row of poplars, a couple strolling beneath. I recognize this: our second date. We met for coffee and it lasted all day.

Shane is looking at me, thinking, *There she is*. He doesn't have to be alone ever again.

Shane's breathing comes hard and fast. So does mine. Sweat pools under my arms, along my backside. My muscles vibrate. So close. We just need one last push.

I reach with every ounce of energy my friends shared, every bit of love I hold for Shane. I grab the problem's core.

Things will never be the same again.

The same as what?

Shane is six years old. He's in his bed, heart racing, bolt upright. He creeps down the hall to his parents' room, wide-eyed and trembling.

Holly's reading in bed, while Frank writes in a journal. They both set their things aside when Shane pads in.

"Come here, honey." Holly pats the bed.

Shane climbs up and slips between them. His mother's warmth and soft vanilla scent envelopes him, along with his father's solid weight, the sharp smell of his aftershave. "I had a bad dream."

"What happened?" Holly ruffles his hair.

"I died." Shane tucks his knees to his chest. "I died and then I was invisible, and none of you could hear me, and I kept shouting I was here, but you only said, 'Guess we lost him,' and nobody was even sad or..." He breaks off in a hiccup.

"Oh, honey." Holly continues to pet his hair. "We will never lose you."

"You promise?"

"Of course." Frank now. "Do you know why? Because we have faith. That's what binds this family together." He continues to murmur, his voice taking on the same soothing fairy-tale quality as when he reads to his grandchildren. The words fade; they aren't what matter. Only the feeling.

Shane's eyelids droop. The nightmare is far away, powerless now. His father is right. He belongs here with his family, all of them together. Nobody ever has to be lost.

Finally, I understand. "You're scared to be alone," I whisper.

Shane tenses, the childhood nightmare fresh. "Don't go."

"I won't." Then I give the cord one final wrench.

He cries out and sags onto all fours. The cord dissolves in my fingers, but it leaves a gaping cavity. A deep, jagged wound in Shane's energy. I have to fill it before...

Energy floods the room. It pours into him from all directions.

At first, I think it's him. Or me, subconsciously. But no, it's ambient, coming from everywhere at once. I sit back, eyes wide, and watch energy bubble up from the earth beneath Shane's knees. The windows slam open and wind whips into the room, sending debris from the shattered bulbs flying. Energy detaches from the shafts of sunlight and spirals up in beads of moisture from our sweat, our mingled breath.

Energy healing itself.

Then, before I fully process what's happening, Shane's body jerks and he slumps to the side, unconscious.

I pace the backyard, mug of tea in hand.

Bea watches from the porch, sipping a cup of something stronger. "You're making me dizzy."

In response, I circle faster. "What if it didn't work? What if he wakes up and he's still angry?"

"He probably will be." She shrugs. She, Holly, Tanya, Chloe, and I spent the better part of the morning cleaning up the living room. Even that stress outlet wasn't enough.

I scowl. "Not helpful."

"If you want sugarcoating, ask somebody else." Bea takes another drink. "Your husband just went through a big energetic change, plus a healing rite he didn't exactly request or prepare for. He's gonna be confused as hell. Possibly also pissed."

I groan.

The back door creaks and my breath catches. *Shane.*

But it's only Holly, emerging in a shawl. She shakes her head. "Still sleeping."

At this rate, he's going to sleep through the night.

Nervously, I glance at Chloe and Tanya. They huddle together on the bench Shane and I bought during our honeymoon. The store in Key West was all beach bungalow decor, so the bench is entirely out of place in our Utah backyard: driftwood edges, embedded seashell kitsch. But we could never bring ourselves to get rid of it.

"What if I messed up?" I ask. "Like last time. What if I broke something in him, or—"

Bea groans. "No amount of angst will change the outcome. All we can do is wait."

"But I hate waiting," I say, mostly to get a reaction.

"Quick, phone the presses," she deadpans. "Local millennial hates waiting."

"To be fair," Holly puts in. "I hate waiting and I'm a boomer."

"Really?" Bea squints. "What year were you born?"

"Sixty-eight."

"Oh, no, you're Gen X. Or maybe that's Xoomer, I forget."

As they start comparing the Lost Generation to Gen X, I wander toward my friends. "You didn't have to wait."

Tanya scoots over to make room on the bench. "We wanted to."

I squeeze in. "This is definitely not made for three."

Chloe snorts. "Here." She flips sideways, slinging her legs over my and Tanya's laps. "Better?"

"For you maybe." Tanya shoves her boot playfully.

I hold out my hands and wait for my friends to take one each. Then I squeeze. "Thank you for coming. Even though I've been a crap friend lately." I glance at Chlo.

She squeezes back. "We've all been the crap friend at one time or another. It was your turn."

I snort.

"You know," Tanya says after a moment, "in the future, if you ever need space or whatnot…just tell us, okay?"

I press my lips together. Nod.

"For the record," Chloe adds. "If Shane doesn't come around, he's the biggest fool on the planet."

"Dunno." I take a deep breath. Release. "When we got married, Shane had a very specific idea of who I was. And I've changed a lot lately. If we don't work this out…I'm not sure I'd blame him."

"You don't have to." Chloe elbows me. "We'll be furious enough for you."

"What are friends for?" Tanya smirks, and I stifle a laugh. "But I get what you mean." Tanya rubs the back of her neck. "We have these ideas about who other people are, and when they don't live up to our expectations, we blame them. Really, we should be blaming our own imaginations."

"Or we're convinced our partner has to be exactly like us," Chloe says. "I was stuck in that trap for ages. But Marisol is, like, my complete opposite. I'm learning so much from her."

My eyebrows climb. "So do we get to meet this opposite sometime soon?"

She bites her lip and ducks her head. The expression is so unfamiliar, it takes both Tanya and me a second to place it.

"Oh my god. Are you shy about this?" Tanya cackles.

Chloe groans. "I don't have any practice with the whole meet-the-friends bit!"

I snort. "What's there to practice? Introductory handshakes?"

"Hey, I would've brought her around if there was anything to invite her to," Chloe grumbles.

"Let's make plans, then." I side-eye them both. "Dinner next week?"

Chloe brightens. "I'd like that."

Holly's voice interrupts. "Lexi?"

My whole body stiffens. Sure enough, a light has flicked on in the upstairs bedroom. He's awake.

Tanya touches my shoulder. "Good luck."

With every step, my stomach knots tighter. I pause on the top stair to listen to the bathroom tap. When it stops, I approach the bedroom. "Shane?"

"In here."

I step inside and shut the door behind me.

He's in the bathroom, fully clothed. Water drips from his stubble, tracing the curve of his mouth. He catches my eye and buries his face in a towel. "How long was I asleep?"

"A few hours." My body aches to move closer. Instead, I perch on the bed. "Your mom and Tanya helped carry you up here. Holly is shockingly strong."

He laughs. "Eight grandkids will keep anyone in good shape." Then he turns and leans back against the sink. The movement makes the veins along his forearms stand out. His head hangs lower, so only the bridge of his nose is visible through a slash of dark hair.

Look at me, I beg.

He doesn't. "So. I owe you several apologies. And a few to that woman—"

"Bea," I supply.

"Right." He drags a hand over his face. "You're right. There was no excuse for treating her the way I did. And this is not an excuse either, but...I haven't felt like myself in a while. For weeks, really." His shoulders stiffen. "At first, I was hurt because you shut me out. But then, I don't know. It was like something outside of me kept feeding it. I was getting angry all the time over the most insignificant shit. At work, at the station. And with you..."

Finally, he raises his head.

There's pain in his eyes. Regret. I feel every ounce of it, a flood as strong as the emotions I sensed earlier. But I don't say anything. Not yet.

"God, Lexi. Sometimes it was hard to even look at you. I didn't want to fight. I kept telling myself to stop, but I couldn't. Because...if I stopped being angry, I would've had to admit I'm fucking terrified."

"And now?" I ease off the bed. Take a step closer. "How do you feel now?"

His throat bobs. "The same."

A fist grips my heart. It didn't work.

"Also not," he says and I breathe again. "I mean, I'm still angry. And worried about you. And I don't know what's going on with us, or why we're suddenly a disaster. But I feel in control now, at least. Whatever you did…" His gaze drifts toward the doorway. He shivers.

I risk another step closer. Then another.

There's still a pull between us, but it's not the twisted, wrenching cord anymore. It's a softer emotion, one that's easier to grasp: longing.

"Did you feel it?" I ask softly. I'm close enough to hear him swallow.

"I felt…something. I don't know." He searches my features. "Lex, I'm not sure I'll ever believe in this stuff you're doing. And the way you've been avoiding me and shutting me out, I can't live like that."

My hand twitches. Every cell in my body yearns to bridge this gap between us. I want to promise it will all be fine, to swear we'll figure it out. But the truth is, I don't know if we will. There's so much to work through.

"We've got our work cut out for us, huh?"

The corner of his mouth twitches. "Good thing we're both stubborn."

"And bad at being told what to do," I agree.

For a moment, neither of us moves. We lock eyes and gaze at each other in a way we haven't done in years. No more hiding, no more walls.

"That thing you said about going back to therapy…"

"I meant it," I say.

He nods, slowly. "Maybe we both should."

My smile inches wider. "I'd like that."

Another long moment passes. Then he lifts his hand to

rest it on my shoulder. The touch is featherlight, not clinging or grasping. This isn't a bond or a promise. We don't know where we go from here. Whether we'll make it. If we even should.

But I reach up and lay my palm over his. This touch says the only thing we can for now: we're both here, in the present.

We'll find out what happens together.

Chapter Thirty-Two
Six Months Later

"With each breath, go deeper into yourself." My breathing syncs to the other six women in the room. We're all cross-legged on cushions, ensconced in the upstairs studio of Bea's Odds and Ends. Downstairs, a new sign hangs out front, right beneath Bea's wooden one.

Energy Lessons with Lexi.

"Let any emotions that arose during this session come to the surface. Feel them, acknowledge them. Allow them to pass." As I speak, my gaze drifts over the women, one by one.

My very first class.

Closest to me is Chloe. Beside her kneels Marisol, the latest addition to our girls' night group. Also Chlo's soon-to-be fiancée—assuming she says yes. Just thinking about the proposal Chloe has planned brings a giddy smile to my face.

Sensing the attention, Mar cracks an eyelid.

Hastily, I rearrange my expression. "Acknowledge the work you did here. Thank yourself for facing it."

The other four students are unfamiliar faces, but I'm eager to get to know them. I can't wait to learn what inspired each woman to sign up for the course. When I first announced it, I wasn't sure anybody would. Neither was Bea, who kept reminding me of the rejection she's faced in Garden Vale.

It was nerve-racking, announcing my new career path. Nobody will view me as the old Lexi anymore: the practical real estate agent; the career-oriented, type-A planner. Once word gets around—which happens fast in Garden Vale— there will be no more pretending to be normal.

But if energy work has taught me anything, it's that "normal" doesn't exist. What a resident of Garden Vale, Utah perceives as "normal" is completely different from what's "normal" in small-town Germany or a big city in China. Even here in Garden Vale, no two people face the same struggles, and we each react to those struggles in our own ways. We have different pasts, unique families and heritages, our own desires and needs.

There's no right way to live.

That used to terrify me. I wanted rules, structure, order. I wanted a guidebook to follow: *Living a Good Life for Dummies*. But the idea of a "good life" was suffocating me. I contorted myself to fit a mold that didn't exist.

Now, I know the only "good life" is my life.

Not everyone will understand me. That's all right. A few people saw my announcement and thought, *I want to learn this*. They're the ones I want to meet—the other people who feel this pull, who want more from life, and dare to reach for it.

A flutter of nerves erupts. I hope I'll be able to help these women, the way Bea helped me.

"All right, ladies." I clasp my hands. "That's it for today. We'll meet back here again next week. In the meantime, practice the meditation technique we went over, even if it's just for a few minutes each day. Oh, did you all get a candle?" I wait for everyone to hold up their tapers. "Great. See you soon."

I lean back on my heels, exchanging murmured thank-you's and answering a few questions. It still doesn't quite feel real. They're trusting me to guide them.

Do they know what they're getting themselves into?

Then I catch myself. *Stop it.* Defeating impostor syndrome is an uphill battle, but I'm getting there.

A blond woman at the back lingers. She was the last to join, a walk-in today right as we were starting. Since Bea was kind enough to let me use her space for classes, I decided we should set a formal schedule. But I'm glad we had room for the surprise arrival, because she seemed the most affected during the session.

I'm about to start toward her when I notice Chlo and Marisol waiting too. "Want to grab lunch?" Chlo asks.

I nod. "Be right out. I just need a minute." While they tromp downstairs, I approach the blond woman. "Thank you for coming."

Her face splits into a smile. There's something so familiar about her, though I can't put my finger on what. "Thank you for squeezing me in. I'm Sophia, by the way."

"Lexi." And then, because it's bothering me. "I'm sorry, I... Have we met? You look really familiar."

Puzzlement creeps into her smile. "I don't think so? I haven't actually been in Garden Vale long. Well, okay." She gestures vaguely. "I grew up here, but I moved away for school. I only came back last winter when my dad..." Her breath hitches. She blinks hard, and sudden tears stand out along her lashes.

On instinct, I open my arms.

She steps into the hug, laughing, shaking her head, and crying all at once. "Shit. Sorry. I don't..."

"It's okay," I murmur.

We break apart again and she sniffs, scrubbing her face with the back of a wrist. "God, sorry. It's been so fucking weird. He passed away suddenly, and I... There was a lot of unresolved stuff between us. I'm not sure why I'm telling you all this." She laughs, breathless. "It's just...I think something drew me to your class. Being here was the first time I really let myself feel it, you know?"

"I do," I say softly. Because it's true. And because I finally recognize her. Or, more accurately, her smile. I've seen its exact duplicate before, in a time-worn photograph. The obituary text swims in my mind's eye. *Survived by his daughter...* "Your father was from Garden Vale?"

I already know. Still, it sends a frisson along my spine when she says, "Henry Jensen." At the recognition in my eyes, she brightens. "Did you know him?"

"Not personally. We worked at the same company. But..." I glance around the studio. "You might say he's the reason I'm here."

Her eyebrows rise. "Really?"

I nod at the exit. "Are you free for lunch? I'll tell you the whole story, but my friends are waiting."

She hesitates. "I don't want to intrude..."

"Don't be silly." I lead her downstairs.

In the shop, Bea is propped on a stool by the counter, nose-deep in a shirtless lifeguard romance. "How'd it go?" she calls without looking up. "Any of your new pupils as frustrating as you were?"

I flash Sophia a grin. "Nah, I lucked out."

"The world remains unjust." Bea turns a page. "By the way, you've got another walk-in."

Only now do I notice the figure at the front of the shop. Backlit by the storefront, Shane looks almost as uncomfortable as Tanya on her first few visits to the store. He crosses his arms, shoulders tensed to his ears.

We talked about my new business venture together for weeks. He went over all the numbers, calculating how much we can afford to risk and all the potential liabilities.

Sometimes it frustrated me, how technical he was being, but he made good points. He sees the pieces I don't notice, and vice versa.

I just don't know how he'll feel now that the plan is actually in motion.

My arm slips from Sophia's as I approach him. "Hi," I say.

His smile is slow. A cloud breaking apart. "Hi."

Behind us, Bea clears her throat. "Told him he missed the first session, but maybe you're willing to make an exception."

I blink, confused.

From his pocket, Shane withdraws a toy metal fire truck. The red paint peels along the top, and one wheel has broken off completely. "You said students should bring something from their childhood, right?"

With a tentative smile, hope burning in my chest, I reach up to take my husband's hand. "It's perfect."

FOLLOW THIS QR CODE TO EXPERIENCE THE
EVERYTHING WE NEVER KNEW PLAYLIST
AND TAKE THE QUIZ TO DISCOVER
YOUR ELEMENTAL CONSTITUTION.

Reading Group Guide

1. In this novel, Lexi is experiencing her Saturn return—an astrological phenomenon that occurs in an individual's life approximately every twenty-nine years when Saturn completes a full orbit since the day of their birth. If you're over the age of twenty-seven, have you noticed any major changes in your life that occurred around the time of your own Saturn return? How do you feel about this concept in general, and does it resonate with your own life experiences?

2. Lexi says that Bea talks about "astrological signs the way other people discuss the weather." Bea believes in astrology and thinks that science just hasn't advanced enough to prove its real-world effects yet. How do you feel about Bea's stance on astrology?

3. Many of the women in this novel have plenty of reasons not to like one another: Bea and Chloe have a mutual disdain, Bea and Tanya have very different beliefs, and many characters assume that Holly wouldn't be accepting of Lexi's journey. However, when these women band together, extraordinary events occur and Lexi's energy is

healed. Is there a moment in your life when being supported by other women—even women who may not like you—resulted in something great? Can you relate to this concept?

4. After learning about the five elements that form a person's energy (earth, air, water, fire, and aether), which elements do you see the most in yourself? Which elements do you see the least of?

5. Throughout the novel, characters like Lexi and Bea discuss the connection between energy and religion. To Lexi and Bea, energy and religion aren't necessarily related; both concepts can exist without intersecting. How do you perceive energy and spirituality? Do you see them only as religious concepts? Do you see them the same way Bea and Lexi do? Or something else entirely?

6. When talking about roots and trauma, Bea says, "You can't recover from a wound until you look it in the eye." How do you feel about this statement? Does this ring true for your own life experiences?

7. Lexi is abundantly polite, regularly repeating mantras to herself like, "Stay positive. Avoid the negative." How does Lexi's past contribute to her need to be polite? How does it contribute to her fear of vulnerability?

A Conversation
with the Authors

What was your motivation for writing *Everything We Never Knew*?

Julianne: For years, people have been curious about my personal story and have been asking me when I'm going to write my own autobiography. It never felt fully right for me to tell my own story, but I wanted to write something that was specific to experiences and lessons that I learned along my journey, without giving too much detail of my own private life. With *Everything We Never Knew*, I went through such a transformation in 2017, one that really informed probably the biggest transformation of my life.

This was around my Saturn return, which is when you go through these cycles of life every thirty years, where the planets are aligned at the same time you were born. It's about having a big life transition and making a decision to unlearn everything you've learned through conditioning, whether it's through environment or religious upbringing, or family conditions, or trauma or healing. If you don't actually work through that during the time that your transition is in Saturn return, then you end up repeating patterns and cycles.

During that time of my life, I went through so much

transformation, shedding and unlearning all the things that I had created to protect myself over the years. This felt like the opportune time to share those experiences, the "how," through this modality that came through me, which was all about the elements and having these "oneness" experiences—I know I'm not the only one. I wanted to be able to create something that, instead of being so grounded in reality, was a bit of a fantasy that would allow and give people permission to escape, maybe the hardships of what it means to transform and change so much and to escape into a world where you have permission to believe anything is possible. That's what this book is about.

Ellen: As soon as I heard Julianne's idea, I fell in love with it. I consider myself a spiritual person, but it's a side I've repressed for a long time—as I'm sure many of us have! But talking about spirituality in a grounded way feels vital right now. So to get the chance to work with someone as knowledgeable as Julianne, who works hard to share her path, her experiences, and her lessons with the world... It was a real privilege.

I believe the best kind of fiction illuminates universal truth. We tried to distill that truth into Lexi's journey. Here's hoping you find it every bit as inspiring as Julianne herself is!

Lexi's journey throughout the novel is a result of her Saturn return—an astrological phenomenon that majorly influences a person's life every twenty-seven to twenty-nine years. When did you learn about the concept of a Saturn return? Did your own Saturn return inspire any part of Lexi's story?

Julianne: My Saturn return was when I had my big transformation, and to my friends and my family, I was shifting dramatically, but nobody really understood what I was going through because it was so hard for me to even understand and articulate that I was having these mystical experiences. So a lot of the time, I was just quiet and kept things to myself.

However, a lot of Lexi's journey is what I went through. We obviously just changed certain situations for my own privacy, and yet I experienced a lot of loss and grief in my life that is very close to what Lexi goes through, which is a trigger and activation point for her to find these innate superpowers that we all possess and have within us.

Instead of suppressing those emotions and those feelings, she was starting to let them come out. That's the only way we can really, truly heal and transform: by allowing those emotions and those dramas to be seen and valued instead of letting them control us or letting them have a voice. It's so that we are now in control and we design our life instead of letting life dictate.

Ellen: I had not heard of a Saturn return until I met Julianne. After she explained the concept, I got my birth chart mapped. Turns out my Saturn return began the same month that I quit my day job to write full-time, gave up my apartment in New York City, and booked a yearlong trip around the world with seventy-nine strangers. So, I definitely relate to Lexi's desire for change!

But I understand Lexi's fear of change, too. Like Lexi, I had a good job, close friends—a comfortable life. Walking away was a huge risk, and I wavered on the decision for months.

In the end, I realized no matter how good my life looked on paper, I wasn't happy. Writing was my dream. Traveling was where I felt alive. So, I took a leap.

Much like Lexi, I've never regretted it.

What was the most challenging scene to write in this novel?

Julianne: I think writing this book, and this novel in general, was challenging because it's exposing parts of ourselves and especially parts of myself that, I think, we try to protect. I think revealing a sense of isolation and loneliness, when the world thinks that you have everything perfectly put together on display, is a very vulnerable thing to do. I think because it's so abstract and fantastical, what she's experiencing, it can be very "woo woo" or "hippity dippity," but it's not to say that it wasn't real and a real experience for me.

I made sure that I stayed integral with my true experience while also making sure that it was relatable to people. I think being vulnerable about loss and grief and feeling alone is a very revealing thing to share, and while doing that, it was therapeutic and healing for me to be able to share those things, almost like therapy. Putting words and feelings on paper and getting them out is exactly what this whole book is about. It's about revealing and expressing your truest self so that you're not hiding or suppressing parts of you that deserve to be seen and valued.

Ellen: This whole novel challenged me more than any other project I've worked on. Julianne had such a clear, strong, inspired vision—I desperately wanted to do it justice. Not to mention, we drafted this during lockdown. So much of the story is about human connection and the importance of community at a time when I had never felt more isolated from my people (albeit for a necessary cause!).

But the most challenging scenes for me were Lexi's emotional confrontations: with her mother, with Shane, even with her friends. I too struggle to recognize my own emotions, to accept and articulate them in the moment.

Forcing Lexi to confront a similar problem, then digging in and refusing to let her suppress it or run away... Let's just say, I learned a lot about my blind spots while unveiling hers.

Which scene was the most fun for you to write?

Julianne: I think what was so fun writing were the lessons that Lexi goes through, the elements with Bea and understanding her own power through the elements, and really seeing the visuals and the mystical experiences that she's having. Because imagination is where, well, we've lost a lot of our imagination over the years. When we're kids, we have an unbelievable—and just inspiring—imagination, one where anything is possible. As adults, we dim that imagination. Being able to create a visual that was so otherworldly, which was really my experience, was so fun to be able to play again. I think we deserve, as adults, to come back to that inner child where we create and dream up the imagination and let it run wild. All the elemental lessons that Lexi goes through, as deep and as impactful as they were emotionally, were also super stimulating as far as the sensory experience, visually, auditorily, and kinesthetically. I was feeling everything that Lexi was going through while writing it, while reading it, and, of course, when I was going through it. It was super fun.

Ellen: The scene at the sand dunes is my personal favorite. It's the first time Lexi lets go of these rigid, self-imposed rules she's been clinging to and just lets herself have *fun*.

All the scenes where Lexi taps into her power were similarly cathartic—whether she's using her energetic power or her everyday power, like when she finally tells off her boss.

307

The setting plays a major role in this book—both in the natural beauty described in the scenery and in the cultural values each character holds. Why did you choose small-town Utah as the setting for this novel?

Julianne: I chose Utah to be the backdrop because it's where I grew up. It's not necessarily where I learned most of my lessons in my formative years, but it's my roots. When you think about epigenetics and family ties and everything, I wanted to go back to the beginning, and Utah is so, so beautiful in its nature. If you go down to southern Utah, it's beautiful—red rocks, the water, and the history there. Then you go up to Salt Lake City and Park City, and it's this crystalline energy that is just bright. It's the juxtaposition of both of those energies—the feminine energy, which is very unknown and very much southern Utah and then the masculine high-spirit energy, which is very much northern Utah. There was a really good polarity, not only for the novel itself but really for my experience as a child growing up there.

Ellen: Confession time: I've never actually been to Utah! Thankfully, Julianne put up with me asking a few thousand questions. She paints such a wonderful picture of her home state, I really felt like I was standing there at times.

What's the most important lesson or idea you hope readers take away from this novel?

Julianne: I think the most important lesson or idea behind this novel is that through individual experiences, we might be going through different things, but a lot of our emotions and things that we are experiencing or dramatically affect us are similar for men and women. But for women specifically, for years we have suppressed that feminine energy and been the person that people need us to be. We've shown up to be

308

the good little girl, do things right, be perfect to be accepted in society the way that has been constructed in the systems that have been set in place.

So, this idea is that it might be hard to let go of those systems and those conditioned beliefs that have been put on us from the environment, society, cultural references, family, whatever it might be. It might be difficult, yet the outcome is so rewarding when you can go through it instead of hiding it, suppressing it, or pushing it down. By doing so, that can lead to years and years of not only pain that we hold in emotionally but physically manifest into certain things, whether it's body aches, ailments, or disease. This is hopefully an opportunity where people feel like I have the space, I have the community, I have the support where I can go on this journey, and I know I'm not alone.

Ellen: As humans, we are hardwired for comparison. We study everyone else, trying to determine how life "should" be or what's "normal." But there is no right way to live. Or rather: there are as many right ways to live as there are people in the world.

I hope Lexi's journey reminds you it's never too late to start over. The most powerful force we possess is change. Use it.

Acknowledgments

Julianne

There are so many incredible humans that contributed to making this book come alive.

Thank you to Sourcebooks—Kate Roddy, Cristina Arreola, Siena Koncsol, Kayleigh George, and Molly Waxman. You have all been such a source of support for me during this process. Without your patience and understanding, this would have never survived. Let's do it again soon!

Thanks to Allie Dyer, Marty Bowen, and everyone over at Temple Hill. You helped me turn a seed of an idea into an actual concept, which led to this book. You have all been my biggest cheerleaders from day one.

Thank you to everyone who had a hand in this project, including Albert Lee, Brooks Butterfield, Maddie McLaughlin, Carrie Gordon, Caroline Stewart, Nikki Bohannon, Jason Weinberg, and Danielle Thomas.

Special thanks to Morgan Pichinson and Rebecca Liaw from Canary House Productions.

Thanks to John and Christina Amaral, Scott Picard, Oliver Niño, Joyce McFadden, and Tony Robbins. You have all helped me heal and connect to my authentic self through your own unique modalities.

Thank you to the KINRGY community—both internal and everyone out there subscribing and taking the classes. During the time this book was written, I especially needed all of you. I experienced firsthand the support, growth, and effort you put into KINRGY—the modality that changed my life and is all over this book. True encoded energy. What KINRGY did for people all over the world, during such a challenging time (COVID) personally and collectively, really kept my spirit alive. Thank YOU!

Thanks to my mom and dad. My early relationship with you was somewhat ruptured because I moved away when I was so young. I obviously have always been independent and have taken care of myself for as long as I can remember, but during my divorce, you really showed up for me when I couldn't do it alone, and we reconnected in a way my younger and current self truly needed. I love you!

Thank you to my sisters, Sharee, Marabeth, and Katherine, for paving the way through your own hardships and challenges before I went through mine. You were all so vulnerable and needed more empathy. I didn't know and couldn't understand that before I went through my own. It has been beautiful to reconnect as adults, and I am forever grateful for you all.

Thanks to Isabel Emrich. Your cover art is breathtaking, and I'm beyond grateful to have it representing this book.

Thanks to Dani and Duddy who cowrote the music with me. I will hold our writing/therapy sessions close to my heart. This book is all about our spiritual senses, so thank you for bringing the characters to life through an auditory experience. I am so proud of what we created together.

To my ex-husband, Brooks—I am grateful for you, our relationship, and our marriage. When we met, I was very much my ten-year-old-child self, and you gave me a protective, stable, and consistent environment. With that safety that you held for me, I was able to go on this healing journey.

To my Mommas, Lexi and Harley—you both taught me unconditional love. Your traumatic passing sent me into a spiral of loss and grief that I have never experienced before. Today, I believe you cannot have joy without sorrow, and that sorrow I felt is due to the true joy that you both brought me in this life. Thank you for all the love I got to experience.

To Sunny, thank you for allowing me to pour my love into you every day. You are my Sunshine!

To Ellen, there are no words to describe my gratitude for taking what my kinesthetic being ideated and articulating it on to the page. Your patience was unwavering; your understanding was known. Thank you for creating magic with me.

I want to say thank you to all the people, places, and things that were a catalyst to the unraveling of my life. It's easy to thank the people that make your life more enjoyable in the moment, but I am grateful for the people, places, and things that made me realize it was time to prioritize my worthiness, uncover all the layers of healing, and claim my authentic self. I have a deeper and greater understanding of who I am and an empathy for myself and others. Because of that, I am able to share that through this book.

It is now yours!

Ellen

This book would not have happened without the coordinated efforts of a huge team.

First and foremost, shout-out to my agent, Bridget Smith, who saw the call for authors on this project and said, "That sounds like Ellen." You were right! And thank you for talking me out of my nerves during the audition process when I (a humble, uncoordinated writer) took a dance class with a pro.

To Kate Roddy, thank you so much for believing in this book and championing our vision. To the rest of the Sourcebooks team—Molly Waxman, Cristina Arreola, Siena Koncsol, and Kayleigh George—thank you for all of the support, encouragement, and willingness to consider at least four time zones to find meeting dates that work for everybody.

Thank you to Alli Dyer and the team at Temple Hill for being there throughout all four of the years it took to bring this book to fruition, and thanks to Morgan Pichinson, Camila Forero, Taylor Sargent, Rebecca Liaw, Meredith Fridline, Payton Mayer, Caroline Stewart, Brooks Butterfield, Maddie McLaughlin, Albert Lee, Mackenzie Rollinson, Nikki Bohannon, and Jamie Batey for the emails and meeting coordination.

Once again, I'm lucky enough to have been blessed by the cover gods—in this case, artist Isabel Emrich. I think we can all agree her work is stunning!

To another talented artist I met at home in Lisbon, Helen Vechurko, thank you for chatting the whole time you were shooting my headshots so I could finally relax and look normal.

Speaking of Lisbon, shout-out to my Escritoras, Chanstay Young and Diana Pinguicha, who kept me sane in the anxiety-inducing early days of the pandemic and who cheered on the first draft of this book. On the other end, much love to Suzanne Walker, who road-tripped through Scotland with me while I struggled through the final draft—the change of scenery was exactly what I needed.

Thank you to Tracy Banghart, my debut twin, for providing text message support and page reads. To Joy

Mitchell, I appreciate all the pep talks and creative industry venting sessions—I'm so glad our paths crossed for as long as they did!

To my family—Mom, Dad, Kev, and Mel—thanks for cheering on my wild endeavors. I'm blessed with more friends than I can possibly fit in one acknowledgments page, but please know that I love you all and I can't wait until we live in a giant seaside manor/villa somewhere scenic, instead of scattered across the globe.

To everyone reading this, it's an enormous privilege to be able to share my writing with you. I hope you enjoyed Lexi's story, but either way, thank you for taking a chance on this book!

Finally, and most importantly, Julianne: I'm so grateful that you trusted me with your brainchild. I had so much fun working together, even if we picked a rough year to start. Isolation felt a little less isolating with Lexi's world to dream up together.

About the Authors

© Elias Tahan

Julianne Hough

© Helen Vechurko

Ellen Goodlett

Emmy Award–winner, entertainer, producer, and entrepreneur **Julianne Hough** is known to audiences globally for her success in film, television, and music. She became a household name as a two-time champion on ABC's top-rated *Dancing with the Stars* before making a seamless transition to award-winning recording artist and accomplished actress. Her acting credits include *Safe Haven* opposite Josh Duhamel, Diablo Cody's *Paradise* with Russell Brand and Octavia Spencer, *Rock of Ages* with Tom Cruise, and Netflix's original Dolly Parton anthology series, *Jolene*. Julianne founded Canary House Productions, which provides storytelling rooted in transformation, self-discovery, and identity, as well as KINRGY, the only trauma-informed dance fitness and energy healing modality backed by neuroscience and evidence-based research. Most recently, she cofounded the low-calorie premium wine company Fresh Vine Wine.

Ellen Goodlett is the author of the young adult duology *Rule* and *Rise*, as well as the fiction podcasts *Elixir* and *Memory Lane*. She grew up in Pittsburgh, spent her twenties in New York City, then left with a single suitcase to explore the world. She currently resides in Lisbon, Portugal.